New Crescent Series

SPIRIT

MARY LOU GEORGE

BookStrand

SPIRIT

New Crescent 2

Mary Lou George

ROMANCE

BookStrand
www.BookStrand.com

GEORGE MARY LOU

A SIREN-BOOKSTRAND TITLE
IMPRINT: Romance

SPIRIT
Copyright © 2008 by Mary Lou George

ISBN-10: 1-60601-339-4
ISBN-13: 978-1-60601-339-7

First Publication: November 2008

Cover design by Jinger Heaston
All cover art and logo copyright © 2008 by Siren-BookStrand, Inc.

Printed in the U.S.A.

PUBLISHER
www.BookStrand.com

DEDICATION

For Kim and Bill. I couldn't do it without you.

SPIRIT

New Crescent 2

MARY LOU GEORGE
Copyright © 2008

Prologue

He hungered. Not for food…but for life. How long had it been? Time was a concept he no longer grasped. A taste here, a taste there. He'd existed on so little, so pathetically little. But change was coming. He'd felt it when he'd fed from that snooping kid. There were always people nosing around. Their curiosity angered him, but it sustained him. Barely. It was time.

Chapter 1

"Bennett House sold?" Regina Stanton swallowed a mouthful of pancake and said, "I was only gone two months. How could it have sold so quickly?"

"I guess there's still a market for large waterfront properties with white elephants on them," Reggie's father replied.

"I happen to like elephants, white or black or even pink. Whatever. I don't discriminate." She looked earnestly at her father "So, it's gone then. My house belongs to someone else. Who bought it?"

Don Stanton glanced over his shoulder at his wife, slicing bananas at the counter. She nodded to him and he said, "Some writer…goes by the name, Pat Somers?"

Reggie choked, and with a grin, her father thumped her on the back. "You've heard of her?"

She rolled her brandy colored eyes at him and gasped. "Only because I've read all of her books! This is amazing! New Crescent is the perfect place for someone like her to live. And in Bennett House?" Her smile dissolved as she said, "Please tell me she doesn't intend to tear the place down."

Her mother stepped in, placing another plate of pancakes and fruit before them. "Apparently not." She sat down and dug in. "She's having it restored. The house, the gardens, the path to the beach, the whole bit."

"The work is well underway," her father said. "Nothing but the best."

"This is great news. Did you meet her?" Reggie licked maple syrup off her finger.

Her mother handed her a napkin. "No one's met her. She made all the arrangements through an agent named Jackie Blake. Your father handled the sale. We debated calling and telling you, but we didn't want to interrupt your trip."

Looking at her plate, Reggie chased a blueberry with her fork and effectively avoided her mother's eye. She wasn't ready to discuss what had happened that past fateful summer. The only sound heard in the kitchen was the familiar burping and sighing of the coffeemaker.

Reggie finally broke the awkward silence. "Thank you both for holding down the fort while I was gone. I especially missed you...my sweetie. It was way too long."

She reached down and gave her beloved dog, Prudence, an enthusiastic mauling. Prudence, or Pru to her nearest and dearest, lapped it up.

After breakfast, Reggie accompanied her father to town. Happiness made her heart beat faster as they drove the familiar streets.

She tilted her head in her father's direction and sighed. "I swear, Dad, for me, New Crescent is a little slice of paradise on earth. It's good to be home."

He nodded. "Yup, that's the way it is, pretty much. Our native sons and daughters always find their way back to us" His face creased with concern. "Does it still bother you that you didn't inherit the Goode family gift?"

Reggie shrugged. "Not so much. I've accepted the fact that I was passed over. I'm just happy that their blood runs through my veins." She waved a hand at the charming main street. "Look what they founded. What kind of courage would it have taken to provide sanctuary during the Salem witch hunts? For that Rebecca, Elizabeth, and Morgan Goode will always be my heroes."

His lips turned up into a gentle smile and he sent it her way. "That's my girl."

"It's enough to be part of this magical town. It still amazes me that some outsiders come here and never even sense the undercurrents. They have no idea that it's so much more—that it's a place where the unexplainable is almost commonplace." Sad for a moment, she shook her head. "They think New Crescent is your run of the mill, uneventful small town. The few who take the time to look into our past think the stories of enchantment are manufactured just to entertain the tourists. They smile and act like they're privy to some sort of inside joke when really they kind of just float on the surface of a calm sea and never dive deeper to explore the wonders beneath the surface. They miss so much."

"Their loss."

"I couldn't agree with you more. My guess is the Goode sisters set it up that way," Reggie nodded as they pulled into the parking space behind the real estate office. "Not everyone can handle the knowledge that there is more to this world than what meets the eye. It's best left to those who are armed with the gifts necessary to comprehend—and the power to act."

Situated on the main street of New Crescent, Stanton Realty had been in business for years, always owned and operated by a descendant of Rebecca Goode. After her father retired, Reggie had taken over the company. She loved it. There was something very satisfying about finding the perfect home for a client. For Reggie, roots ran deep. Land was more than something to be bought or sold if the price was right. Here, in this town, it was a birthright, and it meant everything.

The office was a welcome sight. As soon as she unlocked the door, she felt comfortable. Decorated in shades of white, blue, and green, the subtle colors and whitewashed furniture suited her to a tee. Reggie took the chair behind the desk. Her father sat opposite her.

She looked at him with suspicion. "That's a pretty smug look you've got on your face there, Dad. Care to fill me in?"

He sucked at subterfuge.

Bursting with excitement, he rubbed his hands together and shifted his chair closer. "I have a job for you."

She looked around the office, her eyes wide and said, "I thought I already had a job."

"Of course you do dear and you're very good at it. The business is yours and has been since the day you were born. It's been gratifying to see you make such a success of it."

"I like this work, Dad. Maybe it's in my blood. I had to inherit at least something from Rebecca Goode besides height, right?" Reggie was almost five feet ten in her socks. It was a well-known fact that founding sister Rebecca Goode had been unusually tall, and Reggie picked up where her ancestor had left off. From her mother, she'd inherited lush curves, blonde hair, and warm coloring, a fact she'd never bemoaned even though her looks had often made men forget what they were saying. Perhaps she wasn't beautiful in the conventional sense of the word, but she was sexy and striking.

Don Stanton ignored his daughter's self deprecating comment. "Have you ever considered making use of your more creative abilities?"

"Cut to the chase. What are you asking me exactly?"

"Pat Somers's agent asked me if I knew anyone in town who would be interested in taking on the interior design of Bennett House, and I thought of you. I know of no one in this world who cares more about that house. You took interior design in college. You're the perfect choice."

Regina stared at her father, a look of astonishment on her face. "I don't have the experience. That's an awfully big job."

"The woman wants to hire someone connected to this town. She knows all about you and wants you to take on the project. I must admit, I waxed a bit poetic about your love of the place when I showed the house. I guess my charm held sway. Just call the agent and work out the details. The project is yours if you want it."

She laughed. "Want it? I'd have to be crazy to say no. It's the kind of thing I dreamed about when I was a kid…it seems almost too good to be true."

"Well, honey, sometimes dreams come true." He walked around the desk and kissed the top of her head. Turning on the computer, he said, "I'll continue on here in the office until you're finished with Bennett House. Why don't you go take a look right now, check the place out."

"So, Mick Jagger, is this just an underhanded way of coming out of retirement? Is Mom okay with it?"

"Would I be suggesting it to you if she hadn't already approved the idea? I'm old, not stupid."

She moved from the chair so he could take it. "You're neither. And I love you very much. Mind if I take the car?"

"Stop! Flashback! The first year you had your license…didn't they call you Crash?" He laughed at her expression and said, "Ah, good times…"

He tossed her his keys.

In the driver's seat of her father's car, Reggie sighed. Funny how things work out. Her very first solo voyage behind the wheel had been this exact route. She'd made the trip to Bennett House countless times, by every mode of transportation available to her. From the age of eight, when her only means was a silver Raleigh bicycle, she'd taken this road, made this turn. Every tree and shrub had grown up right along with her, like siblings. She couldn't remember a time when she hadn't longed to live in the big house. But no, now it belonged to someone else, it seemed Bennett House wasn't her destiny and like other disappointments in her life, she'd accepted it with grace.

Nearing the lane that led to the house, Reggie shook off the threat of melancholy and forced her mind to concentrate on the positive. If she couldn't have it, then what a wonderful stroke of luck to be able to make the house over the way she'd always imagined. As a child, late at night when she couldn't sleep, she'd restore the house and grounds in her mind, eventually drifting off to sleep where more vivid dreams awaited her.

Surprisingly, she'd never spent much time inside the house itself. She'd snuck in through boarded up windows a time or two, but for as long as she could remember, Bennett House had been empty and forgotten. When she was younger, she'd resented that the house was ignored by its owners, by outsiders. In her mind, it was despicable to leave such a place abandoned. It deserved life, love, tender-loving care. It gave her satisfaction to know that she'd get her chance to make it a home, even if not for herself.

As she rounded the last curve of the driveway, Reggie smiled at the number of vehicles parked in front. The place was a hive of activity. Her pleasure was short-lived, however, when she spied the all-too-familiar, beat-up Chevy pickup.

Chase McCann. Hell! The last person she was prepared to see right now. For a split second she considered turning the car around and heading for home, but that option slipped away when the man himself stepped out of the house and recognized the car. He headed toward her.

Chapter 2

He moved with an economy of motion that was heartbreakingly familiar to her. It suited him. With Chase, nothing was wasted. Everything counted. He spoke only when something needed to be said and acted only when something needed to get done. She couldn't remember a time when she didn't know him. He was sewn into the fabric of her life like threads of gold woven into a priceless tapestry.

At six feet seven, he was the only person who'd ever truly towered over her. Sometimes he could make her feel so small. And not just because of his height. Like Reggie, her friends Travis Sinclair, Sam Daniels, and Chase McCann were from Old Families. They'd all been close since childhood. Travis and Sam were like brothers to her, but Chase had always stood aside. Things were different with him. He was no brother to her. The difference was subtle and indefinable, but Reggie knew it was there…between them. Still, she couldn't imagine her world without him in it.

Sitting behind the steering wheel of her father's car, Reggie braced for impact. Chase reached the driver's side just as she stepped out. Neither said a word. He held the door open for her, closed it after her, and still they said nothing.

Uncharacteristically, Chase broke the silence. "No one told me you were back."

She looked up at him. Damn, he looked good. A tuft of hair stood up on the crown of his head. The sun shone through it. He'd got a hair cut. Maybe he'd had to because of the head wound he'd suffered on her account that past summer. The summer they'd never talked about.

The sun had lightened the tips of his sandy brown hair and had darkened his skin just enough. Reggie knew that some men these days spent hours and paid a fortune to achieve just a fraction of what Chase McCann came by so effortlessly. The thought irritated her and added an edge to her voice.

"I'm back. There, I told you."

"Good."

His blue eyes held humor as he appeared to wait for Reggie to start talking. She couldn't resist. It's what she did when he was around. She talked.

"I guess I'd never be back officially until I came here. My dad and mom told me that Pat Somers bought the place. She's my favorite writer you know…" They started toward the house.

Reggie had come unprepared, wearing much-loved, but impractical, high-heeled sandals. The gravel made it difficult to walk with dignity. Without uttering a word, he took her elbow and helped steady her. She continued to fill the silence with chatter. His touch sent tiny reverberations through her body and her heart raced.

Abruptly, she stopped walking and talking and paused for a second.

"I came to the hospital the next day to see you, but they told me you'd left against doctor's advice."

"I hate hospitals."

"Who doesn't? You should have listened to the doctors. Head wounds can be serious." She sighed. "The slightest dent and your hair never parts right again."

Her quip scored, and he laughed. She kept talking. "I went to your house and the Garden Center, and you weren't there either. You'd left."

"There was something I had to take care of."

She put a hand on her hip and looked up at him with irritation. "Care to tell me what was so important?"

"No."

She shook her head. "No surprise there, but don't you think I deserve some sort of explanation? I put myself between you and a bullet, cowboy. That should count for something, even to you."

He had a closed look on his face. "It's not my story to tell."

She knew she'd get nothing more from him and sighed with impatience. They were right back to their usual dynamic, Chase calm and stubborn, Reggie angry and frustrated. She had hoped things would be different after what they'd been through together last summer, but nothing had changed. He still maintained that invisible but rock-solid distance between them.

Instinctively, she too slid back into old habits. She put an arm up to push him aside.

"Okay, that's it then. Out of my way, Lawn Boy. I need to take a look around inside. I'm going to bring this house back to life."

He didn't move. She sighed and looked past his shoulder. Rolling her eyes and pasting a bored expression on her face, she pointed. "Oh look, your minions are getting restless, a fight's about to break out."

He turned and swore creatively. She raised her eyebrows and thought, *Profanity. At least something's changed.*

He gave her an apologetic look, and when she waved him off, he said, "This is the third fight this week."

Reggie used the distraction to her advantage and slipped past him into the house. Over her shoulder, she called back to him, "Good luck with that."

Standing in the entrance to Bennett House, Reggie took a deep breath to settle her nerves. There. It was done. She'd seen him and managed to avoid blubbering all over his shirt. With resolve she vowed to bury her feelings. She'd done it before, and she could do it again. *But, damn, he looked hot.* Just being near him, Reggie felt a heat that had nothing to do with the readings on a thermometer.

Why was she shaking? No sense asking the question when she knew exactly why. Damn it! She still wanted Chase McCann. She longed to get her hands on him and to feel his hands on her. She ground her teeth at the thought, and her stomach made its way into her throat. For the hundredth time, she asked herself, how it could have happened and when.

Had it been anyone else, she could have handled the physical desire without question or hesitation…but with Chase? Her skin felt electrified when he was near, and all she wanted to do was get closer. Not for the first time, Reggie cursed her body's wayward response to him.

Squaring her shoulders and pushing Chase from her mind, Reggie glanced around at the renovations made to Bennett House so far. It was remarkable. There must have been a veritable army of craftsmen working round the clock to achieve such results. Excitement pulsed through her veins. At last, someone was doing it justice. All major work to the upper floors had been completed. They just needed to be decorated. She was pleasantly surprised to note that the master bedroom was almost as she'd imagined it could be. Two smaller rooms made into one large one, with a dressing room and private bathroom. It was magnificent. Standing in the spot where she'd envisioned a high, king-size, four-poster bed, Reggie felt a joy she couldn't contain. Her laughter sounded right as it echoed in the empty space.

Still smiling, she descended to the main floor. The grand staircase needed work, but she could see its promise. Through a wall of windows opposite the living room, she caught a glimpse of Chase outside talking to one of his men. He'd successfully broken up the fight, but she could see the tension in his shoulders. He wasn't pleased. She knew the signs. Running her hand over the smooth oak of the window seat in the great room, she watched him. It was a pleasure.

Memories washed over her. She couldn't help wondering what would have happened between them had circumstances been different. Shaking her head, she sighed and stood up. Too much time had been wasted on what-ifs.

Reggie looked down at the paper in her hands and reread her notes. Jotting down a few more thoughts, she moved from the window seat into the hallway that led to the library.

This particular room she approached with anticipation. She'd always imagined it—every wall filled, floor to ceiling, with books of every kind, on every subject. Reggie smiled when she thought of the research she'd have to do to find the right kind of ladder system to provide the best access to the shelves. She had a million ideas and couldn't wait to start hunting down the endless number of old books she'd need to do the room justice. Good thing the new owner was a writer. Reggie had good reason to think Pat Somers would appreciate a room overflowing with books.

The hallway still smelled of neglect. She wrinkled her nose at the odor and shivered in the dampness. Hesitating in front of the library doors, Reggie was filled with an unexpected reluctance she couldn't quite explain.

Disquieted, she had to force her frozen hands to turn the door knobs. Stubbornly, the doors stuck. She used a hip and, with an unladylike grunt, shook them free. Propelled into the room, Reggie stumbled and regretted the decision to force her way inside. What greeted her was unexpected.

Work hadn't begun here yet. She grimaced. The air inside the library was more than stale, it was rancid...aggressively so. It assaulted her senses, disorientating her. Reluctant to breathe the foul smell, she put a hand over her nose and mouth. The thought of filling her lungs with something so putrid was repugnant. But in the end she had no choice. She took a breath and gagged.

Her stomach dropped as something vital inside her drained away, leaving behind a sucking void. It was as if the disgusting air she'd been forced to breathe into her body had chased away all the hope she possessed and left behind a gaping despair. She wanted to crumple to the floor and weep.

The room was very, very wrong. Unnatural? She didn't bother to look around more. She knew she had to get out. Turning on unsteady legs she faced the open and mocking doors. With a burst of speed she rushed out of the library and into the hallway. A sour gust slammed the offending doors shut behind her. She didn't bother to investigate the source. Gasping for untainted air, Reggie sought refuge.

Chapter 3

Chase found her in the kitchen. She reached out to him, and almost before she could register movement, he was by her side. His embrace brought the warmth back to her frozen limbs.

Why was his body so warm when his words could be so cold? Reggie wondered as she rested her head on his shoulder. He could certainly move fast when the situation warranted it. Would it always feel so right in his arms? Perversely, she pulled away from him and stood on her own.

"I'm fine." She ran her hands through her artistically messy, short hair and shook her head. "That's just nasty. There's something really wrong in that room."

"What room?"

"The library. It's sickening, cold, damp…and the smell…whew, it's hard to put words to it except to say that it smells like death in there. Something sucked at me. You know when you haven't eaten anything and your stomach growls?" She didn't wait for him to answer. "Well, my soul felt empty the same way. Only your soul doesn't growl, it whimpers. If I were the dramatic sort, I'd tell you I was lucky to make it out alive." Missing his warmth, she wrapped her arms around herself and rubbed her hands up and down.

"You? Dramatic? Never," he said with sarcasm and pulled her back into his arms.

She struggled for a minute, but he felt so good that she gave up and let his warmth seep into her. Reggie rested there until her nerves got the better of her and she needed to talk or to eat. At that particular moment, with Chase's strong arms around her, she decided food was the more prudent remedy.

"I'm hungry."

"Of course you are," Chase said with a gentle smile. "Come on, I'll share my lunch with you."

Part of her wanted to refuse. It was safer to stay away from him, but as usual, her appetite outweighed her caution. Together, they walked out of the kitchen.

Summer was over, but obviously, the sun hadn't received the memo, because it was a deliciously warm day. Autumn was Reggie's favorite time of the year. When September came around, she'd never wanted to be anywhere but New England. The leaves had just begun to turn color, and the nights held an exhilarating chill that made her heart beat faster. In fact, Reggie reveled in her senses in the fall. The fragrance in the air promised a bountiful harvest. With a palette of colors that could never be reproduced, nature painted her world. Fallen leaves made music as they danced in the breeze. The earth felt moist and rich and mysterious, its gifts sustained and added flavor to all life. Yes, it was good to be home.

Chase, carrying a large bag, two bottles of water, and a carton of milk, joined her in the garden. Her stomach growled as he placed fruit, sandwiches, cut veggies, and cookies before her. They sat on a stone bench that had withstood the test of time and, like the house itself, was just as solid as it had been in the 1700s. Straddling the bench, they faced each other. Chase smoothed a napkin down between them and unwrapped the feast.

Laughing at the huge spread, Reggie said, "You must have known I was coming."

"I eat too, you know."

He looked so cute sitting there, all six feet seven inches of him, munching on p. b. and j, and drinking milk as the cowlick at the back of his head bobbed in the breeze. She half expected him to sport a milk mustache when he put the carton down.

He raised his eyebrows, but said nothing when her hand went straight to the cookies. She paused and gave him her best don't-you-dare look. Reluctantly, she offered him one. With an indulgent smile, he shook his head.

After biting into an apple, he chewed, swallowed, and said, "You looked pretty shaken in the kitchen."

She shuddered. "Don't remind me."

"That bad, huh?" At her nod, he continued. "I'll talk to the contractor and have him clean it up."

"Don't bother, I can do that. I have to talk to him anyway. I see Duncan's company's doing the work on the house."

He nodded and waited for her to continue talking. She didn't disappoint him.

"I'm afraid it might take more than a few of Duncan's men to clear out what's in that room." Between bites, she explained her experience in the library and summed it up by adding, "That room is wrong, on a level we can't even comprehend right now. It's messed up. There's something mad and unnatural in there."

Chase narrowed his eyes and paused before saying, "I believe you. I'll check it out myself after lunch."

Her stomach dropped, and she regretted taking such a big drink of water as her throat clenched. She didn't want him to go near that room, but she didn't know what to say to stop him. She'd sound so stupid, and knowing Chase, he'd surely ignore her concerns.

Inspiration hit. She said, "I'll go with you."

Bless him. He walked right into her trap. "No, you won't."

She almost began to enjoy herself. "Oh, yes I will."

"No, you won't." His voice was firmer this time, and he ignored her provocative smile.

"Oh yeah? If you're going in there, then so am I."

"Reggie, you're not going into that room again." Chase's jaw clenched revealing an agitation that only spurred her on. Excitement flickered in her eyes.

Standing inches from him, and just for the hell of it, she challenged him.

"You can't stop me, so accept it."

"No." He stood.

With her heart racing, she did the same.

"And how in hot and humid hell are you going to stop me?"

The tension between them was a writhing, tacile thing as they faced off. She knew he was just as keyed up as she was. She could see it coming and did nothing to prevent it. Damn it, she wanted it.

He took her by the shoulders. At the same time he pressed her body to his, he took her lips. He wasn't gentle, and Reggie was glad because that was the last thing she wanted. She returned his passion, kiss for kiss. His mouth made love to hers, his tongue, teasing, demanding, exciting, all in one. He even used his teeth. It was glorious. Lost in each other, he was hot and hard and more than ready. Reggie wanted him to sink into her right there in the garden in broad daylight.

A low whistle permeated their sensual haze, and they pulled apart just far enough to peer into each other's dazed eyes. They ignored the whoops and cheers of the amused workers around them and stared at each other.

Without taking his eyes from hers, Chase told their enthusiastic audience to get back to work. After a few more taunts, they moved off. Still, he held Reggie.

Her heart broke just a little when he shook his head as if clearing his mind of something unwanted. When he looked at her again, he'd reverted to the Chase she'd always known, the damnable frustrating one. He backed away from her in embarrassment. She saw the apology in his eyes and before he could say anything she said, "If you apologize, I swear, I will find something really heavy and hit you with it...twice...and just for the hell of it, I'd hit you again. Trust me. I'd go for the triple." She poked his chest with a finger.

He raised his eyebrows and smiled. "What would you have me do then, Reggie?"

"I don't know. Admit that it felt good maybe?"

He looked down at his still-aroused body. "I would have thought that was obvious."

She gave him a little smile. "Good."

His laugh was filled with self deprecation. "For you maybe. But I've got to face my guys like this."

Their shared laughter broke the tension, and they sat down on the bench again.

He avoided her eyes when he said, "I should explain myself."

Amusement gone, she tilted her head and challenged him. "Do you want to?"

"Honestly? No." He held up a hand and prepared to continue.

She didn't want to hear it and ignored his gesture. His grudging desire for her wasn't something Reggie felt up to discussing. She interrupted him and changed the subject before he could say anything that would smart.

"What I felt in the library sure proves I'm back in New Crescent with a vengeance."

"Yeah." he nodded and swept out his arm. "Alas, people, I give you our hometown, the source of all things strange. I still don't want you going into the library again."

"And I still don't want *you* to go there without me."

He nodded with defeat. "How about a compromise?"

When she looked at him, she narrowed her eyes, and he chuckled. "No tricks, I swear. I'll get Duncan's guys to clean it out and we'll go in together when they're done. Deal?" He held out his hand to her. She hesitated a second then placed her palm firmly against his, and they shook on it.

For a split second, she saw her hand and his joining and becoming one. She thought she'd been hallucinating until she looked up and realized that he'd seen it too.

With a frown, he said, "I'll get right on that."

Rubbing his other hand against the back of his neck, he gave his head a shake and walked away.

Alone, sitting on the bench, Reggie looked around. Left to grow wild, the garden still held an undeniable beauty. She closed her eyes and turned her face to the sun. A feeling of homecoming wafted over her—the antithesis of what she'd felt in the library.

Tearing her face away from the sun, Reggie looked over the vast gardens. Chase had his work cut out for him. They seemed to go on forever reaching out to the rocky shore. Catching a brief flicker of movement in her peripheral vision, Reggie turned her head with a quick snap. Was she imagining things now? She could have sworn she'd seen the graceful movements of a woman out the corner of her eye, but now there was nothing. Where had she gone? Around the corner of the house?

"Enough of this." Irritation tinged her voice when she spoke aloud.

Reggie acted. Kicking off her inconvenient shoes, she sped off after the woman. Careening around the corner of the house, she was brought to a sudden stop by a solid wall that was Chase's broad back. She bounced off him with a grunt Facing the opposite direction, he hadn't seen her coming but his quick reflexes enabled him to catch her just before she crashed to the ground.

Frustrated to have her pursuit thwarted, she looked up at him without apology or gratitude. "Did you see her?"

Gripping her arms, Chase frowned and shook his head. The three men he had been talking to lumbered off, leaving them alone.

"A woman. There was a woman. I saw her!"

"I didn't."

Angry, she rolled her eyes at him and just barely managed not to stamp her foot in frustration.

"It was probably something blowing in the breeze," he said.

Reggie frowned for a moment. "Puhhh. That wasn't what I saw."

His touch spread that special warmth she couldn't ignore. "Let me go." She shook his hands off. "I'm fine. I know who I need to talk to."

Effectively dismissing him, she walked away and moved toward the driveway. Urgency gripped her as she started the car.

She wasn't crazy. She'd seen a woman vanish into thin air and of course there was the library. What was it in there that had made her feel so hopeless? Just remembering it made her flinch. The library had stood untouched for over one hundred years. Was that what made it feel so different? She shook her head. No way. There was more to it than that. There had to be. Standing in that room, Reggie had never felt so empty. Something had sucked at her spirit and she intended to find out what.

* * * *

Mmm…the woman. She'd been so lush, ripe, filled to the brim. What a revelation. She had plenty. Ah, it would be sweet to use her up, leave her spent...wasted. It wouldn't be long now. He was getting stronger every day. She'd be back, and he'd take more. When the other realized what was happening, it would be too late.

Chapter 4

Sprawled in the yellow chair in her friend's living room, Reggie told Gillian Watson about the strange phenomenon she'd experienced. She left out the part about the kiss. She wanted to hang on to that for a while. It hit too close to home. Still shoeless, she used one bare foot to stroke Gillian's uncanny dog, Hank.

Gillian looked at her friend and smiled. "You felt nothing unusual when you were sharing Chase's lunch?"

Reggie avoided her eyes. "Nothing during lunch." She wasn't ready to share yet, even with Gillian.

"Come to think of it, it's not so surprising." Gillian nodded her head, speculating. "You've always been deeply connected to that house, and it's coming alive at last. It's stirred up, I'll bet. There's a lot of history there, you're New Crescent born, and so is Chase. Maybe your connection to the place is so strong that you've drawn him in with you." Gillian raised a hand to fend off Reggie's vehement reaction. "Actually, that makes more sense than you'd think. Chase is a landscaper. He works with the earth, gets his hands dirty. He's been there for weeks. He's already connected, whether you like it or not."

Reggie counted the butterflies in her stomach, and for a moment, considered naming each one. She figured, since they were going to be spending a lot of time together, they may as well be on a first-name basis. Hank whined and put his head in her lap. Stroking his head, Reggie remembered he liked to chase butterflies, an uncanny dog indeed.

Gillian smiled at the look on her friend's face and said, "Chocolate?"

Reggie's eyes widened with avarice. "Chocolate is my love-ah."

Gillian laughed and Reggie added. "Sadly, the only lover I have at the moment."

"I baked brownies with nuts and marshmallows. If you weren't so keyed up when you walked in, you would have smelled them. I'll just get you a plate, shall I?" Gillian left the living room.

Unwilling to let her out of her sight, Reggie followed. A little less than patient, she leaned against the counter. She snagged the first brownie Gillian put on the plate and stuffed it in her mouth. She rolled her eyes. Bliss.

Sheriff Travis Sinclair burst through the kitchen door. He tended to do that when he was riled up.

He pinned Reggie with a dark look. "What the hell are you thinking?" He was followed by Chase, who pulled up a kitchen chair and calmly straddled it. He handed Reggie her forgotten shoes.

Figures, he'd find the sandals. Damn it, how did he make the simple act of sitting, look so sexy? Reggie shifted uncomfortably. She grabbed another brownie with one hand and used the other to slip her sandals back on.

To Chase, she said, "Stoolie, rat fink."

She turned to Travis with shoulders back and head held high. Coquettishly, she smiled and in perfect Scarlett O'Hara inflection, she said, "Why, Sheriff, you do tend to burst into a room and overwhelm a girl, lordy, my...my...my...I'll get the vapors, I swear I will..." She fanned herself with her hand.

Gillian and Chase laughed.

Travis ignored them. "You're not going near that damn Bennett library alone, do you hear me? My gut tells me there's something stewing up at that place and it's not good."

Reggie wasn't impressed. "Your gut sure is a blabber mouth, and so is your friend here." She wrinkled her nose at Chase and said, "What? Did you rat me out as soon as I pulled out of the driveway?"

"You'd just started the car actually. I told Sam too," Chase said implacably. She couldn't help but smile.

Travis failed to see the humor. "Stop it, both of you. This is no joke. I'm going to call Aunt Ernestine and get her take on all of this."

In a quiet tone that brooked no argument, Chase said, "No, you're not. This is something Reggie and I will handle. If Ernestine's counsel as Guardian is needed, Reggie and I will seek it. I just thought you needed to know, you being Sheriff and all."

Travis, never one to take no for an answer, confronted his buddy. "Not bloody good enough, Chase. You know Reggie has no special abilities, she'd be virtually helpless if things go the way I'm afraid they will."

Gillian cringed at Travis's words. Instinctively, as if trying to cushion the blow, she reached out as Reggie looked down at her hands, shoulders stooped.

Oblivious, Chase faced off with Travis, "Back off, Sheriff. She's never needed Rebecca Goode's gift in order to be powerful. So what? On her fourteenth birthday, she didn't wake with some mysterious gift like everyone hoped...expected even. I was with her today, she did just fine."

Regret showed in Travis's handsome face as he addressed Reggie. "I didn't mean it like it sounded, Reg. I'm sorry. I just don't want anything to happen to you."

With grace, Reggie accepted his apology. "I understand Travis and I appreciate your concern, but you can't stop me from pursuing this thing. If it concerns Bennett House, I couldn't ignore it, even if I wanted to. We're connected."

As if to support her statement, Hank chose that moment to bark. Travis looked at him and scowled.

Gillian walked to the man she loved and stroked his face. "By the way, Travis, honey, I'm with Reggie and Chase."

He looked down at her with love written over every inch of him and sighed. "I know. You didn't have to waste time putting it into words. I got it." He put an arm around Gillian and said to Chase, "Don't let her do anything stupid."

Reggie looked outraged, "Oh, since—"

"I promise, she'll be safe," Chase said, ignoring her. We'll get to the bottom of this."

* * * *

His kiss had been just as she'd remembered it. Why did it have to feel so right to be in his arms? Her body had responded as if it belonged there. Behind the wheel of her car, Reggie couldn't help but take out that other memory from so many years ago and savor it just for a minute.

Aunt Ernestine's annual birthday bash. As a descendant of the founding sisters and the town's Guardian, Ernestine Sinclair commanded a great deal of love and respect. It showed in the elaborate preparations for the event and the feeling of anticipation that permeated the whole town. For the first time ever, Reggie had been reluctant to attend. Another fight with her boyfriend had led to an impasse, and she'd ended the relationship. Still feeling raw, the last thing she wanted to do was make merry, but she loved Ernestine too much to miss her big day. The champagne tasted so good and went down so easily, she started to feel better. Dancing with every young man there, she was the life of the party, until Chase stepped in and soberly claimed her for a slow dance.

"Had enough yet?" he said, his chin grazing the top of her head.

"If you're asking me if I've had enough of you, the answer is yes. If you're asking me if I've had enough fun, I'd have to say not by a long shot."

Tipsy, she tried to pull away from him, but he held her fast. He was quiet for a few moments and Reggie wondered if he'd ever respond. She took a breath and opened her mouth to say something, but he interrupted her.

"For once, Reggie, just shut up and dance with me."

The emotion in his voice took her by surprise, and she tilted her head back to look at him. With a hand on the back of her head, he rested her cheek against his chest. They danced as one. She closed her eyes and enjoyed the sensation. She could feel the muscles in his chest flex and it felt wonderful against her sensitive breasts.

The song ended and another started, but still they clung to each other, ignoring their surroundings. In that moment, the world consisted of Chase and Reggie alone. Slowly, he bent his head and kissed her. There was nothing brotherly about how he took her lips, and she responded without thought. He splayed a large hand on her lower back and pressed her body closer to his. He used the other to cup her face. The close contact made it impossible for him to hide his body's response to her. It thrilled her, and she moved her hips against his. Her thighs trembled. He stopped, dragging his mouth from hers. She made a sound of protest and followed his talented lips wanting more, but he stopped her. Grasping her upper arms, he gave her a little shake.

Reggie looked up at him, mystified. She couldn't interpret what she saw in his eyes. Was it pity, regret? The champagne haze dissolved, and all that was left was cold, harsh reality. She shook her head, much preferring the hazy world to this new, stark one. The one where Chase McCann kissed her then rejected her.

"I think that's enough, Reggie. I'll get Sam to take you home." He backed away and left her standing alone. She wanted to go after him, demand an explanation, but she was rooted to the spot. She hadn't moved an inch when Sam found her, and she made no objections when he drove her home.

Chase had never again shown any inclination to kiss her until a few months ago when both their lives had been threatened. He'd come to rescue her, and she'd been so happy to see him alive that she had launched herself at him. They had kissed each other with relief and with growing passion, or at least that's what Reggie had thought, until the next day when she'd gone to the hospital to see him and found him gone. They still hadn't talked about what had happened.

But just yesterday at Bennett House, he'd kissed her again. And what a kiss! She touched her tongue to her top lip, remembering the taste of him. It was essence of Chase McCann, gourmet cuisine. She closed her eyes and took a deep breath. She was spiraling out of control.

With well-practiced self-discipline, Reggie forced all thoughts of him aside and parked the car close to the front entrance. Her dog, Pru, knew exactly where they were headed and showed her excitement by wagging her tail and looking over her shoulder with doggy impatience.

"I'm going as fast as I can, so calm down, will you?" Reggie's entreaty was ignored as Pru barked at her. Finally, she opened the passenger door. The little dog jettisoned out of the car and ran to her favorite spot. Reggie didn't bother to enter the lobby of the Seniors Residence. Like Pru, she knew exactly where Ernestine Sinclair would be at this time of the morning. She made her way there, but with a little less haste.

When she rounded the last bend in the pathway, she couldn't help but smile. Her little dog lay splayed on the ground, her pink belly exposed as Ernestine made a great fuss over her.

The old lady looked up. She smiled widely, and the lines on her face deepened but somehow that smile made her look younger, immortal. Of course she wasn't, though with power like hers, Reggie wouldn't have been surprised if the old girl did live forever.

Ernestine Sinclair was Guardian of New Crescent. She'd inherited her power from her ancestor Elizabeth Goode. She watched over the people of the town, protecting their secrets from outsiders. Ernestine always knew when trouble was brewing and guided the town to safety. Her advice was followed, her word was respected, and her wisdom was unfailing. Most New England towns had histories filled with tragedy, hurricanes, bigotry, shipwrecks, disease, financial disaster or juicy scandal, but not New Crescent. The Guardians had always protected their little town from such things. Ernestine had been Guardian since her twenties, just after her mother died. Like so many before her, she'd inherited her gift on the morning of her fourteenth birthday. Six a.m. on that fateful day, she had woken feeling different. There had been a potency to the air she'd never felt before. She'd laughed in wonder as Mother Nature's intentions became clear to her and she knew that one day she'd be a Guardian of New Crescent. As she grew up she'd accepted her awesome responsibility. There was potential for good and evil in the town's future. Ernestine had a duty to steer it in the right direction, and at the tender age of fourteen, she'd embraced the awesome responsibility of safeguarding the fate of the town and its citizens. For years, Ernestine had prepared herself for what was to come. The old lady knew what Reggie needed from her.

For Ernestine, as for all Guardians, free will was sacrosanct and as such she'd learned not to influence others too directly. She'd tried to let events play out naturally without interference.

As the last female child in Rebecca Goode's direct line, much had been expected of Regina Stanton. The Old Families had anxiously awaited her fourteenth birthday. She'd received many gifts, but not the most desired of all. Everyone tried not to let her see it, but the tension in the town grew to mammoth proportions in the days leading up to the fateful birthday. At last they'd heard the sad news. She'd been passed over. Their collective disappointment had been palpable. Young Reggie had felt like she'd failed all those she cared about, and she'd carried that guilt around with her every day since.

Ernestine wisely understood that in an effort to lighten her burden, Reggie used humor as a defense mechanism. She didn't even bother to try and make lemonade out of lemons. Instead, she made orange juice. Reggie decided that since she'd never have supernatural abilities, she'd make sure no one could fault her *natural* abilities. No one worked harder than Reggie. And no one cared more about New Crescent or knew more about what made the town tick than Reggie did. Even the ladies of the New Crescent Historical Society or those who ran the Wicca Museum on Main Street, used her as a source when they sought information about New Crescent. She had the knowledge and dedication, but not the gift.

Sitting on the bench beside Ernestine, Reggie wanted details. She'd never asked for this kind of favor before because she'd never felt it was her place and Ernestine hadn't offered it up, but today, she'd have to insist. She needed information that wasn't recorded, the kind passed down verbally from Guardian to Guardian

Dispensing with small talk, Reggie got right to it. "I know everything there is to know about the history of Bennett House, Aunt Ernestine. Now you have to tell me what's not written down."

The old lady sighed and closed her eyes. When she opened them, there was a light in them that awed Reggie.

"You know I can't interfere don't you?" Reggie nodded and Ernestine continued in a clear but soft voice. "I'm not certain why or how you're connected to Bennett House yet, but you are, so I'll tell you what you need to know at this point in time."

Reggie's thick black eyelashes almost cloaked her eyes as she gave her a narrow look. She knew Ernestine would be cagey. "Quit with the inscrutable, out with it…"

Ernestine took a deep breath then let it out slowly. "Let's start with what you know already." Reggie rolled her eyes but the grand old lady ignored her impatience.

"The first Bennett built the house using money he'd made in the shipping business. Even I can't tell you whether Vincent Bennett made his fortune through fair or foul means. There's always been speculation about it. The one person who could tell us is long dead, almost forgotten." Ernestine smiled and took Reggie's hand. "Constance McCann. Yes, my dear, Chase's ancestor, was one of the Guardians. She married Vincent Bennett against her family's wishes. He was an outsider, and there'd always been rumors about his business dealings and his personal predilections. Even Constance herself could see that he wasn't meant for her. You see, on her fourteenth birthday she'd inherited the gift of precognition. She could see more than the present, see beneath what appeared to be reality. Like me, she could interpret and sometimes influence nature's plan."

Reggie nodded. "By nature's plan, you mean destiny."

"You could call it that."

"But if Constance had that kind of ability, why would she ignore it and marry Vincent? Surely, she could tell if he was a good man or not."

"I'm sure on some level she knew exactly the kind of man he was. But you of all people should know, one's heart doesn't always listen to one's head. Strangely compelling, Vincent Bennett had a reputation for getting what he wanted, and he wanted Constance from the moment he'd laid eyes on her. She was like a fever in his blood." Ernestine shook her head sadly. "Much younger than Vincent, Constance was an innocent in many respects, despite her position as Guardian. She allowed herself to get caught up in Vincent's urgency."

"There's no sign of a marriage ceremony or hand fasting in our record books. They didn't marry here in New Crescent," Reggie said.

"They eloped." Ernestine nodded. "She shocked everyone by running off with him in the middle of the night. They married in Salem. There's an official record of it there, so at least her family knew he'd indeed married her. The Old Families had no choice but to accept what she'd done. Afterward, no one talked of it. She became just Constance Bennett. She turned her back on her gift, rejecting her role as Guardian."

Reggie watched as finches landed on the bench near Ernestine and wondered as nature itself was drawn to the old lady. She paused, enjoying the phenomenon for a second then remembered her mission. "Constance and Vincent had no children."

"The McCann gift was lost to that part of the family. It turned up in a distant cousin who'd made her way to New Crescent unaware of her heritage. That's a whole other story. But, as you know, people with unusual abilities are drawn to this place."

"Like Gillian."

The old lady nodded, and the sun reflected off her silver hair. "Yes, just like Gillian."

"So Constance Bennett was from one of the Old Families. I noticed a Connie McCann in the records, but she just faded away. There were other gaps and anomalies around the same time so I blamed it on poor record keeping."

Ernestine shook her head. "Constance Bennett pulled away from her family, the town, and everything that means so much to a Guardian."

"As I recall, there's no record of her death, so the cause was never noted. Anything could have happened to her." She looked at Ernestine hopefully.

"I'm sure you'll find what you need to know dear. Vincent Bennett died of syphilis years after his wife's death." Effectively closing the subject, Ernestine grabbed her walking stick. "I'm glad you're home. I missed you."

Reggie knew she'd get nothing more from her. Secretly, she congratulated herself on anticipating this turn of events. Chase promised to check the archives while she pumped Ernestine for information. They were to meet back at Bennett house for lunch and share what information they'd gathered. Her self congratulations were short-lived, however, when she bid Ernestine good-bye. The old girl never missed a thing.

As Reggie turned to leave, Ernestine said, "Tell Chase he needs to open up and relax a little. Enjoy your lunch. He's sticking with the peanut butter, but he's got Belgian chocolates for you this time."

Reggie called out to the old woman as she and Pru walked away, "You're a witch, Ernestine Sinclair." Still walking, she turned and smiled at the old woman. "An absolute witch…the very best kind."

Ernestine's laughter was carried on the breeze and out to sea.

With a little time to spare, Reggie swung by her office and signed the contract Pat Somers's agent had sent over. The terms were generous, and Reggie was excited by the challenge ahead of her. Bennett House would finally fulfill the potential she'd always seen in it. She'd get to the bottom of the strange energy or impulses that echoed throughout the place. If she had to accept help from Chase to do it, then so be it. They were supposed to be friends, there was no reason he couldn't be of some assistance. He was a permanent fixture in her life. She had to get used to dealing with him and her feelings for him. No time like the present.

Chase was there in the garden waiting for her. At first, he appeared unaware of her presence. Stretched out on the bench, with his long legs crossed at the ankles and his arms resting along the back, he had his face turned up to the sun. Reggie paused to admire the sight. It shocked her to realize that for once, she wasn't hungry for food. She hungered for him. He was a month's worth of comfort food to a starving woman. And just for a moment, Reggie feasted.

The sound of his amused voice startled her when, without even opening his eyes, he said, "Are you going to stand there all day, Reggie?"

Embarrassed, she walked toward him and started babbling. "You're making progress with the gardens, I see. I never realized they were so extensive. The path to the beach is terribly overgrown. I guess the lion's share of the work will have to be done in the spring, but there's no time like the present to prepare. Ernestine thinks you need to relax more." She was distracted by an iron gate that looked perfect in the garden. She smiled. "I never noticed that little gate before. It's charming. Was that always here or did you find it somewhere else?"

Chase tilted his head and said, "Yes." When she looked confused, he added, "I found the gate here on the property and restored it myself."

Reggie sat on the bench beside him. He'd set their lunch on a napkin between them. Of course, Ernestine had been right. He'd brought her Belgian chocolate. She met his smile with her own when he placed the package in front of her.

She breathed deeply and could swear she'd caught his scent much like a female animal does when seeking out her mate. It was a heady experience, and instead of trying to shake it off, she welcomed it, gave herself over to it. Once she'd stopped fighting the temptation, more sensations washed over her. She could feel his heart pound in his chest, and her breath caught as her own heart beat in rhythm with his. When their eyes locked, she could see the desire in his and wondered if he saw the same in hers.

"Will you two kiss already?"

The words were filled with petulance. Reggie snapped her head around to see who spoke to them so sharply.

There was no one there.

Chapter 5

"Did you hear that?" Reggie asked Chase.

"Uh huh," he said, while turning his head and searching for the source of the impatient voice.

Reggie sighed. "Good, because I thought it was just me."

In unspoken agreement, they sat motionless listening intently. No one was there. They were alone in the garden. Finally, Chase stood up and began to look around. "Is someone there?" He called out with impatience. They were greeted with an odd sort of suspended silence. No birds chirped. No leaves rustled in the breeze. They exchanged a look of confusion.

"Do you feel that?" Reggie asked him.

"If you mean do I feel the bloody air thicken, then, yes, I damn well do. If I didn't know better, I'd swear we were underwater, but I can still hear you."

"Me too. I can hear you speak, but everything else sounds muffled."

Chase continued to look around. In a loud voice, he said, "Okay, you've got our attention. Stop playing games."

There was no response, and Chase shrugged. "You try."

Taking a deep breath and relishing the subtle rush the altered air induced, she said, "Is there someone here? Please, do something. Give us a sign." She treated Chase to her best it's-worth-a-try look.

"Is that the best you can do?" the voice said. Chase nodded to her indicating that he heard the voice, too. "No wonder it took me so long to connect. You lack imagination."

The voice hit a sore spot. Now Reggie was irritated too. "And just who are you to judge? You don't even exist. In fact, maybe my imagination is so vivid I made you up. How's that for creativity?"

She heard the soft chime of feminine laughter as a misty shape appeared. "Do you see that?" Reggie asked under her breath, indicating a spot with a tip of her head and a meaningful look.

Bemused, Chase shook his head. "I don't know what you're talking about, I see nothing unusual. I heard laughter though."

Reggie pointed to the garden gate Chase had restored. "You mean you don't see the woman standing by the gate?"

Frowning, Chase said, "No."

With a long, suffering sigh, Reggie cocked a hip and slapped her hands to her waist. "Well that's just great! Now I see dead people."

The otherworldly laughter continued.

Chase said, "That's good, Reg. Whoever she is, she's in a good mood."

Reggie rolled her eyes. "Sure, everything's fine until the laughter turns maniacal."

When she looked back at the gate, the misty woman was gone. They could hear the birds sing again and the breeze played with Chase's cowlick.

Stunned, she sat down on the bench and put a hand to her forehead. She popped a chocolate into her mouth. She bit down and was momentarily distracted. "Mmmm, chocolaty goodness."

Chase stayed silent and watched her for a full minute. Then he asked, "Was that anything like what you felt in the library?"

Reggie shook her head with feeling. "Nothing whatsoever. This feels exciting…exhilarating even. No, the library made me feel hopeless. It sucked something from me. Here, this thing seemed to fill me up. This was giving, despite the obvious irritation in the voice." She laughed self-consciously.

"It's gone now, isn't it?"

"Yeah, I feel completely normal. I'm starving, but completely normal."

He laughed. "Starving is normal for you."

She nodded and popped another chocolate in her mouth.

By silent agreement, they turned to a safer subject. Neither seemed ready to discuss the specter's demand that they kiss each other.

"Ernestine was helpful up to a point." Reggie proceeded to tell him what the sly old lady had to say.

He nodded. "My research backs up her story. Constance McCann just fades from the history books."

"It was worth a try. I had hoped that fresh eyes might find something I missed. Is there any record of how she died?"

"No real information. The household accounts show the purchase of a coffin at the time. It could have been for her, but it's hard to tell. If I've interpreted it correctly, a female servant went missing that year as well. I'm going to go over some of the journals from that period, see if anyone mentions Constance's death."

Reggie nodded as she grabbed half of his sandwich. After taking a bite, chewing and swallowing, she said, "Let me know if you need help with that. I've read them all, but that was some time ago and I wasn't looking for anything specific."

"How 'bout we meet here at eight o'clock tonight? Some furniture was delivered this morning. We can use it to make ourselves comfortable while we search."

She looked at him with surprise. "You can get your hands on the journals? The ladies at the Historical Society don't let that stuff out of their sights. How'd you manage it?"

Leaning over her, he invaded her space and said, "I can be very persuasive." He kissed the top of her head and moved away. "See you tonight. And remember, don't go near the library."

Speechless, she sat back on the bench and watched him go.

* * * *

The main floor of the house was humming with activity, and she smiled when she saw how the place was shaping up. The owner, Pat Somers, had selected some pieces of furniture and wanted them incorporated into the interior designs for the house. Reggie crossed her fingers praying that she'd approve of Ms. Somers's choices.

It was a great relief when she saw the beautiful living room furniture. She smiled. Wow, even better than what she'd had in mind for this room. She opened her notebook and jotted down her thoughts on the ideal colors and accessories. She chose some paint chips that might work and made note of the numbers. Larger samples would be painted and delivered so she could better determine what worked best in the space. The design work was going so well so far she didn't want to make a mistake.

When she was done, she moved through the other rooms on the main floor. There was still a lot of work to be done. As she walked, she greeted the workmen she recognized and introduced herself to those she didn't. As for the library, she avoided it, but she could hear a number of male voices coming from that direction and knew that Chase was as good as his word. He'd arranged to have it cleaned out, and by the tone of the voices coming from that part of the house, it wasn't a pleasant job.

In the second-floor master bedroom, Reggie was delighted by the huge bed she found there. It, too, was perfect, maybe even better than perfect because she suspected it had been custom made. It was larger than any bed she'd ever seen and inspired all kinds of ideas for the room. With determination she pushed aside all carnal thoughts the bed had conjured.

The sound of men yelling had Reggie rushing to one of the windows to see what had happened. A group of men stood over a prone young man. Chase was pushing aside a fallen ladder in order to get to his man. Discarded tree branches littered the ground. The poor man must have fallen off the ladder he'd been using. She opened the window and called out to Chase.

"Is he all right?"

Shielding his eyes from the sun, he squinted up at her. "Yeah, he says he's just shaken up. I'm taking him to the hospital, just in case." He helped the young man to his feet and called up at her. "Eight o'clock tonight. Don't be late or I'll start without you. Stay away from the library." He didn't wait for a response.

As always, Chase had meant what he'd said. When she arrived at Bennett House at five after eight, she found him sitting on one of the new couches in the living room flipping through one of the many journals laid out beside him. It surprised her to note that he wore glasses.

"I see you've made yourself at home, Poindexter."

Without looking up at her, he ignored her jibe. "I see you've finally made it, Crash."

It was a young Chase who'd given her the nickname when she'd run over the garbage cans at school. "Yeah, traffic was hell." Her sarcasm finally made him look up at her. He made room for her at the other end of the couch and put a pile of journals between them. The books didn't provide much of a barrier, but Reggie was glad they were there. The words *sexy nerd* came to mind. Wearing those glasses, Chase looked so appealing that she found it hard not to stare at him. He smelled good, too. Her intense reaction to him made her nervous and that in turn made her hungry. Chase looked up from the journal he was reading and smiled as she fidgeted. She stopped when their eyes met.

"Gillian sent pie," he said with a knowing smile.

She didn't bother to deny it or to ask him how he knew. She looked around the room and found no pie. She frowned.

"It's in the kitchen. I'm brewing coffee."

"I'll bring you a cup." She swept out of the room.

In the kitchen, she cut a modest piece and ate it with her fingers. It was good. Trust Gillian to know just what she'd need. After licking her fingers, she poured two cups of coffee and walked back into the living room. She got down to work.

After two hours, they'd found nothing of significance in the journals. Chase stood up and stretched with feeling. With his arms in the air, his t-shirt rode up and exposed his abdomen to her.

Watching him, Reggie bit down on her cheek. *Calvin Klein called. He wants his underwear model back.* The jury was in, Chase McCann was beautiful. She wondered what it would feel like to run her tongue down all those bumps on his stomach. She fancied a row boat riding the waves on the ocean, up one swell and down the next. Shaking her head, she looked away.

"Do you want more?" he lifted his coffee cup..

She looked at him stunned for a second then found her voice. It was shaky. "No, if I do, I'll never sleep tonight."

"Join me then, while I have another."

He offered her his hand, but she pretended not to notice. She didn't want to touch him for fear she'd come undone.

She followed him. Together, they paused just outside the library. At a constant temperature that was consistently colder than the outdoors, this part of the house was damp and unwelcoming. It felt wrong, like something unnatural, the antithesis of the phenomenon she'd felt in the garden. Reggie stood rooted to the spot as the foul odor wafted around them. Chase looked down at her and nodded. He could feel it, smell it too. She wasn't alone. Despite the warmth Chase's body provided as she stepped closer to him, she felt chilled to the bone. Never had Reggie known such despair. Everything inside her that held optimism or hope was drained from her, and she tasted bile. That was the only warning she got before they were thrown against the library doors with such force they gasped for air. She looked up helplessly at Chase.

With Herculean effort, he breathed the thick, rancid air into his lungs and forced it out again. On the exhale, he grabbed Reggie's arm and yanked her away from the doors. Whatever it was that held her eased up slightly enabling Reggie to push off and stagger to the opposite wall. She leaned heavily against the paneling struggling to catch her breath. Then she started back to help Chase break away.

"No!" he yelled at her, and with one final effort, he tore himself away from the doors, severing its hold on him. With surprising speed, Chase ran from the hallway and swept Reggie with him.

Standing in the living room breathing heavily, he said, "On second thought, maybe I shouldn't have that coffee after all."

They burst out laughing. Laughter was the perfect tonic. When their amusement petered out, they huddled beside each other on the couch. Chase put an arm around her, and she rested her head on his shoulder for a moment.

"What the hell was that? Did you see anything?" he asked.

"No, not this time, and judging by the way that thing made me feel, I'd rather not put a face on it."

"Yeah, I know what you mean. It defies imagination, and call me a creative wasteland if you will, but I kind of like it that way."

"The guys working in the library today didn't seem to feel anything like what we did just now."

He rubbed the back of his neck. "No, but I talked to Duncan. He said that every guy who'd been in that room today complained about one thing or another."

"I think we need to figure out what it is and fast. It was stronger tonight than it was before."

"Reggie, you've always been connected to this place. Before now, have you ever felt uneasy here?"

She shook her head. "No, I've felt nothing but good vibes from this place."

"It's possible that it's been here all along but was too weak to surface. Since the house was sold, there's been a steady stream of people around the place. What if that thing feeds off human energy or something?"

Impressed by his theory, she said, "Creative wasteland my eye. Thank you Stephen King. What you're suggesting fits, but it doesn't help us to figure out what to do about it. If you're right, then it will continue to get stronger. If tonight is any indication of its power, I don't want to think about what it could do at full blast."

"We have to talk to Ernestine and Gillian. As Guardians, they may be able to tell us more."

Reggie sat forward on the couch and glanced over her shoulder at him. She missed his warmth, and the temptation to curl up with him forever was strong, but she resisted.

"Ernestine wasn't much help to me this morning."

As if he knew she was cold without his touch, he rubbed a hand up and down her back. She shivered, but not from the cold.

"She may have felt we needed to confront this thing by ourselves. You know she's like that." She nodded with a sigh, and he continued. "Maybe we should talk to Ernestine and Gillian at the same time. Gillian's new to all of this. She may not be as cautious as Ernestine and let something slip. And while that something might be information we shouldn't have, it could still prove useful."

"You're right. Aunt Ernestine is stubborn and frustrating, but I trust her to help us with this."

"Me, too."

"Do you want to set up this summit or shall I?"

He looked around the room and said, "I'll call Gillian right now, but why don't we step outside and get some fresh air?"

She agreed and he helped her put her sweater on. The autumn air had that chill Reggie loved so much. While Chase talked on his cell, Reggie stared at the iron gate she'd noticed earlier that day. She'd seen the apparition standing there. The mysterious woman by the garden gate had startled Reggie, but she'd felt no fear. If anything, she'd felt excitement. The mystical charm of it had filled her with wonder. It was so different from what she felt whenever she ventured near the library.

When Chase had finished talking to Gillian, he told Reggie that the arrangements were made. They were invited to lunch the next day. Travis offered to barbeque. Gillian would pick up Ernestine.

Nodding, Reggie finally relaxed in the cool night air. "Good." He sat on the bench beside her as she continued. "Chase, did *you* feel any malice in the phenomenon today at lunch?"

He thought about it for so long that Reggie wondered if he'd heard her question. Finally, moving closer to her, he said softly, "No. That thing earlier today, I found it...*exciting*."

When he said the word she felt that very same emotion swell in her chest, and her heart started to pound. He muttered something unintelligible and pulled her into his arms. His kiss defined the word *exciting*.

Chapter 6

Reggie was stunned. He stopped kissing her but she moved not a muscle. Riveted to the bench, she struggled to open her eyes. When she finally succeeded, there was an odd mist around the edges of her vision. She blinked a few times to clear it away, but to no avail. Again, she caught his scent and completely forgot her clouded vision. She didn't care, so carried away was she by the sensuous fragrance and the exquisite feeling of being held safe in Chase's arms.

It was the most natural thing in the world to turn her face to his and welcome the crush of his lips on hers once more. It was a soul-surrendering experience. Magic. He gently teased her mouth with his, playfully drawing her into him inch by slow inch. His lips married hers over and over again and drugged her senses. He touched the tip of his tongue to the center of her top lip and tasted her with obvious pleasure. A soft sound of satisfaction that originated low in his throat escaped and she felt like food for the Gods. With the simplest touch, he made her acutely aware of every inch of her body and her eager response to him. When he pressed his hard body against her, she reveled in her own femininity. As he became more aggressive, she matched him move for move, clutching at his back and shoulders desperate to get closer to him. She wanted to tear at his clothing and her own. Skin against skin was her only goal. She ignored the sensible side of her nature that urged caution. Desire, hunger was all she knew.

The sound of distant, musical laughter brought her to her senses. She snapped her head back just as Chase's eyes flew open. He'd experienced it too—all of it, the spell, the passion, and laughter. He looked at her with confusion, as if surprised to find her there in his arms. Awkwardly, he straightened, stuffed his hands in his pockets, and took a step back. He seemed lost for words. Embarrassed, Reggie pushed off the bench and tried to flee.

Lightning quick, Chase grabbed her wrist. They looked at each other. At long last, he spoke in a very measured tone. "Reggie. Let me explain." He shook his head. "Or rather, I wish I could explain. I don't really know what just happened here, but I stepped way out of line. I'm sorry. It was so strange. I wasn't myself."

She stood staring at him, completely flattened by his words. Yes, it was strange, otherworldly even, but for Reggie it had been magical and here he was apologizing for it. He claimed he wasn't himself, and she understood him perfectly…he wasn't normally tempted to do such a thing with her. He was making lame excuses, tripping all over himself to apologize, to dismiss it. Damn him!

As Chase continued to fumble for the right words, Reggie ceased listening to him. Feeling battered and raw, she pulled away and lashed out.

"Enough McCann! Stop babbling. You act as if I've never been kissed before. Forget it. No big deal. So you haven't had any in a while. I get it. Maybe you should find yourself a regular squeeze and lay off me. Forget it. It was nothing. I'm going home." She pushed past him.

"The hell you are! Is this nothing?" He pulled her into his arms and kissed her fiercely. This time, there was nothing other-worldly about it. In fact, this kiss was as earthy as it gets. He mated with his mouth, and Reggie felt her knees give out for the second time that day. With one hand entangled in her hair and the other around her waist, he pressed her closer and closer to him. Chase tilted his head back and inspected his handiwork. Her eyes were glazed, and her lips were swollen and moist.

"There, that's better," he said with a satisfied smile.

He was gloating! Actually gloating. Reggie wanted to punch him hard, but she knew she didn't have the strength to make a dent, so she drew her dignity around her like a cloak and said, "So you can kiss. I never said you couldn't." Pleased with how unaffected she had managed to sound, she pushed away and walked around him, giving him plenty of room.

He tried to reach for her again, but she put up a hand to forestall him. "I'm going home. I've had enough."

"I'll walk you to your car." When she started to object, he said, "Don't argue with me."

She didn't get a chance to. The crash startled them both. It came from the other side of the house. It sounded like someone was boldly poking around. Chase put a finger to his lips and silently moved around the corner of the house in what Reggie assumed was an attempt to catch the intruder red-handed.

For a split second, Reggie considered staying put, but that thought didn't please her at all, so she crept around the other side. If she played this right, maybe they could trap the guy between them. She was as tall as many men. Surely she could use the element of surprise to gain advantage. For once in her life, she was grateful she'd worn flats. Navigating the grounds would have been impossible in heels. She heard a scuffle, a grunt, and then the sound of running feet. Without thinking, she took off after the fleeing figures. He had a good head start and lost her easily. Defeated, she made her way back to the house. Chase came back shortly after her, empty-handed as well.

He shook his head and gave her a dark look. In her own defense, she said, "I was running, and it occurred to me that I had no idea what I was gonna do if I caught him." She made a theatrical gesture. "Take it away Chase."

Instead of berating her for chasing after the prowler, he laughed. "We've had some petty thefts around here lately. Nothing major. I just thought maybe I'd catch whoever was doing it, but he was too fast for me."

"You're always were a better long distance man than sprinter. I guess some things never change." When their eyes met, she knew without a doubt that he'd picked up the double meaning in her comment. Before he could say anything that would make her uncomfortable, she said. "I was on my way out. Still intent on walking me to my car?"

Without saying a word, he bowed and let her lead the way.

* * * *

"That went well." Chase muttered to himself as he got behind the wheel of his truck. He followed Reggie until she parked her car outside her parents' front door. Instead of turning and waving to him in appreciation for his concern, she pretended he wasn't there. He smiled. She wasn't so unpredictable after all. He was glad she was home.

To Chase, she looked as beautiful as ever. He couldn't remember Regina Stanton looking anything but breathtaking, even at her worst. He'd had to force himself not to stare at her with raw hunger in his eyes. He'd missed her these past months. He couldn't get enough of the sight of her. She defined the word animation. No still photography could ever capture that woman's glory. Just when he thought he'd seen her every expression, he'd glimpse something new and be enchanted all over again. He sighed heavily.

Driving home to his place, he remembered how she'd looked in the garden. Her golden eyes had mesmerized him. He'd longed to drink them in like he would a fine whiskey. She certainly intoxicated like fine spirits, he thought as he pulled up in front of his house.

Chase didn't live on an estate like most of the other Old Families. He owned a garden center and lived in a small bungalow on the property. The money meant nothing to him. The principle, however, had gnawed at him for years. He supposed he should be grateful in a twisted way. By frittering away all of the McCann family money, his stepfather had done him a favor in the long run. Chase knew what a good hard day's work meant, and he was proud of his ability to stand on his own. He'd refused help from Travis and Sam, who'd both offered whatever he needed. He was proud that he did it on his own.

The only thing he'd managed to keep out of creditors' hands was his mother's garden center. When she was still alive, it had been merely a hobby business, an indulgent gift from Chase's father. After her death, Chase had struggled long and hard to make it turn a tidy profit, but he loved the work.

Standing on the step, he opened the mailbox and took out a stack of flyers and trade catalogues. Before entering the house, he ran a hand over the childishly painted mailbox. His stepsister Jade had painted it and everyday when he got the mail, he thought of her. She'd been such a roly-poly little thing when her father married his mother. Chase had fallen in love with her on the spot. She was six years his junior, but they'd adored each other from day one. Her father, Robert Adams, was an abusive son of a bitch who'd gambled away all they had. Adams had charmed his way into Mary McCann's life, but soon after the wedding, his charm wore off, and the emotional abuse started. A fact she'd kept hidden from her son. Jade was helplessly aware of it because he'd been the same to her for her entire life.

After his mother's death, Chase did everything possible to get custody of Jade, but he'd had no legal rights over her biological father. In the end, it was Jade herself who'd made him stop the fight. With a world-weary look in her eyes, she'd told him that she needed to stay with her father. When he started to argue with her, she silenced him, displaying a maturity far beyond her fifteen years.

"It has to be this way Chase."

He could still remember how she'd cried in his arms before saying goodbye.

Distance hadn't severed their bond however. Over the years, they didn't see much of each other, but they'd stayed in touch. Jade would never discuss her father with him, and Chase couldn't touch the man without hurting her, his sister. His hands were tied.

He looked down at the mail in his hand and smiled. *Of course, think of Jade and there she is.* Her fluid handwriting was impossible to miss. She stubbornly insisted on writing letters. She used the phone and e-mail sometimes, but she saved the good stuff for her letters. Chase looked forward to reading this one.

A huge cat wound around his legs almost tripping him, and he frowned.

"Still here huh?" He bent and scooped up the enormous creature. *Damn he was heavy.*

"Well, you may as well spend the night then. Just this once." He'd been saying those exact words to this cat for months now. It just showed up one day and walked in as bold as brass. And it stayed. It wouldn't leave. Utterly comfortable in Chase's home, the cat wouldn't even go outside. Chase installed a cat door in hope of encouraging him to venture out, but to no avail. Yet, everyday when Chase came home, part of him dreaded the thought that the cat might actually be gone. He refused to admit it, though, so he and the cat lived in a sort of suspended commitment to each other.

He saved Jade's letter until he was ready to go to bed. With the cat curled up beside him on the bed, he savored the moment. It was a pleasure to read for enjoyment for a change. He glanced over at the proofs couriered to him that day and refused to feel guilty for not looking at them. He'd had a big day. Didn't Ernestine ask Reggie to tell him to relax? Tonight he planned to take her advice. Jade's letter was the perfect distraction, but when he'd finished and turned out the light, all he could think about was the look on Reggie's face after he'd kissed her. He knew sleep would be very elusive that night.

Chapter 7

"You'd better turn that one over, man." Sam Daniels pointed to a hamburger on the grill.

Travis frowned at him. "What would you know, Trust Fund, you've never cooked a meal your entire life."

"That may be so, but I've eaten many times and to me, charcoal isn't a condiment." Sam took a deep gulp of beer and turned away. Travis looked at Chase for support, but got none when Chase shrugged and stayed silent.

The three men stood on the patio in the backyard. Reggie and Gillian each set huge bowls of cold salads on the table. Ernestine sat at the head of the table with her eyes closed, her face turned up to the autumn sun.

Having agreed to get down to business after they'd eaten, they conversed happily over lunch. Finally, Ernestine pushed her dessert plate away and said, "Gillian, that was delicious as usual."

Travis looked hurt. "Hey, I did the cooking. Don't I deserve some credit?"

Reggie lifted a shoulder and said, "So you burned a couple of hamburgers for us, big deal. But since you insist..." She patted his always disheveled hair. "That'll do, pig."

Gillian laughed. "Oh, *Babe*, I loved that movie! I haven't eaten pork since I saw it. Neither has Hank." She looked down at the big white dog with apology.

"That's one of things I love most about you, Gill, your soft heart." Travis leaned over and planted a kiss on her lips.

Gillian smiled. "It's my extraordinary mind you really love, though." She turned to Reggie "We may as well get this thing started. What's going on up at Bennett house?"

There was no question as to who would do the talking. Reggie explained in detail what she and Chase had experienced. She made no direct reference to the passion ignited between them, but she knew Gillian could read between the lines. Chase acknowledged Reggie's discretion with a small, private smirk. She pretended not to notice.

When she finished, her audience said not a word. All eyes turned to Aunt Ernestine, who sighed deeply.

"Has anyone else working there experienced anything like what the two of you have?" the old lady asked.

Reggie looked to Chase, and he said, "No. There's been an unusual rise in the number of small accidents and fights on site, but there've been no reports of anything like what we felt."

"Okay, that could mean you're the only ones who can feel the energies. Others may be affected by them, but on a much more shallow level. And Reggie, my dear, it's definitely directed at you."

"Since I'm the only one who saw something visual manifest?"

Ernestine nodded.

Reggie raised a fist in the air without enthusiasm and grumbled, "Hurray for me."

Her sarcasm was ignored.

"By the sounds of it," Ernestine said, "the spirit in the garden is Constance McCann. It makes sense that she'd hang around given the mystery surrounding her life and death. She was a Guardian at one time; all that power had to go somewhere. She's chosen you Reggie. Probably did so a very long time ago and that's why you've always felt so connected to the place."

"She's manifesting to me now because she doesn't want Bennett House restored?"

Ernestine shook her head. "I don't think so. She's not angry. She's playful. She's doing this because she can. Constance finally has the power now and doesn't care how she got it. Fool. Reggie, you are going to have to communicate with her and warn her."

"Warn her? Of what exactly?" Chase asked.

"A spirit doesn't just suddenly find power. It's taken from someone or something. If my guess is right, that other entity in the library has something to do with Constance's renewed strength, and she's ignoring it. She always was a bit too selfish and naïve to be an effective Guardian."

"Just how do I communicate with her?" Reggie asked. "The human race has made great strides in technology but I don't think we've cracked the whole, talking to dead people thing just yet."

Gillian said, "I could try. I can do it easily enough with the living, conscious or unconscious. Maybe I could connect with Constance?"

Travis started to object, but Ernestine silenced him with a look. "No. Gillian, you must stay away from that place until Reggie and Chase have dealt with the energy in the library. You and I as Guardians would be an irresistible temptation to the entity. I'm too old, and your power is too new. No. This is Reggie's destiny."

Travis looked at Chase and Sam in silent agreement. He said, "That settles it then. The three of *us* will help Reggie."

"No." Ernestine shook her head earnestly. "Chase alone can help her. He is Constance's descendant, and as such, he's connected to Bennett House too. Anyone else runs the risk of becoming food for that entity. Chase has already faced it and broken free. That gives him a slight upper hand. We can't risk anyone else."

Sam said, "Since no one else is going to ask the question, I will. So what's the Big Bad in the library?"

Reggie answered with certainty. "Vincent Bennett, Constance's husband."

"You're right, Regina." Ernestine took a sip of her coffee. "It can only be him. I've long suspected he used some pretty powerful dark magic to win Constance. Even she wouldn't have married him without some sort of unnatural manipulation."

Chase asked, "Do you think she has any idea of what Vincent's up to?"

"On some level, she does, but she doesn't want to deal with it. She's probably too blinded by the recent infusion of power to think straight. It's up to you, Reggie. You'll have to snap her out of it."

"And just how do you suggest I do that, oh great swami?" Reggie bowed.

"Insolence doesn't help, dear, but since you seem to need to make silly jokes, I'll overlook it this time." She patted Reggie's hand. The rest of them had to resist the urge to laugh. Ernestine continued. "I can't tell you how. You'll know or she could never have appeared to you in the first place."

"No disrespect, Aunt Ernestine, but that's not good enough. You have to tell us more." Sam said.

"I can't answer all your questions." She nodded her head at Gillian. "And neither can Gillian. Regina, my girl, I suggest that you connect with Constance as soon as possible. Leave the library alone. The time will come when you will have to face that evil, but for now, don't let anyone go near it." Then the grand old lady dropped the bomb. "Reggie, you should move into Bennett House for the time being."

"Are you crazy?"

"Hell no!"

"Over my dead body!"

Chase, Travis and Sam all answered at the same time. Reggie and Gillian couldn't help giggling as the old woman put the three of them in their place. When she was done, they looked like three very unhappy chastised little boys, and she continued uninterrupted.

"Reggie, you were right to seek advice. I know I haven't told you much, but trust me, it's best you act on your own instincts without any more interference from me or Gillian. This thing is powerful, and if it's not handled right, it could spell disaster. One that could send shock waves farther than any of us can imagine. Reggie, you have the strength. Trust yourself. I believe in you."

Ernestine smiled gently. "Sam, You may take me home now." He opened his mouth to object, but thought better of it when Ernestine arched an eyebrow.

After they'd left, Chase pinned Reggie with a blue-eyed stare. "If you're moving in, then so am I."

"Yeah, good luck with that," Reggie said casually.

"Luck has nothing to do with it."

She narrowed her eyes at him and affected a bored sigh. "Ernestine seems to think it's *the* thing to do, moving into a haunted house. All the kids are doing it."

"Not funny, Reg," said Travis. "I'm with Chase. Since he's the only one Ernestine thinks can help you, then you're stuck with him. It's either Chase or all of us and Ernestine can go to hell." He was deadly serious.

Serenely, Gillian said, "Chase is right, Reggie."

The next day, Reggie moved into Bennett House. *Not quite a dream come true,* Reggie mused. Chase had helped her bring her stuff upstairs to the master bedroom. It was positively painful to act naturally around him with that huge bed standing between them. She cursed her vivid imagination and refused to look him in the eye.

Nervous, she filled the room with chatter.

"I called Pat Somers's agent, and she said it was fine that I stay here. She knew about the thefts and vandalism. I guess Duncan told her. I said nothing about you staying too. You'll have to do that yourself. That's not my responsibility." She stopped talking for a second and smoothed a sheet over the bed. He grabbed the other end of it and tucked it in. It was a very domestic little scene, and it disturbed her more than she cared to acknowledge. He hadn't told her where he intended to sleep, and she was afraid to ask.

Instead, she stated, "I feel like chips," and walked out of the room and down the stairs. She had to get away. Chase's proximity was starting to erode her self discipline. He didn't speak much, so she couldn't take umbrage with anything he said. The tension was palpable. Reggie's hold on her temper was slipping, and his presence was unsettling. She couldn't stop remembering what it felt like to be kissed by him, and in a few hours, they'd be spending the night together. She was becoming a nervous wreck. Soon she'd weigh two hundred and fifty pounds if she didn't find something other than food to alleviate her stress.

After grabbing a bag of potato chips from the kitchen, she rushed outside to the garden. She was glad she'd thought to bring groceries. At this rate, she'd be forced to replenish her supplies on a daily basis. She'd frowned when she noted that Chase had brought supplies of his own. It all felt a little too domestic.

The work on the house and grounds was moving right along despite her distraction. Desperately, she clung to her work, trying to take her mind off Chase. She'd selected most of the interior paint colors and looked forward to seeing the final samples. So far, all of her plans had been approved without question. Part of her wondered if the owner ever really saw any of her ideas, but she refused to look a gift horse in the mouth. This was her opportunity to do what she'd always dreamed of doing, and in its way, it was very rewarding.

"Why are you running away from him?" the voice asked, startling her.

Without realizing she'd done it, in her agitation, Reggie had sought out the section of the garden with the iron gate. To top it off, she had pathetic timing. Unprepared to face the apparition, Reggie responded instinctively.

"I have to run away from him or I'll do something stupid," she said under her breath.

"Coward."

"What would you know about it?" Irritated, her temper got the better of her. "You're not even here. Find the light already and head toward it."

The spirit laughed lightly. Reggie could see Constance McCann plain as day, but she could also see the gate through her, a perfect reminder that this wasn't going to be a normal conversation.

"Constance?"

The woman continued to laugh. "So you finally know." She danced around the little gate with grace.

"What are you doing here Constance? Why me?"

She continued to laugh at Reggie's sober expression. "I'm here because I'm here, but I have no idea why it has to be you. So far, you're the only one who can see me. Trust me, I've tried to appear to some of those very handsome workmen over there, but they have no more imagination than a tree stump."

"Don't you wonder why you're here, at this particular point in time?"

"Time doesn't matter. You're too concerned about the things that don't matter, and you ignore the things that do." The woman, almost singing the words, refused to grasp what Reggie was trying to say. "I'd much rather talk about that very impressive man I see you with so often."

"Chase McCann. He's your distant relative, so you might want to keep that in mind before you say anything you'll regret later."

"Thanks for the advice." Constance stopped moving and frowned. "Why do you resist your feelings for this man?"

"That's none of your business."

Constance smiled. "You're wrong Regina Stanton. Unfortunately, everything about you is my business."

Confused, Reggie said, "What's that supposed to mean?"

"Just that I know all about you and I find you boring."

Reggie was insulted. "Oh, easy for you to be all interesting, what with the being dead thing."

"I was interesting in life too, my dear."

Her comment brought Reggie to her senses, pushing her irritation aside, she asked, "Will you tell me about your life? What made you marry Vincent Bennett?"

The apparition shook her head then appeared still and awkward for the first time. She put her hands to her ears. In a strident voice, she said, "No! I won't listen to you…no!"

She vanished.

Constance stubbornly refused to reappear, despite Reggie's pleas. Reggie chided herself for blowing it. Her own issues had distracted her, and she'd learned nothing from the spirit except that she was indeed Constance McCann. She definitely wasn't prepared to talk about Vincent, but Reggie knew that at their next encounter, she'd have to insist.

"Reggie?" Standing about ten feet away, Chase looked concerned. "Are you okay?"

Nemesis in the flesh, but such tempting flesh, she thought. She took a moment before she answered him. He moved and didn't stop until he stood directly in front of her. Before he could reach out a hand to touch her, Reggie sat down heavily.

"I just had a conversation with Constance."

The excitement in his eyes was unmistakable. "What happened?"

Reggie provided him with an edited version of the experience, careful to leave out any embarrassing bits about him.

When she was done, he said, "So she said she knows all about you. Did she give any indication of how?"

Guilty, she said, "No, I was so unprepared I didn't think to ask. Damn it! How stupid of me!"

He smiled and tried to reassure her, "Don't berate yourself. Conversations with dead people can rattle a person."

"I just want to get this show on the road. The suspense is killing me. It gives me the creeps to know that the Big Bad is in the library, not so far away."

He nodded, "Who can blame you? Rest assured, if it takes to wandering in the night it'll come for me first. I'm going to bed down on one of those couches in the living room tonight. I'll be closer. I don't suppose you'd take pity on a fella and offer to share that big bed upstairs?"

Uncharacteristically lost for words, Regina stood and walked away from him. It was her only defense.

Chapter 8

Work on Bennett House sped along despite a number of minor accidents and the odd disagreement. Reggie had made great strides decorating the upper levels of the house. She'd decided that the main level had to wait a little longer because they still hadn't found a way to safely confront the entity in the library. Living in the same house as Chase had turned out to be much easier than she'd thought. For the most part they stayed out of each other's way. He slept downstairs; she slept upstairs. Once the sun went down, Reggie saw very little of him.

"He's the anti-vampire." She rolled her eyes at her own lame attempt at humor. She was walking through the garden hoping to catch a glimpse of Constance. Lately, Reggie had been singularly unsuccessful in her attempt to contact her. With virtually no direction, Reggie didn't know what to do. Every day, she walked in the gardens trying to spy something that might indicate Constance was still lurking about.

"Vampire? Who is?" Blushing, she turned to see the contractor, Duncan Taggert, smiling at her.

She laughed. "You don't want to know."

He shrugged. "Probably not. I just came back here to tell you that the paint you ordered has arrived. Did you want to check it before signing the invoice?"

Reggie walked with him to the front of the house where she double checked the paint delivery. She'd always liked Duncan. She'd even dated him a few times, but he was more taken with her than she was with him, so they'd settled for friendship. It was nice to be in his undemanding company. There was no tension between them, and Reggie was able to relax. He was a great contractor. It was amusing to see his reactions to her more creative ideas, but in the end, they'd both been happy with the results of their collaboration. She signed the invoice and handed it to Duncan.

"How's Tom?" she asked, referring to one of his men who'd cut himself the day before.

Duncan smiled. "He's going to be fine. The emergency room was packed, but in the end, I think he kinda liked the pain killers the doctor gave him after stitching him up. He'll be back in no time."

They walked together through the house and noted the progress made in each room.

"Duncan, have you had more accidents on this job than on others? I know Chase has had problems with his crew. It seems that just about every day someone either gets hurt or starts a fight."

He nodded and paused with her in the doorway to the master bedroom, "Yeah, there have been some pretty near misses too. I've done big jobs like this before where I've had twice as many men and had half the problems. I'm glad it won't be too much longer before we'll be done. I'm starting to run out of men."

She nodded. Leaning against the doorjamb, she rested her hands on the framing behind her. Duncan looked down at her with a smile that told her he was still interested if she was, but she'd have to make the first move. She didn't.

"You've had some materials stolen, too. I haven't heard anything since I've been spending nights here. Have the thefts stopped?"

He hesitated a second before he answered. "Yeah, if memory serves me right, we haven't had a theft since you moved in. Maybe you should go into the security business."

She laughed. "I have a job already and another one in the wings. Thanks."

They were smiling at each other when Chase found them. With a frown, he said, "You're needed outside, some delivery."

Reggie straightened and started to move with Duncan. Chase stalled her. "I was talking to Duncan."

Taking the grand staircase, Duncan looked back at Reggie and shrugged innocently.

While working in the house, Reggie never wore heels, so Chase towered over her. She wasn't accustomed to feeling small. But he managed to make an astonishing success of it. The thought irritated her, and she didn't bother trying to keep it out of her voice when she said, "That was rude."

He ignored her and walked into the master bedroom. Reggie refused to follow. The sight of him so close to that massive bed ratcheted the tension up another notch. One more turn and she feared she'd spin off into the stratosphere.

"Have you tried to connect with Constance today?" he asked.

"Yes, as a matter of fact I have. I was doing just that when Duncan came. He found me in the garden and told me about the paint delivery."

"And you ended up in the doorway to your bedroom. That makes perfect sense."

His harsh tone failed to anger her. Instead, it exhilarated her, and she almost thanked him for it. She'd needed an outlet for her tension. She was ready for a fight, and he'd just given her the perfect opportunity to let it rip.

"I don't know what the hell you're trying to get at, but my relationship with Duncan is no one's business, least of all yours."

He raised his eyebrows. "Relationship?"

She walked into the bedroom and stood in front of him. She wanted to hit him, make contact, anything to crack his calm.

She settled on sarcasm, a rash decision. "You caught us, Chase. A second later and you would have caught us grabbing a quickie." With theatrical exaggeration, she sighed. "Mmm, Duncan is insatiable. He can't get enough. We've been doing it behind everyone's back the whole time. That's part of the thrill." Feigning ecstasy, she ran her hand up her thigh, between her breasts to her neck, with her eyes half closed. "Duncan's so hot. Other men can be so cold." She stopped the provocative act immediately when she caught the look on his face.

His eyes flashed blue fury at her. He laughed without humor and said, "Cold? You think I'm cold? For a smart woman Reggie, you are almost pathologically stupid."

His use of the word *stupid* fueled her already raging fire and she prepared to retaliate. Instead, he grabbed her elbows, and pulled her against him with force.

The flood gates opened. She fought back. At almost six feet, Reggie was not an ineffectual fighter, and at some point during her enraged attack, she knew she'd landed some pretty good blows. But she kept struggling until she realized Chase wasn't fighting back. It was no good when he didn't fight back. She chanced a quick look at him and was horrified to see genuine amusement in his face. For a split second, she considered wiping the smirk off his face by grabbing a most carefully guarded part of his anatomy. Then the absurdity of the situation struck her, and she started to laugh with him. They ended up collapsing on the end of the bed breathless, side by side.

Laying on his back and looking up at the ceiling, Chase said, "Better?"

Reggie nodded. "Much."

He turned, propped his head up with an elbow, and said, "I came up here looking for you. I have an idea of how to make Constance appear again."

She looked at him, the laughter still vivid in her eyes.

He said, "I'm going to make dinner for both of us tonight. We'll even eat in the dining room. After dinner, we'll take a walk in the gardens. It's supposed to be a full moon tonight."

She understood immediately. She didn't like what he was suggesting but she wasn't having much success contacting Constance on her own and Chase's idea had merit. It was dangerous for her peace of mind but it just might work.

"Constance likes to see us together. If she thinks she's made some progress, she won't be able to resist giving us another push."

Reggie raised an eyebrow at him. "Devious, but not bad."

"Good. So we have a date?" He put his hand out to her.

She nodded and put her hand is his. He stood and pulled her with him. Bending his head toward hers, he kissed her lips quickly. As he walked away, over his shoulder, he said, "Thanks for the tussle."

In a loud voice, she said, "Damn it, there's never a hammer around when you need one."

His full-bodied laughter echoed as he descended the grand staircase.

He was a good cook. As if it were a real date, they'd both showered and dressed in "date" clothes. Reggie wore a cream-colored dress with matching heels, and Chase wore a dark blue dress shirt and slacks that fit him just right. He left off the tie and Reggie was glad of it. She liked to see that little hollow at the base of his throat.

He'd turned the lights low and lit candles in the dining room. Reggie had to remind herself that this wasn't an actual date. The music he'd turned on after he'd seated her didn't help either. In an attempt to distract herself, she looked around the beautiful room. She was proud of what she'd done so far. It wasn't complete, but with the lights low, it didn't matter. An evening such as this in Bennett House was just what she'd always dreamed of, but with sadness, she reminded herself that tonight it wasn't for real. It never would be. Bennett House wasn't hers, and neither was Chase. She took a sip of the wine he had poured. It was delicious, damn him.

In a bright voice, she said, "Everything is so beautiful, Chase. When did you find time to do all of this?"

"When you do something, it's always more satisfying to do it well. I'm glad I took the trouble. The room almost does you justice." He smiled at her over his wine.

She wanted to be seduced by his words, to forget the charade, but in that direction, danger awaited, so she said, "Good line, Chase. The candlelight provides just the right ambience."

He feigned a hurt look and shook his head at her. "Aren't you going to tell me that I look good too?"

"You don't need to hear it from me."

He leaned toward her and in a low voice said, "Maybe I do."

She forced a laugh and leaned back. "Oh, that was really good. I'll have to remember the soft voice and earnest look. Very effective."

For the first time in her life, Reggie wasn't hungry. Using a fork to push food around the plate, it dawned on her that she couldn't finish the wonderful meal because her stomach was filled with butterflies. There was no room left for food, no matter how well prepared.

Chase looked at her with concern as he took the dishes away, "Are you okay, Reggie?"

"Yeah," she said, lying. "I wasn't sure if you could cook, so I had a burger before dinner. Sorry."

He shook his head. "Bet you're sorry you misjudged me now, huh? Leftovers won't be nearly as good. Did you want some brandy?"

"Sure." She hoped the alcohol would help her to relax. Of course, just like everything else, it was excellent, and she closed her eyes as her first sip warmed her from the inside. Glasses in hand, they rose from the table and walked out of the dining room.

Without a word, they judiciously skirted the library hallway and made their way out to the garden.

Awkwardly, Reggie sat beside Chase on a bench. Her heart pounded. Would he now pretend to want her? The thought made her sick, and for a second, she was glad she hadn't eaten much.

From the side of her mouth, she whispered, "What now?"

He leaned back and looked up at the moon. "Now we relax. Come here." He put his arm around her, pulled her to his chest, and gently held her there.

With her heart in her throat, Reggie closed her eyes. The night was clear, the strong breeze they'd had all day faded away, and all was still. The garden was earthy and fragrant but instead she inhaled his scent. Savoring it, she cautiously opened her eyes.

Constance was there! Reggie grabbed a handful of the shirt covering Chase's chest. He took hold of her chin, tipped her head up, and took her lips in a thrilling kiss.

Everything was forgotten as she responded with enthusiasm. This couldn't possibly be a make-believe kiss. Could it? He made a provocative noise in his throat when she ran her tongue along the ridge of his top teeth. His tongue followed hers, and they got lost in each other. Reggie dug her nails into the muscles on his chest when he applied lips and tongue to her throat. With both hands she grabbed his hair, and pulled his lips back to hers. She sucked his bottom lip into her mouth, and he moaned. He pulled her on his lap, and she gasped when she felt his hardness. She'd never wanted anything so badly in her whole life.

"Shouldn't you retire to more private accommodations?" Constance teased. She laughed when they jumped apart guiltily. Reggie looked right at her with glazed eyes. Chase couldn't see her, but he tried to follow Reggie's gaze.

Chase straightened and Reggie slipped off his lap. "Constance."

The spirit teased them. "Funny, usually your voice is so steady Regina. I like it this way better. Good for you, Chase. It looks like you know what you're doing after all. For a minute there today, Regina, when you were in the garden talking about vampires, I thought the other man might make a claim."

Reggie looked at her in confusion. Vampires? She shook her head. This time, she wasn't going to let the little minx distract her.

"Why are you here Constance?" She asked.

"Just because…" She almost sang the words.

"Tell me. You were once a Guardian. You know more than you're saying."

"No," Constance said. The music in her voice faded.

Reggie persisted. "Oh yes, Constance. You know there's work for you to do or you wouldn't be here. You have to help us."

"I have helped you. Without me, the two of you would still be circling each other under the impression you can keep your hands off each other."

Chase and Reggie exchanged a look. "Yeah, thanks for that," Reggie said ruefully, "But that's not all we need. The library, Constance, what do we do about the library, and what's in there?"

Constance's voice was filled with very human panic when she said, "I don't know what you're talking about."

Reggie could see the fear on her face as she started to fade. "Don't go, damn you! We need your help…" Her words had no effect as Constance disappeared and the breeze started up again.

Chapter 9

Under her breath, she said, "Bloody fool, talking to her is like nailing Jell-O to the wall."

Chase disagreed. "Don't expect too much Reggie. At least she showed. It worked. She appears more readily when we're together. Now we know that's how to get to her."

Regina raised her eyebrows and shrugged. "Yeah. But how does that help us? Do we mock date every night in hopes of stirring her? That's ridiculous." She also knew she'd never keep her distance or her sanity.

Chase sat back, resting his large hands on his knees. "We should stop fighting it."

She eyed him with suspicion. "Careful where you go with this."

Exasperated, he said, "How much longer are you going to pretend this thing between us doesn't exist?" When she didn't respond, he said, "Okay, since you lack the courage, I'll say it. I want you and you want me. If Constance hadn't interrupted us tonight, we wouldn't have stopped. Yes, she's manipulating us, but I don't care!" He heaved a sigh, for once losing all patience. "We've been dancing around this for too long, to hell with it! I want you bad. I'm not prepared to ignore it any longer. And I'm not going to hold back, so tonight, Reggie, I put you on notice. I'm coming for you, and I know exactly what I want."

With a hand on either side of her head, he brought her lips to his. There was no question in her mind; he knew what he was doing. She was devastated. A passion like this was completely new to her. The pleasure was so intense it bordered on pain. She wanted to grab handfuls of his hair and drag him back when he pulled away and calmly looked down at her. What he saw in her face must have pleased him because he smiled with triumph.

Standing, he took her hands and walked with her into the house. He surprised her by stopping at the bottom of the grand staircase. His eyes flared, but he blinked and with visible effort, got hold of himself. There was no question about what he'd rather be doing. Instead, he took a step back and said, "Go to bed, Reggie. I think I've given you enough to think about for one evening." He ran a hand through his hair, then stuffed his hands in his pockets, which drew her attention to the notch between his legs.

He gave her a warning look and said, "Go. Now."

Like an automaton, she walked up the stairs and into the master bedroom. Chase watched from the foot of the staircase. Before she shut the bedroom door, he called out, "Sweet dreams."

Safely inside, Reggie dropped like a bowling ball on the enormous bed and looked up at the familiar ceiling. A trembling hand rested on the pulse in her neck. He heart was beating so fast that she couldn't tell one beat from the next. From some part of her brain came the thought, *"I can't blame the stairs for this."* Chase was the only person who could affect her this way. The man was worse than a ninety-minute cardio routine. What was she going to do now? He'd brought it out into the open. There was no way she could pretend this thing between them didn't exist. He'd made it patently clear that he intended to deal with it.

He wanted to have sex. Hell, she did too, but that didn't stop her from considering the consequences. They were an integral part of each other's life. How could sex fit into that equation? What happens after they burn out the passion they feel right now? The awkwardness would impact upon the whole town. They'd make everyone uncomfortable. When their affair ended, could she still live in New Crescent and see Chase platonically without dying a little inside, every day? The answer frightened her. In her heart, she knew he loved her but he wasn't *in* love with her. Like every woman in the world, she knew the difference between the two.

Yet, what choice did she have? Before long, Reggie knew she'd give in to her own needs and take him to her bed. But she didn't have to do it mindlessly. He'd given her the chance to set terms, and she'd do just that. The problem was, exactly what were her terms? Trying to work that out in her mind, Reggie got very little sleep that night. Downstairs shifting on the couch, Chase shared her pain.

The next day, the weather mimicked Reggie's foul mood. Rain dominated the entire day. Sitting across the table from Gillian, she played with her food without enthusiasm. Her appetite, usually a constant and dependable presence in her life, deserted her completely.

"Are you sure you're all right?" Gillian's brow furrowed with concern. Picking up on the emotion with unfailing accuracy, Hank laid his fluffy white head in Reggie's lap. His dense black eyes communicated a world of tenderness. He was truly miraculous.

Reggie looked at her friend and then down at the dog. "You two are good."

"Ah, all is not lost. You might be down, but you're not out. You still have your sense of humor." Gillian pushed her plate away. They'd agreed to meet at the little diner on the main street of New Crescent. The diner served deliciously unhealthy food. As a rule, Reggie loved it. But today, for the first time ever, she couldn't finish her fish and chips.

Even Susie the waitress looked at her with concern as she said under her breath, "Flu season is starting early this year."

Taking a deep breath, Gillian held Reggie's hand in hers. At once Reggie felt her friend's compassion. With a simple touch, Gillian Watson could read a person's thoughts and feelings. That was her gift. It had helped make her a Guardian. Trusting her completely, Reggie didn't pull away. She knew that Gillian would never invade her privacy or take any information that Reggie wouldn't offer freely. Her gift was impressive, but what was really incredible was what she'd done with it. She'd taken her ability, worked with it, suffered for it, and could now use it to bring solace to a troubled mind.

Comforted, Reggie said, "Hey, Gillian, you're better than drugs. Wow. Don't go too far away, I might need you the next time they don't have my size in the perfect shoe."

Letting go of her hand, Gillian said, "I save the really good stuff for special occasions. Shoe shopping definitely qualifies."

"You're getting stronger," Reggie commented on Gillian's impressive power.

"Yeah, I've stopped trying to control it and accepted it as part of who I am. I guess in a way I'm not stunting its growth anymore."

"I'm glad, Gillian. You seem so happy."

"Travis has a lot to do with that." She smiled serenely.

Slipping into familiar habits, Reggie said, "He's been a busy little boy. You don't *have* to marry him, you know. He'd have sex with you anyway."

Gillian paused for a second and played along. "True. The poor boy has pitifully little self-control."

"You own him, girl." She grabbed a chip. Her appetite was starting to reassert itself, thanks to Gillian. "Let's make him do something really outrageous like River Dance."

Their healthy imaginations took over from there and they started to laugh. The waitress glanced over her shoulder and smiled.

"At the risk of sending you spiraling into a relapse, can I ask you how it's going with Constance?"

"She's being difficult. At least when she appeared last night, I had the presence of mind to tell her we needed her help. Not that she was very forthcoming. The naked fear on her face when I mentioned the library was entirely genuine. She's terrified of what's in there. I can't tell you how thrilled I am about that."

"I wish Ernestine would let me help."

"No way, Gill, that thing could wipe you out. You're just too tasty a tidbit. It couldn't resist a gift like yours. I'm uniquely ungifted, and it drains me."

Gillian shook her head. "Don't be silly. You're more gifted than you know."

"Nice of you to say, but I've accepted the fact that I'm outstandingly normal. I can't waste my life wishing for what I can't have." The words had more meaning than Reggie wanted to examine at the moment, so she rushed on. "Even without precognition, I know that I will live here in New Crescent and work in my family's real estate business. I'm not meant to do anything else. I know my destiny, and I'm fine with it."

"How fortunate for you." Gillian humored her.

Reggie shook her blonde hair. "Really."

"So you don't need help dealing with Constance and Vincent because you know your destiny." She leaned over the table eager to hear Reggie's response.

She laughed. "That's not what I meant."

"Well, all I can say is that I'm glad Chase is in this with you. Maybe he can shake your complacency. For a man who's always so cool and collected, he can be remarkably unpredictable, I think."

"You think too much." Reggie grabbed a menu. "What shall we have for dessert?" She refused to discuss Chase with Gillian or anyone. Her nerves were still too exposed from the previous night.

Too sensitive to press her, Gillian changed the subject. "Travis says that there have been some petty thefts around Bennett House recently."

Reggie nodded. "Yeah, and that's not all. We've had a number of little accidents or narrowly averted big accidents. Guys who usually never exchange a cross word are at each other's throats. I know it's the Big Bad in the Library. It's getting stronger." She closed the menu with a snap. "I'm so frustrated. Chase and I have made so little progress figuring out how to get rid of it."

"I know I'm not supposed to get involved, Reggie, but as I understand it, I can still give you guidance. So here it is. Trust Chase, even when your insecurity makes you want to turn away from him."

Stunned, Reggie looked at her friend. Gillian refused to elaborate and smoothly changed the subject.

* * * *

The pouring rain forced Chase indoors. He didn't mind too much. It gave him an opportunity to go over the proofs he'd been ignoring. Duty called. The task was almost distracting enough to keep him from obsessing over the challenge he'd laid at Reggie's feet the night before. A small part of him regretted his words, fearing that he'd pushed her too far, too soon. But a bigger part of him acknowledged that one of them had to do something. Spending so much time close to her was grinding him into sawdust. He had to press his advantage.

She wanted him. Sweet Mother of God, for that, he was grateful. He was finally worthy and in a position to offer her what she deserved. He was no longer skating on the thin ice of shame and potential bankruptcy. Yes, his stepfather had tarnished his family's reputation, his mother's memory, and his own sense of self-worth, but that was the past. He couldn't step back in time and kick the abusive bastard out of his mother's life. She'd made a choice when she'd hidden the abuse from her son. Chase had berated himself endlessly for not seeing what was happening, for being so self-absorbed. In typical adolescent male fashion, he'd been oblivious to the classic signs of abuse.

On her death bed, Annie McCann Adams had told her son that she'd made her own choices and hadn't regretted them. Jade was worth it all. The emotional abuse she'd suffered at the hands of her second husband hadn't mattered. His stepsister was worth it. Of course, she'd been right. Jade belonged in his life. She belonged in New Crescent. He'd never given up hope that she'd find her way back home.

When Jade had called him that morning in the hospital, she'd been almost incoherent. He'd been waiting for Reggie to come so they could talk about what they'd been through the day before, how they'd saved each other's lives. But Jade's call for help put all of that on the back burner. Gone was his intention to stay put until Reggie came back so they could talk over what they'd been through together. Fate had stepped in and made that impossible. Robert Adams, Chase's foul stepfather had died, and the fallout wasn't pretty. Jade needed him. For once in her life, she'd reached out to him. He couldn't let her down. So many years ago, he'd ignored his mother when she'd needed him. That was the worst way to learn a life lesson, but he'd learned it. Disappointing Jade was something he'd vowed never to do.

Unaware of Jade's situation and her cry for help, Reggie had found an empty bed when she'd returned to the hospital to see him. Misunderstanding his absence, she'd reacted impulsively, called her girlfriend who lived in Italy and boarded a flight to Europe without a word. Until Jade was able to clear up the circumstances surrounding her father's death, Chase had to respect her privacy and stay quiet. He couldn't tell Reggie his reasons for leaving so precipitously.

Now he had another chance with her, and he wasn't about to screw it up. The two of them would just have to triumph over this latest madness at Bennett House. His instinct told him they'd have to or be crushed. She was understandably skittish around him, but if he stayed the course, he prayed she'd trust him enough to let her guard down. After a long absence, his self-confidence had slowly returned. He was determined to succeed in shaping his own and Reggie's destiny, but he knew, given her nature, she'd fight him every step of the way.

* * * *

The rain didn't stall work on the interior of Bennett House. The pickings weren't nearly as rich though, without the men working outside. He'd have to be satisfied with less. That fact didn't please him, but he'd learned to be patient. A great power was within his grasp. He could smell it, taste it. He'd wait. The anticipation would make his triumph that much sweeter. The other was still foolish and stubborn. He would take it all in the end. For now, knowledge was power.

Chapter 10

Before heading back to Bennett House, Reggie stopped by her parents' home and picked up Prudence. She'd spent too much time away from the little dog. Her father had been right. The work taking place at Bennett House made it a less than ideal place for a dog, but Reggie didn't want to spend another night without Pru. In New Crescent, all animals were considered Mother Nature's gift. In the Wicca tradition, that belief had been passed down generation to generation by the Old Families. Many pets could trace their lineage back to the three Goode sisters and their animals. Pru, bless her heart, couldn't claim such auspicious origins, but that didn't make Reggie love her any less.

Driving back to Bennett House, Reggie hadn't fully realized how much she'd missed the dog. Just having her furry little body around made Reggie feel better. The sight of her furry little face helped to brighten up a day that was still rainy and melancholy.

The house stood moody and majestic against the infinite shades of gray in the sky. It truly was the perfect setting for a gothic novel. The slight feeling of expectation Reggie felt as she walked in the front door supported the impression.

She could hear the kind of noise and chatter she'd grown accustomed to while working on the house and headed in the direction of Duncan's voice. Pru followed close behind. The contractor was talking to two of his most reliable men. It sounded like they'd had a disagreement and Duncan was helping them to smooth it out. Standing in the doorway, Reggie leaned against the unstained trim and waited for him to finish. He caught sight of her in his peripheral vision, nodded, and held up a finger, indicating he'd be right with her.

With the disagreement ironed out, Duncan turned to Reggie. He recognized Pru and bent to pat her. Reggie had questions for him regarding the tile work in the kitchen. Their discussion became detailed. Growing impatient with inactivity, Pru began to explore. Reggie called her to heel. When her conversation with Duncan wound down, Reggie made her way upstairs using the back staircase. Her ever present sidekick, Pru stayed just a step behind.

Once in the master bedroom, she changed into old jeans and a wrinkled SPCA T-shirt. Pru sniffed around familiarizing herself with such enthusiasm that Reggie could hear her snorting like a pig hunting truffles. She smiled and said, "Come on, you blood hound, we're going to take a look at the kitchen."

This time, she used the grand staircase. The progress they'd made with the renovations brought a smile to her face. The kitchen was a dream. Reggie wasn't much of a cook, but she knew how best to outfit a kitchen and she'd never been afraid to ask the experts. Disappointed with the quality of tile delivered for the floor, she decided to have it sent back. She made a note to call the supplier. She glanced at her watch and decided to call tomorrow. She looked around for Pru, but the little dog was gone. She'd followed Reggie down the stairs. Doggie nails sliding across the slippery new floors weren't a sound Reggie could ignore. But now Pru was nowhere to be found. Reggie began to feel panic in the pit of her stomach.

Calling out to Pru, Reggie moved from room to room. The workmen looked up at Reggie in surprise. No one had seen the little dog. She'd vanished. Reggie's stomach churned, and she was afraid to imagine what could have happened to the little dog. Bennett House under construction wasn't the best place for Pru . Given recent events, Reggie realized she'd been irresponsible and selfish by putting her in the middle of everything. With determination, she walked to the hallway that led to the library. If that evil thing had a hold of her baby, she vowed to destroy it or die trying.

She'd been prepared for the cold but had forgotten the oppressive odor. She gagged as she breathed the foul air, but she pressed on desperately. Both doors to the library stood ajar. That was new. With a dead weight crushing her chest, she walked into hell.

Pru lay on the floor, her legs twitching. Foam oozed from her mouth. Reggie ran to her and dropped to the floor. Everything but the little dog's welfare drained from her mind. The doors slammed behind her with a tremendous bang. The sound made her jump but failed to distract her from her goal. Poor Pru was convulsing ever more violently. Reggie had to get her out. After Reggie gathered Pru in her arms, the little dog went limp. She wanted to scream and shake the dog when she remained unresponsive, but controlled the impulse. Panic would serve no purpose other than to give the advantage to her invisible enemy. A strange pounding reverberated in Reggie's eardrums like corporeal evil demanding entrance.

Shivering with cold and shock, Reggie struggled to stand. It was no use. Pru was dead. It was hopeless. Overcome with savage despair, Reggie longed to sink to the damp and clammy floor and keen with grief. The thing with her in the room was powerful beyond their paltry imaginings. How pathetic she'd been to think she could survive it, let alone conquer it. Depression sucked at her will to fight. With Pru still held tightly in her arms, she started to sink back down to the floor in defeat.

No! A voice from somewhere deep inside her commanded and forced her to resist the temptation to give way. This was all a cruel, but clever illusion. There was always hope. That certainty was branded into Reggie's character. She called upon an unknown reserve of energy locked within and struggled to break free from the depressive spiral. She willed life into Pru and pushed back at the entity with focused strength of will. Stumbling twice, she dragged her feet to the double doors. Prepared for more resistance, Reggie was surprised when they opened easily. As she carried poor Pru out, the doors slammed shut behind them, a last show of power. Reggie ignored it.

Once again, she could hear the natural sounds of human voices in the house and the otherworldly banging in her eardrums faded away. Reggie was aware only of Pru and her condition. The little dog stirred and started to come out of whatever spell had claimed her. Reggie sobbed with relief as she sat beside her on the floor outside the library hallway.

From somewhere in the house, there was a great crash, loud voices, and running footsteps. Weak, Reggie used the wall to help find her feet. There was silence. Another accident. *My God, when would it stop?* Pru regained consciousness but Reggie couldn't leave her and she called out. "What's going on?"

An apologetic voice said, "It's okay. One of the ladders tipped over. It's a mess, but no one was hurt."

Reggie breathed a sigh of relief.

Her encounter in the library had sapped her strength, but she refused to succumb to exhaustion. Pru had recovered at last. Now Reggie's rage drove her on. With determination, she walked through the garden, ignoring the rain.

"Constance, show yourself now!" A faint rumble of thunder punctuated her demand. Nature's synchronicity gave her a jolt of confidence. Staring at the iron gate, she willed Constance to comply.

She felt an almost imperceptible change in the air and knew she could be heard.

"I know you're there, Constance. No more games. Someone very dear to me almost died today. You have to help me!"

"You weakened it," Constance whispered, but still she refused to appear. "Your strength during your little rescue mission today was a surprise, but you're going to need more than that to vanquish what's in that room."

"Tell me what I have to do."

"You're not ready yet. First, I suggest you catch the petty thief who steals from this place every night. You don't want lawmen here. They are acquainted with violence and would only feed that thing in there. You and Chase have to do this alone." And the spirit was gone, the air changed.

Soaked to the skin, Reggie pulled together a string of cuss words as long as her right leg. She was still swearing when she walked back into the house and straight into Chase's arms. While in conversation with Constance, she'd had no idea he'd arrived.

He smiled as he steadied her. "Whoa there, Crash, your vocabulary is impressive."

His use of her nickname drained some of her anger, and she sighed. "I'm highly motivated."

Chase nodded. "You always were an overachiever."

She started to shiver, and he said, "Go upstairs and run a hot bath. We'll have dinner when you're warm again. I'll start a fire."

"What…"

He silenced her by putting a finger to her lips. "Get out of those wet clothes or I'll do it myself." Wiggling his eyebrows, he said, "And we both know how that'll end." With the same finger he'd pressed against her lips, he pointed up the stairs. "Go."

Reggie took her time, not only because the warmth was heaven sent but also because she was terrified of what this night might bring. After getting so little sleep the night before and her experience with Pru, she knew she'd have no defenses. "I'm Belgium," she muttered, "and look what happened to it in the First and Second World Wars." Glancing down at Pru curled up on the fluffy bath mat, she said, "Don't look at me that way. I'm operating without sleep or food. It's the best I could do." The ridiculousness of her conversation made her laugh. She'd coasted right past exhausted to punch-drunk.

Her punchy condition explained Reggie's choice of apparel as she dressed in a terry cloth robe, enormous flannel pajamas, and fluffy slippers. The not-so-subtle message wouldn't be lost on Chase. Tonight, she was no sex kitten. She pulled the elastic waistband of her voluminous pajama bottoms and let it snap back.

Satisfied, she smiled. "Ah, clothes to eat in. I'm starving."

Her slippers made navigating the stairs very awkward and she giggled. Safely on the main floor, she followed her nose. He'd lit a fire in the living room and had set food on trays in front of it. She looked around for him, but the room was empty. Pru made for the food but stopped when Reggie gave her a warning look. Chase came into the room, his arms filled with pillows. He dropped them on the floor in front of the fire.

He took one all-encompassing look at her and slapped the heel of his hand on his forehead like he should have had a V8. "Flannel! So *that's* Victoria's secret."

She shared his laughter.

He nodded at the pillows. "These will make eating on the floor nice and comfy. Here..." After helping her to get settled, he turned the lights off and joined her in front of the fire.

Reggie bit into a drumstick, chewed with relish, and said, "I get it. This is the third act, seduction scene." She looked at her slippers. "Damn, wardrobe got it all wrong, again."

He laughed. "Don't be so sure. I think you look adorable. Overkill though, the jammies could actually fit me."

She looked at him with exaggerated innocence. "And have you enjoyed wearing women's clothing since puberty?"

His laughter rang out, genuine and heartfelt. "Relax, Reggie, neither the wardrobe nor the humor was needed. I get the message. You're dead on your feet. Trust me, when I take you to bed, you'll need every ounce of strength you have. Tonight, you're just not up to it."

She didn't look at him. Instead, she stuffed her mouth with pasta salad. Damn, but the man knew comfort food. She closed her eyes with ecstasy.

"Knock it off, Reggie. When you look like that, I want to change my mind and jump you after all."

She swallowed and still said nothing. Silence filled the air. They could hear the house settling in for the night. Reggie loved the little sounds. This house deserved to be lived in. It cried out for it.

"Talk." Chase's voice interrupted her thoughts.

She shrugged. "I think that's the first time you've ever said that to me."

He ignored her quip and pressed her. "What happened today that drained you so completely?"

Reggie revisited her experience with Pru. As she spoke, Chase's frown deepened.

He closed his eyes. "I'm not even going to bother berating you for going in that room alone. Let's not, but say we did. Shall we?" He stoked Pru's back. "I'd have done the same thing. Are you both okay?"

She nodded and filled him in on her conversation with Constance. "I think we have no choice but to follow her advice for the time being. We have to catch the thief."

Chase looked around. "I feel like I'm being punk'd, but go on, Nancy Drew."

"It's raining pretty hard outside. I doubt the thief will venture out tonight. But tomorrow night, I want to set a trap for him. He takes the bait, we take him."

"And this is Constance's idea?" Chase was calm..

"Yes. Well, no, not exactly. The idea is hers, but the plan is mine. Will you help me?"

"Of course," he said with resignation. "If I don't, you'll do it by yourself."

"Good man. What's for dessert?"

The next night, the weather cooperated up to a point. It didn't rain, but what little sun they'd had all day hadn't even come close to drying the sodden earth. Reggie loved the variety a New England change of season offered, but standing an inch deep in mud, behind a smallish pine tree, in autumn, was pushing it, even for her.

She couldn't see Chase from her hiding place, but she knew he was there. They waited. Earlier, Chase left some tools out in hopes of tempting the thief. He'd rolled his eyes about the whole thing, but told Reggie he'd chosen the kind of easily carried materials that their thief seemed to find irresistible.

At first, when she'd crouched down behind the pine tree, she'd been startled by every shadow, every noise. After a couple of hours spent waiting on tenterhooks, her legs started to cramp. She was cursing silently and massaging her thigh in abject misery when she heard the noise.

Maybe she hadn't wasted their time after all. The dark figure moved with surprisingly little stealth. He was short too, a fact Reggie noted with a smug smile. She could take him. In the darkness, it was difficult to see exactly what he'd picked up and slipped inside his jacket, but she could see Chase moving into perfect position to trap him. Earlier, Chase had tried to tell Reggie to stay hidden until he'd caught the guy, but that suggestion was not well met. In the end, they'd agreed. He'd come up from behind while Reggie approached from the front, cutting off the thief's exit.

Waiting for Chase to make his move Reggie grew impatient. What's wrong with him? Why isn't he moving? Instead of following the plan, Chase spoke to the intruder. Furious at him, Reggie didn't bother to listen to his words. She stood and ran toward them. She was less than eight feet away when the thief turned to flee. Without hesitation, Reggie checked him with her hip, and he went flying into the mud. He grunted loudly. Chase hauled him to his feet, and it was then that Reggie got her first good look at their criminal mastermind.

She wanted to laugh. He looked barely older than twelve, and she was being generous. She should have known. The thefts had been more of a nuisance than a threat. They were simply childish pranks. What the hell was Constance up to? She'd intimated that the thief was significant in some way. Feeling foolish, Reggie exchanged a look with Chase.

Her amusement died, and her blood ran cold when she saw the look on the kid's face and the knife in his small but steady hand.

Chapter 11

Burning with fever, the kid looked right through her. These were not the eyes of a child. Chase didn't hesitate. He grabbed the boy's wrist and forced the knife from his hand. Reggie watched with concern when an emotion flickered in the thief's eyes. He blinked at her as if seeing her for the first time and dropped to the ground in a dead faint.

Reggie crouched beside Chase as he checked the kid's pulse.

"Bring your car around. We need to get him to a hospital. He's burning up."

She didn't waste time with words. Running into the house for her keys, she spared a reassuring word for Pru. Somehow, understanding the weight of the situation, the little dog made not a peep. Chase carried the boy as if he weighed no more than a doll. He was so young he probably didn't weigh much more.

Reggie drove while Chase watched over him in the back seat. Familiar with the roads, she got them to the hospital in excellent time. Chase carried him in, calling out for help as he moved.

The emergency room was busy, but the unconscious boy got immediate attention. Chase and Reggie waited impatiently for news from the doctor. In sync, their heads turned when the doctor came out.

"He's conscious, and he's going to be all right." He smiled when they sighed. "He has a fever. Flu season seems to have started early this year. It's making its way through the school. It's intense, but remarkably short lived. He'll feel better in a matter of hours." His gaze shifted to other beds in the unit.

"What about his parents?" Reggie asked.

"I've called them. They didn't even know his was out tonight…thought he was tucked safely in his bed. They're going to want to talk to you, so if you don't mind, please stick around."

Chase said, "Can we see him?"

"I'd rather you wait until his parents get here."

"We'll wait. Thanks, Doctor." Chase nodded.

"The nurse will let you know when they're here." He moved away. There were other patients to tend to.

"I'm glad he's okay. The look on his face when he confronted me with the knife..." She shook her head. "I wish I could describe it. He had the deadest eyes I've ever seen. No question, he looked perfectly capable of stabbing me in that split second... but then he changed. It was like an alternate personality took over. In that moment, he transformed from potential, cold-blooded killer into scared, sick kid."

"We need to talk with his parents. I don't think we should bother the sheriff's office with this just yet."

She nodded her agreement.

It wasn't long before a frantic man and woman rushed in asking about Todd, an eleven-year-old boy brought in earlier. The parents had arrived. A very busy nurse took a moment and showed them to their son's bed.

About fifteen minutes later, the boy's father came out and introduced himself to Chase and Reggie.

"I understand we have you two to thank for getting him here." He put out his hand. "I'm John Marks."

Chase took his hand and introduced Reggie. She didn't waste time and immediately asked if she could see Todd. The man nodded and showed them to his son's hospital bed.

His skin looked gray against the white sheets. Brown hair stuck up in every direction as his mother repeatedly ran a shaking hand over his head. He looked at Reggie and Chase without recognition. They exchanged a look.

John Marks made introductions. His wife, Tammy, smiled down at her son. "Todd, these are the people who brought you to the hospital tonight."

The kid looked confused for a second, and then he looked away. A stain of red stood out on his cheeks as he blushed. Reggie could see that he'd remembered.

Quietly, Chase talked to his parents, explaining what their son had been up to. Reggie stood by Todd's bed and said, "Tell me what you remember."

He looked frightened for a moment and Reggie reassured him. "It's okay, Todd. I'm not mad. I just want to know what you were doing up at Bennett House tonight."

His father spoke, "Tell her son."

In a tiny voice that underlined his tender age, Todd said. "It was Aidan and the guys.. They told me I had to go to the scary house and take something so I could hang with the gang."

"What guys?" Reggie asked

"All the really cool guys in school hang out together. If you're with them, you're okay. Aidan said I could hang too if I passed the initiation."

With a knowing look, Chase said, "And stealing something from Bennett House in the middle of the night was the initiation."

"Yeah, a bunch of the guys have already done it. They told me I had to prove I had guts, prove I was a man." He started to cry. "I don't have guts, Mom. I'm just a kid. I was scared and gonna turn around, and I got sorta sick. I remember seeing you."

He looked at Reggie. Her heart broke for the boy and she took hold of his hand. "Well, don't worry about it, Todd. No harm done. You just get better. When you're up to it, we'll have a talk."

"He's never done anything like this before. He's a good kid," John Marks said as he walked out with them.

Chase shook his hand. "Don't worry about it. We're just glad he's okay. I insist, however, that you get the names of all the boys involved from Todd and contact their parents. Bennett House is no place for kids at the moment."

"I intend to do exactly that. Everything that was stolen will be returned to you. Thank you both for being so understanding."

* * * *

Back at Bennett House, Reggie went straight to the kitchen. She opened the fridge and asked, "Do you want a sandwich?"

Chase laughed. "Sure, since you're making one."

"I should have got a candy bar from the vending machine, but I didn't want to miss anything." She pulled out some cold cuts, grabbed the bread and very efficiently started to build two hearty sandwiches. She hesitated for a second and looked across the kitchen island at Chase, "I'm not making you a peanut butter and jelly sandwich by the way. Speak now or forever hold your peace."

He laughed. "Whatever you make will be fine with me. Just no pickles."

They ate at the table. Chase poured them both large glasses of ice-cold milk.

"I'll call Travis in the morning." When Reggie started to object, he continued. "Not as Sheriff. Just as an FYI thing so he knows we don't expect anymore petty thefts around the place. That should keep the cops away from here like Constance hoped."

"I don't have to tell you what this means, do I?"

"No, but you're going to anyway, aren't you?"

"Kids, Chase, that thing has been feeding off innocent kids. That's what was wrong with Todd tonight. He doesn't have the flu, and neither do any of the other kids in school. I'm willing to bet every kid who's come down with this virus has a souvenir from Bennett House."

"It's possible."

"So I guess there was a method to Constance's madness after all. We had to stop the thefts in order to cut off the supply. That's why the evil's been getting so much stronger, even though we've kept everyone away from that room."

Chase nodded. "Yeah. From my hiding place, I could see Todd hesitate outside the Library window. At the time I thought he was just being cautious."

Reggie said, "No, that thing in the library did something to him. You talk to Travis. I'll connect with Gillian and Aunt Ernestine. They can at least confirm what we already suspect. I'm sure they can do that much at least."

She started to get up, but Chase put a hand over hers. "Tomorrow, Reggie. Do you have any idea what time it is?" She looked at him crossly. "It's after 2. Go to bed. Get some sleep. We can do all of that in the morning."

The late, or rather early, hour took Reggie by surprise. It felt like she'd spent days hunched behind that damn pine tree. However, she'd been oblivious to the passage of time during the events following Todd's appearance. She wasn't tired, but the more practical side of her character told her that once she got between the covers, the exhaustion would hit her. Hard.

He took their plates to the sink and walked back to her. With a hand on each of her chair's arm rests, he bent towards her. A fraction of an inch from her lips he said, "I haven't done this all day." He kissed her thoroughly, and she quietly lost her sanity. He pulled back and said, "Go to bed, Reggie, before we both lose control. Yes, I want to share that big bed with you, but sleeping is not what I had in mind. And sleep is what we both need." Patting Pru on the head, he walked out of the kitchen.

* * * *

The sun shone brightly the next day, but there was still a chill in the air. Some of the trees on the Bennett property had already changed color, some had resisted the temptation, and some stood naked, with their leaves gathered on the ground. Reggie caught a glimpse of Chase talking with a group of his guys. The work on the garden was almost done for the autumn. She felt a twinge when she thought of leaving this house to its new owner, but resolutely, she pushed it aside. She'd called Gillian first thing in the morning and had been immediately invited to brunch. They planned to talk about what happened last night over Gillian's blueberry waffles. Reggie couldn't wait.

When she pulled into Gillian's driveway, Hank came running. He worshipped Pru and waited patiently for her to jump out of the car. The two ran off into the herb garden together.

Reggie could smell the waffles as soon as she entered the house. Her mouth watered. Gillian smiled at her.

"Good morning. I'm just about done."

Reggie asked why Travis wasn't at home, and Gillian told her that he'd got a call from the FBI, asking him to consult on a case. Lines of worry creased Gillian's brow. Reggie knew that these cases weren't easy for Travis, but since leaving the FBI, he'd been asked to consult on two serial murder cases. He'd come home drained, a look of deep sadness on his face and they'd talked it out together. They made a good team. Reggie envied them.

"Don't worry, Gill, he knows what he's doing. A least he's not heading the task force like he used to."

Gillian nodded. "Yeah, I know. I also know he feels a deep sense of responsibility when he thinks he can be of some help. I'd never stop him. It's just always so sad." She walked to the door and called Hank and Pru inside.

Reggie understood that Gillian would need Hank nearby. He was Gillian's familiar and he helped her to handle her gift. She'd need his support when she learned about the children.

Reggie needn't have worried. After she'd told her story, Reggie noted that Gillian looked surprisingly calm stroking Hank's side silently.

Reggie said, "Todd's parents will get the names of all the kids involved. I'm going to talk to Todd again later this week. He may be able to tell me more."

"He won't," Gillian said with certainty.

"He'll refuse? Or he won't have any more information."

"He's told you all he knows. Now that you know about the children, you can keep them away from Bennett House."

"Will that make the Big Bad weaker?"

"No. But at least it won't make it stronger. You're going to need to talk to Constance again," Gillian said.

"Aunt Ernestine wouldn't even take my call this morning."

Gillian touched Reggie's hand lightly, "She can't. This thing with the children has hit her hard. She's an old woman, Reggie, though she hates to admit it."

"Did she know all along?"

Gillian shook her head. "Not exactly, but she knew power was being drained from a potent source. Think about it, Reggie. This could help you to figure out how to defeat this thing."

"And that thing in the library and our Constance are linked. It likes children, so perhaps children are the way to get to Constance," Reggie said as she licked maple syrup off her thumb. "That might be the way to convince her to stop playing games and help us."

Gillian nodded, but said nothing more.

"I guess I'll have a little chat with Constance this afternoon. It's kind of tough trying to connect with her with Chase's guys around everywhere.. They give me the strangest looks when they see me talking to myself in the garden."

"Reggie, all men look at you, and it has nothing to do with Constance."

She laughed. "You should have heard their reaction when they interrupted Chase and me kissing…" Reggie didn't have to wait long for Gillian's reaction.

"Ah! You and Chase?" She threw her hands up in the air. "That's wonderful." She giggled like a schoolgirl and demanded more detail.

It was nice to have a woman around to confide in.

* * * *

The night had been a disappointment to him. He couldn't get enough. The boy had wandered off too soon. He'd barely begun to suckle when, somehow, the child moved away. Had he been too greedy sucking, too much too fast? Better be more careful. He'd have to find more today. The more he got, the more he wanted. His need was a bottomless pit that required almost constant sustenance. Another host body would have to be located. He was hungry.

Chapter 12

"I don't think he even told Sam or Travis why he'd disappeared from the hospital the next day," Gillian said. "I know Travis tried to get it out of him, but Chase told him that it wasn't his story to tell."

"That's exactly what he told me. I've given up hope of ever hearing that story." Reggie sighed.

"Are you okay with that?"

"No, but what choice do I have? Chase has always been a little distant with me. Sam and Travis always let me in. I can get a beat on what they're thinking, but not Chase. He's never let me get too close."

"Are you sure you haven't misinterpreted him? He's not a big talker. But, I don't think he's cold…just reserved. And actually, he shows more emotion around you than anyone else." Gillian looked at Reggie with encouragement.

Reggie laughed. "That's probably because I'm usually goading him. I do that on purpose to provoke him."

"I kinda got that. It works." Gillian smiled.

"A little too well these days." She gave her friend a knowing look.

Gillian picked up her coffee mug and leaned back in her chair. "Do tell."

"My relationship with Chase has changed since we started working together on Bennett House. I can have a conversation with him now. We connect. We laugh together. Hell, we want to jump each other's bones."

"Good. Do it. It'll be good for both of you." Gillian's eyes lit with excitement.

"That's easy for you to say, but what happens when it burns out and we feel awkward around each other? How do we get the comfort back? It would make everyone uncomfortable. One of us doesn't get invited to things? One of us loses? And I don't think I could take it. We could never go back to where we used to be." Reggie leaned her chin on her hand and sighed.

"You don't know that it won't work for the two of you. No one knows that. If you want guarantees, Reggie, you'd have better luck with late-night infomercials."

She'd given her an opportunity Reggie just couldn't resist. "I don't know. I never did get my money back on those cans of spray-on hair."

Gillian rolled her eyes. "You know you do that a lot."

Reggie frowned. "What?"

"Cover your feelings with humor." She shook her head and held up a hand. "Don't get me wrong, it's one of your most endearing qualities, but don't ever let fear of failure keep you from fighting for what you want."

"And if what I want is Chase?" Reggie ventured uncertainly.

"Don't push him away. Don't break it yourself and then moon over the fact that it's wrecked. Enjoy it. And him, something tells me he's a sexual dynamo."

Reggie looked at her friend with amusement. She could remember not so long ago, having a conversation very much like this with Gillian about her and Travis. She narrowed her eyes. "I'll think about it."

Gillian laughed. "You do that, and while you're at it, think of how it might help with Constance."

"Hmm, interesting, you may have a good point. Constance is eager to warm things up between Chase and me. That would give me an excuse to go for it."

Shaking her head crossly, Gillian said, "Don't play games and don't look for excuses. You have too much at stake."

"Yeah, I know," Reggie said soberly. "You're right. By playing games, I do us both a disservice. I'm just not sure I'm equipped to deal with this right now."

"I've learned that when it comes to human emotion, it's never the right time. You have no choice but to deal with it as it comes to you." Gillian said.

Reggie groaned and using a whining adolescent voice said, "Aww…Can't you do that for me?"

Driving back to Bennett house, Reggie tried to work out what she needed to say to Constance. Tackling the illusive spirit was the first thing

Reggie intended to do upon returning to the house. Constance had to learn about what had happened last night. She probably knew all along about the children and that's why she wanted the thefts solved. In her way, Constance was already helping them. It wasn't enough though. Reggie knew she'd have to give the little vixen a push...well, figuratively speaking.

She was pleased that she'd timed her return to coincide with lunch break. She had the garden to herself. That this time when she communicated with Constance, she wouldn't have an amused audience was a relief. She took Prudence up to the bedroom. She wasn't sure how the little dog would react to Constance, and she couldn't afford to take her chances. Pru didn't seem to mind because she curled up on a pillow and rested her head on her front paws. Assured that she was safe, Reggie closed the door and made her way to the garden.

Standing beside the iron gate, Reggie concentrated. She started with a low voice. "Constance? Can you hear me? Please, Constance I need to talk to you."

She waited. No response. "Thank you for urging me to figure out who was stealing at night. It was good advice." In life, Constance Bennett had been spoiled and vain. Would death have changed her? Who knew? Perhaps it was prudent to start with a compliment.

"Of course it was good advice. I was a Guardian, you know. I'm not an imbecile." Constance's voice had an impatient and sharp edge. The air had taken on that otherworldly feeling and Reggie could hear her own heart beat quicken. There was silence. Constance appeared.

Reggie laughed. "I didn't mean to insinuate anything. I just wanted to thank you."

The spirit didn't smile. She nodded her head with regal grace. "You're welcome."

"I don't think we'll catch kids creeping around the place again, but Chase and I will be vigilant from here on out. We still need your help with the library." She put up a hand when Constance frowned. "I know you want to pretend you don't know anything about what's in there, but I know you do. You can't escape it. I can't do it without you."

"You can't do it without that man either." With a nod, she indicated a spot beyond Reggie's right shoulder. Reggie spun around, surprised to see Chase.

He walked to her side. "Good afternoon, Constance. I know you're here, but forgive me if I can't see you."

"Yes, well…you wouldn't, would you? I'm here for Regina."

"You're here for more than me, Constance. You're here for a purpose. I need you to think about that purpose. It's not for fun and games. You have information I must know."

"No." Constance voice lost its mystical quality. She looked fearful and started to fade away.

Desperate to make her stay, Reggie turned to Chase. "I'll explain later." She reached up with both hands and brought his head down to hers. She captured his lips in a long kiss. Bless his heart, the man didn't resist. Instead, he responded with gusto, pulling her into his arms, pressing her against his much bigger, harder body. With no thought in her head but finding some way to get closer to Chase, Reggie forgot Constance.

"Very clever, Regina. You know I can't resist romance." Her image reappeared. Still in Chase's arms, Reggie rested her forehead on his chest and sighed.

Under her breath, Reggie said, "I told you I'd explain later." She turned to Constance and smiled. "The presence in the library is Vincent Bennett, isn't it?"

Hesitantly Constance nodded. "Yes. He hangs on, greedy for more. He was my husband. I was a fool."

There was no magic or music in Constance's tone when she explained. "My own hubris blinded me to his deception. My weakness gave him the power he needed to make me fall in love with him." She walked around the little iron gate slowly. "I was in love with love and looking for adventure. I'd never known anyone like him, and he wanted me. He was exciting, and my parents didn't approve. My willingness to rebel gave his dark magic added power, and he used it against me. I fell in love, hard, fast. I would have done anything to have him. And I did." She was quiet for a moment. Reggie's heart broke for the naïve young girl she had been.

"I turned my back on my family, my gift, and my responsibilities. I gave him my virginity willingly. He took it with violence. My innocent pain and loss gave him what he needed. He grew stronger. My humiliation gave him pleasure. He was drunk on his own success. In the end, it was his own lust for power that defeated him."

Reggie asked, "What do we need to do to exorcize him? What do the children have to do with it?"

"I won't talk about the children! Not in the same breath!" Constance's face twisted with rage, and she started to fade.

This time Chase tried to stop her. "Please, don't go yet. What can we do?"

Her singsong tone returned when she answered him. "You're doing it, descendant mine. You're doing it…" She faded away. The air around them returned to normal.

Reggie started to move away from him. He grasped her hand. "Explain."

Reggie blushed. Holding his hand, she dragged him to a bench and they both sat down. "I'm sorry, Chase. I had to do something. She was leaving, and kissing you was all I could think of to keep her here."

Chase frowned. Reggie shuddered, and she could feel his tension. He was angry. The emotion swirled around him so clearly, she could almost taste it. It was bitter.

"You go too far sometimes, Reggie. You can't turn another person on and off to serve your own ends." He took a breath and continued in a cold voice. "I don't even want to look at you right now. I'm leaving. I'll be back later, but I suggest you stay out of my way." He stood and looked down at her with disappointment. He walked away, leaving her alone in the garden. It wasn't her imagination when a dark cloud diffused the sunlight and the shadows crept toward her.

Gillian had warned her not to play games. She'd intended to heed the advice, but instead, she'd acted without thought. He was furious with her now, and she didn't blame him. She'd taken advantage of their growing attraction to each other and ended up hurting them both. The disappointment in his eyes had shamed her, and she had no idea how to make it right again. She wanted to cry.

* * * *

The rest of the day was a nightmare for her. Nothing seemed to go right as she found fault with everything in the house. Finally realizing that she'd been terrorizing everyone all day, she offered her victims an apology and called it quits.

Soaking in the huge tub in the master bedroom suite, Reggie heard the front door slam. She'd taken Chase at his word and made sure she was scarce when he got back to Bennett House. She felt sick when she remembered the look on his face. She crossed her arms over her breasts and slipped under the warm water. Unfortunately, she knew she couldn't stay there forever and finally came up for air. The hot bath had not served its purpose. Relaxation wasn't possible when guilt was eating at her. Her heart pounded, and she knew that sleep would be particularly elusive if she didn't do something. She couldn't leave it this way. Flumbling her way out of the tub, she grabbed a towel and began to dry off., Giving up with a sigh, she pulled on her terry robe and fluffy slippers. She opened the bathroom door and prepared to face the music.

He was just starting a fire in the grate as she walked into the living room. He didn't look her way when he said in a clipped voice, "Go away, Reggie."

"I can't. Please, Chase, you have to look at me."

She stood before him, still dripping from the tub, with her robe tightly tied and her feet swallowed by the ridiculous slippers. She knew this was not a stellar moment for her in the glamour department, but she hoped her genuine regret would show through.

Reggie sat on the couch and patted the spot beside her. "Please sit down. I can't do this with you way over there." With a sigh, he joined her on the couch, skepticism written all over his face. He wasn't going to make it easy.

"I am sorry Chase, more sorry than I can say. It was wrong to use you that way. I wish I had a better explanation, but all I can say is that I wasn't thinking." She looked down at her hands. Chase was silent.

Playing awkwardly with the belt of her robe she tried again. "This thing between us is making me crazy. You were right the other night. I do want you." She looked up at him, tears in her eyes. "But I'm scared. It's all happening so fast. The kidnapping last summer, Europe, Constance, that thing in the library, those children...you, I'm overwhelmed. Please be patient with me. I haven't come to terms with it all." She smiled tentatively through her tears.

"I can understand that," Chase said in a soft voice.

She smiled again, a little more confident now that he'd stopped frowning at her so fiercely.

"I appreciate it. I also want you to think about what sex would mean for us. We've been almost like family to each other our whole lives. Family is precious to us both. I can't risk it all without considering the consequences."

"I don't see it that way at all, Reggie." He took her hand. "We have some kind of chemical reaction here. I don't want to waste it. I like it too much." He smiled at her.

"Me, too." She blushed and smiled back at him.

"Good. So can we not worry about what happens next and just enjoy what's happening now? No one would blame us. Just give it a chance."

She shook her head with uncertainty. "There's a lot of potential for hurt here. I know we feel drawn to each other. That's physical. I can handle that, but who's to say we're not being manipulated by other forces. We spend all day here at Bennett House. We already know that there are two entities at work manipulating us. We can't trust our feelings." She hated the weakness in her voice, hated her vulnerability to him.

Nodding, he said, "You make a good point. Yes, we could be under some sort of spell." He threw up his hands. "But I don't care! We have to work together. I don't want to fight my attraction to you along with whatever is in that library. I choose to trust the feeling. It's perfectly natural. Will you try to trust me?"

Tired of fighting it, she gave in. "Okay, but don't rush me."

He nodded. "I deserve that. The other night, I'm sorry. I came on too strong." He laughed self-deprecatingly. "I am a little sexually frustrated. Nothing is going to happen between us until you want it to. Something tells me it will be worth the wait."

"I know what you mean."

Chapter 13

The next morning, in the diner packed with people and a table full of food between her and Chase, Reggie felt optimistic. They were making progress…sort of.

"At least Constance is taking this thing a little more seriously." She said.

Chase swallowed a mouthful of scrambled egg and said, "I think she's always taken it seriously, but pretended otherwise."

"Do you think she's been tied to Bennett House for all these years, in a constant battle with Vincent?" Reggie scooped up a forkful of his eggs and ignored his irritated look.

"Maybe not a battle as such, more like a stalemate. I think she's been keeping Vincent at bay for decades. She's maintained a delicate balance, her powers versus his." Chase popped a piece of sausage in his mouth and talked around it. "He's been feeding off the people around the place. He's grown in strength. As a former Guardian, she'd never take strength from anyone without their consent, so Constance needs our help to defeat him."

"Without kids available to him, maybe we can restore the balance of power. I say we capitalize on our success and face him today. The two of us should start to clean out what's left inside that room. Find his source of power and destroy it." Reggie looked at him fiercely.

It didn't surprise her much when Chase shook his head. "One step at a time, Reggie. I'm up for exploring that room together, but let's be very careful. Neither of us have been near that room and walked out completely unscathed. We've cut off one of his sources, but that doesn't mean we're stronger than him yet."

"Go on," she said reluctantly.

"Research. We need more information about Vincent Bennett. Knowledge is power. The more we have on the man he was, the more we'll understand what it takes to defeat the entity he's become."

Reggie bestowed upon him one of her most brilliant smiles. She was not without powers of her own. She speared a sausage from his plate with her fork, took a tiny bite, chewed, and swallowed. "Not bad, Sherlock."

He ignored her. "No one seems to know much about him. I doubt Constance will be forthcoming, besides there's no guarantee that she can give us anything. No, let's use our own resources this time."

"I can tell you right now, there's nothing about him in this town's records beyond what we already know. I've checked."

"I know, but he had to come from somewhere, and there's a record of him. I just love the Internet, you know. So much information is available at your fingertips if you know what you're looking for."

With her elbows on the table, her head resting in her palms, Reggie smiled. "And you know what you're looking for. Damn, it's nice to have a geek around when you need one. Take it away, Poindexter."

He rolled his eyes at her. "I'll get it started, but you're going to help me if there's a lot of digging to be done. I'll use my computer at home and let you know what I find."

"I was joking, Chase, I'm not a complete airhead. Despite my absolutely drop-dead gorgeous looks." They shared a smile. "I know how to use a computer, but I'll find the same stuff you will, in the beginning, so there's no sense us both spending the day researching."

He looked at her suspiciously. "Ooookaaay."

Before she could assuage his doubts, Todd's father, John Marks approached their table. "Hi, Chase, Reggie, thanks again for helping Todd the other night."

"Don't mention it. How is he?" Reggie asked. She moved so he could sit at the booth with them.

"He snapped right back in a matter of hours. Feel free to have that chat with him you talked about."

"Thanks, I'll call. Maybe take him out for ice cream," she said.

John smiled and shook his head. "That's more than he deserves after his recent behavior."

Chase said, "Don't be too hard on him. Peer pressure can be hell. You might be grateful he learned his lesson at such an early age."

"True. Todd gave me the names of all the other kids involved. I've spoken to their parents. There were mixed reactions, of course. Some people didn't seem too concerned." He reached into a pocket and handed Chase a piece of folded paper. "Here's the list of names Todd gave me. My wife put their phone numbers down so you can call them yourself."

"Thank you, but I doubt that will be necessary. We just want them to know that until further notice, Bennett House is off limits. It's dangerous," Chase said.

He nodded. "They know. I spoke to Tom Weatherby, the principal, and he's promised to add the information to his latest newsletter to parents."

"Oh, that's a great idea." Reggie said.

"Tom said it's the best way to inform everyone. Well, my wife is probably finished grocery shopping so I'd better go help with the bags." He left them with a wave.

Chase asked, "Are you going to talk to Todd?"

Reggie nodded. "Yeah, as soon as possible. Not because I think he has any more to tell us, but rather, I want to hear from him how he'd felt that night. I'll ask him about the other boys as well…Maybe talk to a few of them, too. I'd like to know if they experienced the same feeling of despair and hopelessness that I did, when I came into contact with the Big Bad."

"Good idea. Are you finished eating my breakfast? Want my coffee?"

"You could have had some of mine!" she said defensively.

He held up his hands, wiggling his fingers at her. "I don't come between your fork and food. I have a finely tuned sense of self-preservation, I value my digits."

She looked at him seriously and used her fork to harpoon a potato from his plate and dip it into ketchup, "You are a wise man, Chase McCann." Delicately, she took the home fry off her fork and bit down decisively.

* * * *

Since yesterday had been such a bust, Reggie planned to make up for it today and focused tirelessly on her work restoring Bennett House. The owner, Pat Somers was still incommunicado. Reggie submitted all her ideas to the writer's agent, Jackie Blake. To a large extent, Reggie was given free rein to do what she determined was necessary. Every day, she'd received a delivery of furniture, though; some of it, she'd ordered herself, but many pieces had come from the owner or the agent. Someone must have informed

Jackie Blake that they'd not started on the library because nothing came for that room.

The rest of the work was going well. The results so far made Regina proud. She wondered if Pat Somers had a family. She hoped so. It was time to shake loose the shadowy echoes of the past and fill the house with laughter, that is, if she and Chase were successful in vanquishing Vincent. Reggie mused. Would Constance stick around once he was gone? Reggie doubted it. She'd done penance. Maybe she'd finally find some peace.

Without realizing it, thoughts of Constance drew Reggie into the garden. She sat on the bench near the iron gate that Constance seemed to haunt. Prudence stayed close and sat at Reggie's feet.

Constance came without being summoned. The air changed as it always did when she put in an appearance. Prudence looked up at the apparition without concern.

"I had a cat. I left her behind when I went to Vincent." She looked infinitely sad. "Picket, that was her name, Picket didn't like Vincent. There was a part of me that understood why, but I ignored it. His spell was too strong."

Reggie's face softened with sympathy. "I'm sorry."

"Kind of you to say, Regina, but I've come to terms with that part of my past. My sister took good care of little Picket. I could never have put an innocent creature under Vincent's influence." Her face expressed such excruciating loss, Reggie wanted to reach out and comfort her. "At least not intentionally..." Constance disappeared.

The air cleared, but the profound sadness lingered, and Reggie shed tears for all that Constance had endured and all she'd lost. Her suffering made Reggie even more determined to defeat Vincent. An evil like his, if loosed, could infect the entire town, and from there, who knows what it could do. The Guardians of New Crescent had protected the world from evils such as this in the past. The Old Families' history, with its tales of epic battles of good and evil, had always fascinated Reggie. Sometimes, the battles weren't so epic, but even those had been important because if not checked, evil always grows. Every single struggle against it was important.

With irritation, Reggie said, "If I'm supposed to take this on, why the hell didn't I get some help from my ancestors? You know? Some sort of gift? Like I was supposed to inherit? Duh!" She spoke to no one in particular. For years, she'd lamented that the gift had passed her over and had even accepted a measure of guilt because of it. The very thought of the injustice made her mad. She looked up, unsure of whom she was addressing exactly, but she did it anyway.

Raising her hand pointing her index finger at the sky, she said, "If I get through this, some way, some how, you're going to have to make this up to me! Do you hear me?" She was met with silence. She stalked off.

Unable to concentrate, Reggie decided that she'd spent enough of her day working on the house. She dialed the number John Marks had given her and talked to Todd. She could use some ice cream.

* * * *

Sitting beside the eleven-year-old at the ice cream parlor counter, Reggie scanned the menu on the board.

"I can't decide whether to go for the untried but tempting, or the tried but true. Oh, I'm feeling adventurous today. I'll have a double scoop of Bahama Mama in a waffle cone." She turned to her companion. "What'll you have?"

Todd looked at the young server and said, "I'll have one scoop of bubble gum and one chocolate fudge in a waffle cone, please."

"Ah, the ever-popular split decision…a safe choice." Reggie said. "I swear if I like the Bahama Mama, I'm getting a carton to take home for emergencies."

Todd nodded. In fact, his order had been the first thing he'd said since she'd picked him up. Reggie spun around on her stool twice. Todd looked at her in surprise.

"What? Just because I'm old doesn't mean I don't have fun anymore."

She got her first smile from him. He had a couple of crooked teeth and she wondered if he'd be sporting braces some time in the future.

He finally said, "I'm really sorry about what I did, Miss Stanton."

"It's Reggie, and I know, Todd. I accept your apology. It's not so easy being a kid."

He nodded.

She accepted her cone with thanks, and Todd did the same. For a few moments, they were silent as they gave the ice cream the attention it deserved.

"How's yours?" He ventured.

"Not bad, but I think I'll bring Rocky Road home tonight. How's yours?"

He closed his eyes with reverence. "Mmmm, perfect. Thank you."

Fleetingly, Reggie wondered if she'd just found the man of her dreams. They had so much in common.

"I'm glad you're feeling better. Todd, can you tell me about that night? I know what happened, but I need to know how you felt."

He took another lick of ice cream and then finally responded. "Mostly I was scared. I didn't want to do it." He applied himself to the cone once again.

Reggie did the same. She had long ago mastered the art of talking and eating ice cream at the same time. Deciding to demonstrate those skills, she continued to ask questions.

"In the hospital, you said you'd decided not to go through with it. Can you tell me what happened to change your mind?"

Unaware of the ice cream on his chin, Todd said, "I was gonna turn around and go home. It got real cold. I just wanted to go home. I felt real sad. I think I started to cry." Embarrassed, he ignored his cone for the moment. "I don't cry much anymore, but I wanted to curl up like a baby and cry. I wanted my parents."

"You don't remember taking anything or running away?"

"Nope. My mom says I pulled a knife."

"Yes, but you were clearly not yourself. Where did you get it?"

"It's my dad's from when he was a kid. I'm not supposed to ever play with it. I got in big trouble for taking it." His ice cream cone started to drip onto his fist but he didn't notice.

Reggie handed him a napkin and said, "It's okay now, Todd. It's over, and no one got hurt. You're never going to do something like that again, are you?"

He shook his head. "No way. I don't care what the guys say."

"Good." Reggie smiled. "What have the guys said to you so far?"

"Well, Jeremy, he's my best friend, he was cool. His dad was real mad at him, but Jer was okay with me tellin' and all, seeing as how I got so sick."

Reggie smiled at Jeremy's juvenile justice system…it made a certain amount of sense to her. "Did Jeremy get sick too?"

"Nah, but Aidan did., He got the flu, but was okay the next day. He probably gave it to me."

Reggie nodded, "It happens."

"The whole thing was Aidan's idea. He's the toughest guy in school. He's cool."

She continued to talk with Todd, gently questioning him about the other boys and Bennett House. From what she understood, Todd and his friends had felt the same kind of thing from the Big Bad. They just weren't aware of it, and the aftereffects were blamed on the flu.

When she dropped Todd back at his house, she warned his mother that the ice cream she'd bought him might have ruined his supper. Tammy Marks smiled. "Don't worry, nothing spoils his appetite."

As Reggie drove away, she decided that Todd Marks really was the man of her dreams but was way too young…as usual, her timing sucked.

Chapter 14

Reggie drove by Chase's place before heading back to Bennett House. His battered old truck was parked in front of the bungalow. He was still home. She pulled into the driveway. She'd been to Chase's house once or twice before with Sam or Travis, so it wasn't completely unfamiliar to her. She was anxious to find out what he'd been able to uncover about Vincent. She rapped sharply on the front door.

"It's open," Chase called out from inside.

Seeing him at the computer, Reggie thought, *Ah, the glasses again. Damn he has that sexy, geek look nailed.* He looked distracted and absent-minded professor-ish. She loved it. The sight of him gave her a familiar feeling of excitement.

His welcoming smile made her warm inside. "Hey there, Crash. I've found some information about Vincent Bennett. I don't know if it's going to help us, but it's a start." He was all business as he motioned with his hand to bring her to his side. He stood when she moved closer and absently picked up a stack of papers. Smiling, he swooped down and kissed her lingeringly. He didn't stop until she was breathless.

He licked his lips and said, "You taste fruity. What have you been eating?"

"Blame it on the Bahama Mama at the ice cream shop. I just dropped Todd off."

"How'd it go with our criminal mastermind?"

"Oh, he made a much smarter choice, bubble gum and chocolate fudge." She smiled at him happily.

Chase humored her instead of responding as she'd expected. "I'm glad he's showing at least some good judgment after his foray into a life of crime."

She smiled and shrugged. "He described pretty much the same sense of loss that I felt in the library. We were right. He was under Vincent's influence."

"Did he say anything about the other boys?"

"Yeah, I don't think we'll have further trouble from them. Apparently, the ring leader is a kid named Aidan." Reggie frowned. "I wonder what his story is."

Chase unfolded the list of names John Marks had given him. He pointed to one of the names. "Aidan Scott, here's his phone number." He passed her the sheet of paper.

"Thanks, but I'm not sure I want to go through the parents on this one. John said that some of them weren't so concerned about what their sons were doing. Maybe Todd can point Aidan out to me. I want to see how the other boys relate to him before we meet."

Chase frowned. "Clever, but be careful. Your actions have to be above reproach." He narrowed his eyes at her. "We're talking about children here."

"Exactly. I have to tread lightly. I want to get a feel for the kind of kid he is before talking to him."

He nodded. "Sounds reasonable." With a hopeful tone, he said, "I don't suppose you thought to bring me any ice cream."

"Ah-ha! That's where you're wrong. I've got a tub of Rocky Road in the car. I'll go get it." He stopped her by putting a hand on her back and saying: "I'll get it." He handed her the papers he'd been holding. "You take a look at these. I'll be right back."

Distracted by what was printed on the page, she said, "Yeah, thanks." She sat on the chair he'd just vacated.

After Chase left the room, Reggie, engrossed in the papers, heard rather than felt an unfamiliar vibration. She stopped reading and looked around the room. Nowhere was anything that could have been causing the strange sensation. She pushed the chair away from the desk slowly.

She heard an inhuman growling sound and a large weight landed on her. The flash of quick movement shocked Reggie, and she cried out as sharp little needles pierced the fabric of her jeans.

Chase came running when he heard her cry. He froze in the doorway. Reggie sat pinned to the chair, her lap overflowing with thirty pounds of purring cat. She looked crossly at the feline and pulled his claws out of her thighs with annoyance.

She cast a glance at her host. "My God, Chase, you should warn a person. I almost had a heart attack." She tentatively stroked the huge cat's back. "I didn't know you had a sabertooth. What do you call him?"

"Inconvenient," he said with irritation. "Or how 'bout Pain-In-the-Ass?"

She looked the cat in the face and spoke softly.. "So you don't have a name, huh? Figures, men just don't understand that sort of thing. Maybe you should have selected a female companion to bond with." She scratched behind his ear, and the purring grew louder as he closed his eyes and pressed against Reggie's hand. She looked at Chase standing in the doorway. "Pain in the ass, huh? Well, P.I.T.A. it is then." Addressing the cat, she said, "No complaints Pita. You have no one to blame but yourself…you're the one who picked him."

"He's not my cat. He just showed up one day and never left."

"Did you try to locate his owner?"

He rolled his eyes at her, "Of course I did. I'm still trying in fact."

"He's a Maine Coon cat, I think, the largest and heaviest breed. You should be honored. You're no outsider. You know better than to take an animal's spontaneous attachment so lightly. Be grateful he chose you." She shifted under Pita's weight and declared, "He belongs here in New Crescent. He belongs with you. He knows it, even if you don't. I like your cat Chase. He's a beauty." She laughed as he walked into the kitchen. "I want a bowl too," she called out.

After a few moments, he returned carrying a bowl and two spoons. He opened the ice cream tub and handed her the spoon.

"Since when do you use a bowl?"

"Mmm." She closed her eyes with pleasure after her first spoonful of ice cream. Nodding at the papers on his desk, she said, "You've done a lot of work here. Man, you're set up. I look at this computer system, and I want to ask, how do you fly this thing?"

Moving a chair next to hers, he said, "It works."

"You don't say?"

He ignored her. "I've been able to access the Bennett Family archives in England. That's where Vincent was born. Records show that his parents died when he was six, and he was sent to live with a distant relative.

According to this, he grew up in London and took over his adopted father's shipping business."

"How'd he end up in America?" Reggie asked, looking over his shoulder.

"That's unclear. But I suspect he came for business reasons. He arrived in Boston when he was twenty-nine."

"That would make him at least eleven years older than Constance. Women married young then. Eighteen would have been a perfectly respectable age to wed."

"Yeah, that was normal for the time, but here's the creepy thing. Get a look at the cargo Vincent profited from."

"Oh my God...slaves." Reggie wanted to be sick.

"We really shouldn't be that surprised. It makes sense. The slave trade wasn't so profitable in Britain at that time. He went where the money was, the United States of America. It says here he trafficked in Asian, African, and Native slaves. Our guy didn't discriminate, it seems. He was an equal-opportunity sociopath." Chase's voice dripped with disgust. "A man with his wicked ways would have had a field day trading in human beings. The hell he'd undoubtedly visited upon those poor souls is unimaginable."

Reggie read on. "It looks like the Bennett family didn't approve of his dealings because, here it is, he was disowned. Hmm, that kind of explains why no Bennett ever claimed the house here in America...ill-gotten gains. Maybe somebody had a conscience."

"He'd traveled widely. There's no telling where he picked up the dark magic Constance referred to, could have been anywhere."

Reggie shrugged. "Maybe that won't matter. If we approach Constance as if we already know all about Vincent, she's bound to let something slip." She sat back in frustration. "I feel like we're wasting time. I want to do something."

Chase cupped her chin with his hand and said, "Patience. We're making progress. Let's get back to Bennett House and try to contact Constance with what we've learned."

She nodded. He bent and kissed her lips. Pita complained by digging a claw or two into Reggie's thigh. She pulled away from Chase. "Oww, ow..."

Chase looked confused, then smiled. "For a second there, I thought that was my fault. 'Ow...ow' is not the usual response to my kisses."

"Oh yeah? And just what *is* the usual response, rock star?"

He picked up the cat and put him on the floor. Standing up, he pulled her into his arms. "Let me show you."

He started slowly, taking her mouth with his, gently touching her lips with his tongue then pulling back and doing it all over again. She groaned, and he kissed her with passion. He cradled her head in one hand and paid homage to her neck. She shivered in response and dug her nails into his back. He moved his hips against hers. His hardness, her softness made a perfect balance as he found a multitude of sensitive spots on her body.

She unbuttoned his shirt and nipped his chest. He liked it and let her know it by mimicking her action and pressing his teeth against her shoulder. Desperate to feel skin against skin she helped him pull her t-shirt up and off. The pleasure she felt when her naked belly connected with his, made her want to scream. She rubbed up against him like a cat. And just like a cat she wanted to purr and dig her nails into him. He didn't seem to mind. He unsnapped her bra with ease and cupped a breast in his hand. She was perfect for him and he licked, and sucked and bit her with exactly the right enthusiasm.

Completely lost in him, she responded instinctively. Leveraging herself on his shoulders with each hand, she wrapped her legs around his waist. He held her as if she weighed nothing. Reggie liked that. She tugged desperately at this hair. He looked up, and she smashed her mouth against his, kissing him as if her life depended on it.

Distantly, they registered a gentle vibration and chiming music. They both froze. Their eyes locked. Both their cells phones were ringing. In silent, but oh-so-reluctant agreement, Chase released Reggie, and she put her feet on the floor. At the same moment, they each took a steadying breath and reached for a phone.

If their urgent replies were any indication, they had the exact same conversations. After they hung up, they looked at each other helplessly. Chase was the first person to speak.

"Sam."

She nodded. "We'll probably make it to the hospital just as they do." Grabbing her discarded t-shirt she pulled it over her head. She ignored her bra, picked up her car keys and threw them at Chase. He caught them easily.

She said, "You drive. My nickname is Crash, not a good omen right now."

They rushed out of the house. Chase's unbuttoned shirt flapped in the autumn wind.

In the car, they shared information. There'd been another accident at Bennett House. Somehow, Sam had fallen off the roof and landed on the iron gate in the garden. He was unconscious. Chase had been told that it looked like Sam had broken his back. Reggie had been told he may have broken his neck. Neither option was acceptable to them as they hurried to the hospital.

Reggie said, "How is it possible that he landed on the iron gate? If that's so, then he couldn't have fallen. The trajectory is wrong."

"Yeah. Either he jumped or was thrown." Chase said grimly. "You've always wanted an excuse to use the word 'trajectory' haven't you?" He grabbed her hand and brought it to his lips. He took his eyes off the road just long enough to gently smile at her.

"Yeah, but I could have gone the rest of my life without using it in this context." He squeezed the hand he still held.

* * * *

When they rushed into the emergency unit, they were met by Duncan and four of his guys. Sam was Duncan's friend, too. He looked gray with worry. So far, they'd received no word and he looked at Chase and Reggie helplessly. The hospital had called his next of kin and left a message. It didn't matter. Sam wouldn't want to see his family anyway. His true kin were Reggie, Travis, and Chase.

When the doctor came out, he recognized Chase and Reggie. He walked over to them and said, "Bennett House again?" They nodded, and he said, "Your friend is stable but still unconscious. His leg is badly broken and will need surgery, but right now, we're more concerned about his head injury. I've called in a specialist, and we're doing tests."

Reggie put a hand on Chase's forearm and said, "Gillian's specialist, Doctor Smythe, I wonder if he could help?"

They stepped outside to use her cell phone. Reggie's conversation was brief. "Gillian's calling him. She's pretty sure he'll come."

"Yeah, Smythe has been in New Crescent quite a bit these days, helping the rape victims from last summer." Chase's voice was pitched low.

"That's good of him," Reggie said.

"Yeah, he thinks the world of Gillian, so in my book, that puts him in the good column." Chase opened his arms to her, and she stepped into them.

With her cheek resting against his chest, she said, "This is the last. No more work at Bennett House until we deal with Vincent. I'll call and let Jackie Blake know in the morning."

Shaking his head, Chase said, "Don't worry. Leave it to me."

Chapter 15

Finally back at Bennett House, Reggie flopped down on the couch in the finished living room. It gave her comfort to see what she'd accomplished here. She'd restored its beauty. Fortunately, she'd been able to find the perfect pieces to complement the furniture Pat Somers had selected. Pru was ecstatic to see her, and Reggie apologized for neglecting her that day. After leaving the hospital, she'd dropped Chase off at his house. She knew he'd be right behind her. She didn't even look up when he entered the room.

"You have no one to blame but yourself," he said in an irritated voice as he dumped Pita on her lap. "Figures, the first time he sets foot outside in months, he stows away in my truck. You asked for it."

Reggie laughed and hugged the cat with enthusiasm. Pru looked insulted and walked over to Chase. He bent and patted the little dog. "Don't worry, girl, you'll always have me."

Unconcerned and secure in Pru's devotion to her, Reggie said, "What good is a familiar if he's not with you all the time? Of course Pita wanted to come here. It's his duty to be near you. You'll see."

He gave her a long look and then blinked. "I'm going to make some hot cocoa. I won't bother asking you if you want some. Think you can manage to light the fire while I'm gone?"

"Trust me, baby, I've been lighting fires since puberty." Her provocative glance made him wince.

He cleared his throat and said a pathetic, "Uh, yeah…"

Reggie laughed throatily as he retreated. It was his last line of defense, and she knew it.

He made her dreams come true when he returned with two cups of hot chocolate and fist-sized chunks of Gillian's homemade banana bread.

They sat in silence watching the fire. It felt wonderful curled up to Chase, touching him at will. The indulgence made her sigh. He turned and looked down at her face as she rested her head on his shoulder.

"You okay?" he asked.

"I'm okay. I'm glad Sam's going to be fine. By the sounds of it, he was lucky in a way."

"If we call breaking a leg in three places and severe concussion getting lucky, I agree."

"He's alive Chase. I choose to think that's on the full side."

"Me too."

"We need to find out what happened. Sam is no more likely to throw himself off a roof than you are."

"And I can't imagine what it would take to pitch him off. Sam's tough, no one ever stole his lunch money," Chase said.

"Hopefully, he can tell us something when he regains consciousness. Gillian's Dr. Smythe promises to see him first thing tomorrow."

"I've called all my guys and reassigned them to other jobs for the time being. I've asked Duncan to put his work on hold for now. And I've alerted Jackie."

"You are an army of one, I swear. When did you get time to do all that?" She yawned, exhaustion finally wafting over her.

"I'm good. Very, very good." He had his own version of provocation, and for a second, Reggie regretted her dissipated energy level.

Chase seemed to understand because he leaned forward and helped her to rise. "I think it's time you got some rest. You're dead on your feet." He helped her up the stairs, his arm around her shoulders.

In the doorway to her bedroom, Chase paused and turned her face to him. He kissed her gently. This was a kiss of tenderness and support. He was a magician.

"Call if you need me," he said as he turned toward the stairs.

Reggie couldn't bear to see him go and reached out. He stood completely still, waiting for her to speak.

In a tentative voice, she said, "I don't know if it's fair to ask you this, but I'm going to anyway. Please feel free to say no."

He waited.

"Would you stay with me tonight? I don't want to be alone. Can you just hold me through the night?"

He smiled at her with complete comprehension. "I think that can be arranged." She frowned when he turned to leave again. He shook his head. "I'll just go get something to sleep in. I think tonight might call for it."

She smiled and nodded.

* * * *

She slept well that night. Her dreams were like those she'd had as a child, light and friendly. She smiled in her sleep.

"There. Now you've had some sleep." Reggie could hear Constance's voice so clearly, but she wasn't sure if it had been a dream. She opened her eyes and looked around the room. Chase was still with her. His warmth had made its way into her body and feeling blissful, she wondered if she'd ever feel chilled again.

"Yes, it's me," Constance said in a bored tone.

Reggie snuggled a little closer to Chase's sleeping form. "Go away." She moaned. "The garden is one thing, but I draw the line at the bedroom. Like I said before, if you see a light, head for it. Cross over already."

"Regina Stanton, do you really think I'd be here if it wasn't important?"

Grudgingly, she had to give her that. "Okay. I'm listening."

"Your man friend, Morgan Goode's bloodline. The one you call Sam, I trust he will be healed?"

"Yes. It will take time, but his prognosis is good."

"Blessed be." The relief sounded in her ghostly voice. "You've made a decision about my descendant here I can see."

"How did you know?"

Constance didn't bother to reply. Instead, she said, "The time is now my dear. All you have to do is touch your skin to his. Do it..." Her voice faded away but Reggie could hear the echo of her parting words, "Your skin to his. Do it...do it..."

The words became a mantra and Reggie breathed deeply. She didn't resist. It felt indescribably right. So she did it.

With her heart pounding, she ran her hand up Chase's naked chest. He didn't disguise his response and immediately turned to her. "Reggie?" He said; his voice hoarse and filled with longing.

"Mmm hmm," she murmured.

He captured her wayward hand and brought it to his lips. He said, "Honey, if you do that, you'd better mean it because once I touch you, I won't be able to stop."

She kissed his neck. "I was hoping you'd say exactly that."

He pressed the hand he held to the hardness of his body. There was no hiding his response. He moaned.

Chase was a man who knew how to take his time. And he did, treating her body to endless varieties of sensuality. He helped her to discover new and exciting pleasure zones she'd never known existed. A soft stroke of his fingers on the back of her neck sent shivers rocketing through her entire body.

He did amazing things to her, and she loved every minute of it, but what really affected her was his reaction to *her* touch. She could do to him what he did to her. With reverence, she humbly accepted her feminine power over him and felt blessed.

Their lovemaking was earth-shattering as they drove each other higher and higher. Taking a deep breath, Chase looked down at her in all her wanton glory and visibly forced a shaky control.

Soothing her gently, he said, "Are you sure, Reggie? This is what you want?"

His question surprised her, and she almost responded flippantly until she saw the deadly serious light in his blue eyes. This was not a moment for levity. It was a moment for honesty. She put a hand on either side of his jaw and brought his head closer to hers. With her eyes open, she kissed him. Her pleasure in him was reflected back to her in his shining eyes.

"Yes, a thousand versions of yes."

He took her mouth with enthusiasm. He caressed her body and made her arch ever closer to him. She could feel his amazing hardness, and it thrilled her. She started to guide his body into hers, but he stopped her. His mouth cruised the lush length of her. Hesitating a moment before his lips and tongue moved to the spot on her body that throbbed most for release, he smiled. He didn't make her wait for long. He took her to impossible heights, and just when she thought she could go no further, he'd discover a whole new altitude and take her there.

Reggie wanted to scream. She wanted to do for this man what he'd done for her, but he stopped her with an agonized glance. He kissed her deeply and moved above her. In one sure, hard thrust, he took her. She was more than ready. The joining of their bodies was life. It meant everything. They moved in perfect harmony.

Reggie was thrilled that despite his earlier ministrations she reached another pinnacle right along with him. They both vocalized their release. Bennett House settled itself around their urgent utterances. Pru and Pita discreetly slept through the whole thing.

They didn't talk afterward. They didn't have the breath for it. Naked and wrapped around each other, they drifted off to sleep.

Reggie woke a little while later to discover that they'd started all over again in their sleep. This time, he didn't take it slow and easy but rather possessed her with a ruthlessness she admired. She gave as good as she got. They were matched perfectly.

Afterwards, she knew she'd left marks on him just as he had on her. She didn't mind. For Reggie, such marks were just transient evidence of a passion she hoped would be infinite.

* * * *

There were no workmen the next morning, so they slept in. Waking up with Chase was a treat. He was definitely a morning person, and he proved it to her, twice.

Since she was starving, Reggie offered to make breakfast. She had a little trouble leaving the bed with him still in it, but she managed. Congratulating herself on her will of iron, she took eggs, bacon, and cheese out of the fridge. Scrambled eggs she could do. With a smile, she put peanut butter and jelly on the table just in case Chase needed his fix.

When he came into the kitchen still wet from his shower, Reggie smiled. Somehow, despite the frying bacon, she could smell his unique scent, and a part of her soul yearned to taste him again and again. Was there ever a more effective aphrodisiac?

"And she cooks too? I am a lucky man indeed," he said as he spun her away from the stove and into his arms. With a fork held in the air above his head she returned his kiss.

When he finally let her go, she said, "Of course I cook, seeing as how I'm so hot."

He laughed. "You could liquefy steel, honey."

They sat down at the table together. Pru eyed Pita with suspicion from her spot by the door. Ignoring her, Pita yowled. The sound surprised Reggie. "Does he always sound like that or is something wrong?"

Chase looked a little shamefaced. "He gets fed before I do every morning." He rose and took care of Pita's needs before finishing his breakfast. Reggie noted that for someone who pretended indifference, he sure pampered that cat. Chase scratched Pita's chin before putting a bowl in from of him. The unconscious cooing noises he made brought an indulgent smile to Reggie's already glowing face.

"Just in case you weren't aware of it Crash, I appreciate you remembering the PB and J." He proceeded to slather jelly on one piece of toast and peanut butter on another. Squashing them together, he smiled lustily before taking a huge bite.

"You're just a great big kid, aren't you?"

"After last night, I'd say that's the best way to be." He took another enormous mouthful and smiled.

She blushed and took a dainty bite of a slice of bacon.

"I called the hospital to check on Sam." Chase said. "He's stable but still unconscious. Dr. Smythe was very encouraging."

Reggie breathed a sigh of relief. "That's good news. After breakfast, I want to take a look at the scene of the crime so to speak."

"Me, too. It makes me sick to think Vincent had the kind of power it would take to hurl a man of Sam's size, off the roof."

She nodded. "Maybe Constance can shed some light on what happened. She'll probably know more than Sam himself."

"That's very likely." He cocked his head and furrowed his brow. "This might sound crazy, but did I hear Constance last night?"

Unsure of exactly how much to tell him, Reggie nodded. Taking her time chewing her toast thoroughly, she finally swallowed and said, "She woke me up. She asked about Sam. I think she likes him."

"She's not the first, and she won't be the last."

Reggie smiled. "You can say that again. It'll be interesting to see how he manages to keep his lady friends from running into each other when they visit him. I wouldn't put it past Constance herself to she put in an appearance." She took a sip of the coffee she'd brewed and decided that he definitely made better. "Last night was the first time Constance has contacted me in the house."

"It must have been horrifying for her when Sam came crashing down on the iron gate. She could have been right there watching it, unable to prevent it."

"That's true. I forgot about that. Maybe that's what prompted her to visit me in the house, make the extra effort."

"Believe me, the thought of her gaining strength doesn't chill my blood the way Vincent's does." He made a fist with one large hand. "I'd like to talk to Constance before we go near the library today. We need to tell her what we're going to do."

"If she doesn't already know. She's pretty tapped in."

"I'd feel better being completely straight with her. She tends to beat around the bush, but we can't afford any misunderstandings. Someone we both love very much could have died here yesterday. I don't think it's possible to take that too seriously."

Chapter 16

Reggie put a coat on before going outside. It felt like Indian summer had exhausted itself as autumn returned in earnest. Still, the air smelled rich and promising. She walked with Chase to the spot where Sam must have landed. The gate had done a lot more damage to Sam than he'd done to it.

Looking up at the house, Chase and Reggie exchanged meaningful glances and silently agreed that there was no way Sam fell from the roof. There had to be intent behind his actions. Such intent pointed directly at Vincent. Sam would not have jumped unless some other force had been in control. They knew that without doubt. The idea of Sam committing suicide was positively inconceivable.

Reggie concentrated on Constance and waited for the telltale change in the air. They didn't have to wait long. It seemed Constance was eager to talk this morning.

"Good morning, you two. I hope you had a good breakfast, Regina. You need your strength, now more than ever."

"Well that sounds portentous." Reggie said. "Is that a subtle warning?"

"Of course not, child, but I know you will enter the library today. That is your intent, is it not?" As she spoke, her image became more solid. Reggie gave Chase a quick glance, trying to gage if he could see Constance. He shrugged and shook his head. She was still just a ghostly voice to him.

Chase spoke. "You're right. We're going in the library today."

Instead of resisting, Constance said, "It's time."

Chase and Reggie exchanged a look.

"We know all about Vincent Bennett," Reggie said. "Information is far more easily accessed these days. As a Guardian, you should have seen through him immediately. Why didn't you?" The challenge in her words was intentional.

"Temptation. I inherited a great power when I was just fourteen. My father spoiled me endlessly. I wanted for nothing, so of course I desired what I couldn't or shouldn't have."

She took a deep breath, and Reggie wondered if she performed that mundane human function from need or habit. Constance drew her attention to more important matters. "I was denied so rarely. Vincent Bennett played his hand brilliantly. I was a romantic, a fool for love. Younger, more suitable men fell at my feet, but they bored me. They provided no sport. Vincent Bennett was the perfect challenge in every way." She looked at Chase for a long moment. "Papa disapproved of him, all the Old Families did, even my fellow Guardians. He was much older than I and was inappropriate in so many ways."

"Did you recognize his evil?" Reggie asked.

"Yes, but I pushed it aside. I wanted to rebel, misbehave. The darker side of our nature often vies for supremacy. I was too enamored to resist the temptation. A Guardian's power is strong. When we falter, the repercussions can prove disastrous. I was weak and paid the price, but others paid a price much higher than mine."

Chase said, "I'm sorry Constance, but that's over. The past is dead. We need your help now. Your battle against Vincent took a tremendous toll, but in the end, you prevailed. Vincent Bennett hardly founded a dynasty. It ended here. You did that. Tell us how, so we can end him for good."

She looked at him with annoyance, "I didn't conquer him. No, I wasn't worthy. It was my destiny to hold him here until the one who could defeat him was ready."

"And that's us? Chase and me?" Reggie asked.

"No." Her answer surprised them both. "But the two of you must battle him. That's your destiny."

Chase sighed. "So you're telling us that we have no choice but to fight him, but we're destined to lose?"

"You always win when you fight evil. It is impossible to lose when you do the right thing. You fail only if you do nothing."

Reggie rolled her eyes. "Uh, yeah, thanks for the fortune cookie, Confucius. Care to be a bit more specific?"

Chase smiled at Reggie's flip reply, but he sobered when Constance frowned.

"Do you want my help?" she asked severely.

"Yes." Chase's response was firm.

"You must face him together. Neither of you has the strength alone. Trust each other and believe in your combined strength. Doubt will not win the day." She was gone.

Reggie smiled ruefully. "Sorry about that. You've always warned me that my sense of humor would get me into trouble someday."

He hugged her. "Today is not that day. Don't apologize. Your humor is a part of who you are. It gives you strength. We can't afford to deny our true nature. If we're the ones destined to face this evil, then there's a reason for it. It has to be us. We have to be who we are."

She slapped his hard chest and smiled. "You're absolutely right, Poindexter. You don't happen to have any chocolate on you, do you?"

He pulled a candy bar from his jacket pocket and handed it to her. "I brought provisions."

"Mmm, chocolatey goodness." She smiled up at him as if he'd just gifted her with the moon. If he had, she probably could have eaten it. Despite the large breakfast ,she was starving. He hugged her even closer.

They agreed to meet back at Bennett House to tackle the library together, later in the afternoon. They both had work to do that they felt couldn't be delayed. Chase spent a little more time on the Internet, seeking information about Vincent Bennett and his family. Reggie visited an estate sale in search of a number of items she'd listed in her notebook as must-haves. Estate sales were the perfect place to find the right style and vintage.

* * * *

The backseat of her rental car was full of little treasures when she and Pru pulled up to Gillian's house on the cliff. Getting out of the car, Reggie breathed the sea air and looked out at the ocean for a reverential moment. Halloween was approaching. She could almost smell it in the air. Every season in New Crescent had a fragrance so unique that eluded her descriptive talents. But ask a New Crescent native and they'd agree with Reggie. The place had a different perfume for every autumn, winter, spring and summer. That phenomenon was part of what made the town so magical.

Before walking to Gillian's door, Reggie sent a silent thanks to Mother Nature for her generosity and balance. Trust a woman to get it right.

"Hey, Reggie, Pru, this is a nice surprise." Gillian was in her friend's company for less than ten seconds and knew.

She laughed. "Wow, that man really is a sexual virtuoso. His potency matches his proportions. He got it right the first time out. Lucky you."

Reggie's brandy-colored eyes narrowed. "Oh my God, you know about Chase and me...what was I thinking...of course you're...well...you. If I had any hope of keeping it a secret, I should have known better than to stop by."

Gillian shook her head and, with a brilliant smile, said, "It is always better to stop by. I can't offer you coffee but how about lunch. You hungry?"

Reggie didn't bother to answer. She knew the question was purely rhetorical. Over clam chowder and fat sandwiches, they talked. Hank and Prudence slept at their feet.

It was Gillian's first autumn in New Crescent. Reggie enthusiastically told her all about the traditions of the town. For New Crescent, every holiday was special, and they played it up to the hilt. Travis's parents, Bill and Ruth Sinclair were planning their annual Halloween party. People would come from miles around to attend. Every year, the costumes grew more and more ingenious. It was worth attending just to see what everyone else was wearing. There was endless spirit in their little town.

"I guess Ruth has asked you to design the announcement notices," Reggie said. Invitations weren't needed. Everyone was welcome. But still, reminders were sent out faithfully. The party was always held on the Saturday before October 31. Halloween night itself was saved for a children's party. The Sinclair's Ballroom was open to all trick-or-treaters. Families who lived outside the town limits always drove into town to trick or treat. Many parents swung by the Sinclair house first and dropped off the candy they would have given out had they lived in the town. It was a good way to contribute to the celebration. By the end of the night, in one stop, kids could double their haul by visiting the Sinclair house.

This year, in the spirit of the season, Travis, Sam, and Chase were creating a haunted mansion in the guest house on the Sinclair property. Each new idea topped the last until the project began taking on mammoth proportions. The three men were having so much fun competing with each other over who could create the scariest monster and devising ever more elaborate tricks. It was bound to become an annual thing.

Gillian was a successful graphic designer, so Ruth Sinclair, her future mother-in-law made use of her services. The announcements were beautiful. Gillian showed Reggie the mock-ups and smiled when she guessed which one Ruth had chosen. It wasn't the most elegant design or the most edgy. It was certainly the most fun, and that spirit fit the event to a tee. Gillian and Reggie both approved Ruth's decision.

"Have you decided what costume you're going to wear?" Gillian asked Reggie.

"Yeah. I figured since Chase has resurrected my nickname, Crash, I'd go as a victim of my own driving. Should be easy and comfortable. How about you?"

Gillian grimaced. "Mine's so lame. I'm going to go as a fortune teller."

Reggie laughed with delight. "That's perfect. You've been accepted as a Guardian. What better costume. Ernestine always goes as a witch. She says it's the only day of the year she shows her true self. When we were younger, we believed her."

Gillian laughed. "Not so far from the truth."

Time passed too quickly when they were together, and it wasn't long before Reggie and Pru had to leave. Gillian and Hank walked their guests to the car. Before Reggie opened the car door, Gillian held her hand and said, "Be careful girl. You cannot let your guard down with what's in that library. Please don't drink alcohol. Don't cloud your judgment until this is done."

Reggie frowned at her friend. "Sure. I don't drink much anyway. It won't be tough to resist the demon alcohol. I'll stick to the crack-cocaine." She giggled, raised her right hand and put her left on her heart. "Don't worry, Gillian. I swear to stay absolutely sober until the Voldemort in the library is defeated."

Pru jumped in the backseat and they were off.

Chase was waiting for her when she got back to Bennett House. They talked briefly about strategy before entering the library.

"At first, let's keep physical contact with each other. Since we've been told repeatedly that we have to face this thing together then I want to make our solidarity a physical thing," He said.

Reggie nodded. "I agree. I also think we should be as assertive as possible. You know, act strong and you will be."

"I like that. How do you want to start?"

"Chase, I need you to trust me to speak first. I haven't figured out exactly what I'm going to say yet. Something tells me that when the time comes, I'll know."

He didn't hesitate. "Okay, but if you get into trouble, don't expect me to stand by and hope you can handle him on your own."

"Good, I have no problem with being rescued when necessary."

They smiled at each other. Chase moved to the hallway, but Reggie stopped him. She put her arms around him and turned her face up for his kiss. He didn't disappoint her. When he was done, her lips were swollen, and she blinked more than once. Her heart beat wildly, not with fear, but with excitement. They were ready.

* * * *

The rush had been almost sexual. When that man hit the ground with force, he'd felt a sweet ecstasy not unlike what he'd experienced when taking a young innocent. And there were so many delicious ways to take. Fear and pain gave him pleasure. He'd grown strong from the suffering of others in the past, and he would again. He'd learned that it was always more satisfying when the pain was mental and physical, like taking virginity not freely offered. That was a special agony endured only once in a girl's life…well, almost. With his renewed strength would come memory. For now, he could only vaguely remember what his life had been like. What had pleased him and what had angered him. The other's soul searing anguish had been exquisite, but merely recalling it wasn't enough. He had to have more. His craven yearning was a bottomless bowel that had raged impotently when he'd sensed a coming light, a glistening hope that could end him and others of his ilk. For now, he'd not rise to their challenge. Discipline. He didn't like the word when applied to his own desires, but power needed to be conserved and used when it was most advantageous. And unexpected. He would not underestimate his enemies. Triumph would soon be within his grasp. He would be unstoppable.

Chapter 17

Standing at the threshold of the hallway that led to the library, Reggie held onto Chase's hand and savored the adrenalin. She smiled at him and bravely walked to the double doors. She'd forgotten what the rancid air had felt like as she breathed it in and gasped. It felt infectious. A part of her mind cringed and gagged in reaction, but she pushed it away. She would not let the feeling take hold. It was just a trick, pathetic really. Sharing a glance with Chase, she could tell he felt the same way.

"It's not so bad. It gets easier. Maybe the Big Bad isn't nearly so big nor so bad."

She laughed and Chase joined her. Their laughter gave them a small rush of power. Excitement crackled between them. Everything shared made them stronger, and that knowledge helped them to open both doors with ease

Forcing herself to resist the temptation to turn tail and run, Reggie concentrated on what she could see. At one time, the library must have been the most beautiful room in the house. A majestic curved mahogany staircase led to the second level, and every wall was lined with shelves from floor to ceiling. Most of the books were gone or completely beyond redemption, but the shelves had withstood the harsh test of time. They could be salvaged. The fireplace was made of the same mahogany as the stairs and the shelves. The creative side of Reggie's nature imagined just how impressive it would look when restored properly. Once she'd filled the shelves with books, Reggie knew she'd have to hire someone who could design a system of sliding ladders. When fully renovated and decorated, this room would be her masterpiece.

Clutching Chase's hand, Reggie shook her head with sadness. What once must have been glorious was now covered in mold, mildew, and a strange greasy dust. Work on this room would be a mission of mercy.

Surprised that she could think of anything other than what they were about to face, Reggie forced her wayward mind to concentrate on what was to come. Just stepping over the threshold took courage. She heard a strange hissing noise and looked at Chase to see if he'd heard it too. She didn't have to ask him. His look told her everything. He could hear it, and he didn't like it.

"Duncan's guys sure didn't make much progress in here," Chase said.

"They were only in here one day. I think they tossed out a truckload of books damaged beyond repair. Anything worth money had been cleared out long ago."

Feeling chilled to the bone, Reggie shivered. Chase pulled her close and put his arm around her, trying to warm her. She shook her head. "I feel chilled from the inside. Don't you?"

He nodded. "Strange, it's like an emotional and physical cold. How can that be?"

"I don't know, but I'm not giving in to it even if I have to drag out my parka and earmuffs."

She looked up at him. His jaw was set. He nodded at her.

She took a deep breath and spoke loudly with purpose. "This house belongs to the living. Life will restore it. The past is done. You hold no sway over the future. Vincent Bennett, we will not let you take from us. You will get no more power from the living. You must go."

The hissing got louder, almost deafening. It felt like it came from inside her head. For a split second, she imagined a snake wrapping itself around her head and sliding into her ears, nose, and mouth. She rejected the vision. She was inviolate. The only warmth she could feel came from where Chase's body maintained contact with hers, but she didn't shiver. She wouldn't give it the satisfaction of seeing her react.

Taking strength from Chase's solid form, Reggie resisted the depressing weight of hopelessness that settled around her. She wanted to give up, to leave this room to whatever force possessed it. That urge was almost irresistible, but she fought it back. The effort sapped her energy, and she felt weak and dizzy. The room swam before her eyes, and wave after wave of black sorrow struck her like battering rams. She understood that it was an attack, a battle plan. This feeling didn't come from within her. Clever how the enemy used her own emotions to defeat her, she thought absently.

Stalemate? No, she wasn't alone in this. She had a secret weapon. She looked up at Chase and could see the trust he had in her. He believed in her, and that confidence shone in his eyes.

Her eyes locked with his and she knew she could do it. From deep in her belly, she dragged out a burgeoning power and pushed back hard, throwing the depression off and out. The blood rushed through her veins. She imagined a lightning type force and threw it at the source of the hissing. They heard a deafening crack, then silence.

Chase spoke in a whisper. "Either the air cleared a little or I'm getting used to it because I find it easier to breath now. The smell isn't quite so strong." He looked down at Reggie and reacted immediately. She was dead on her feet, using his solid stance like a life preserver.

He swept her up in his arms. In a deep and firm voice, he addressed the entity. "You do not belong here! Go, or be destroyed! You will grow weaker every day, and we will grow stronger. We will never give up. You will never win!" His words were met with silence, but this time, the air cleared completely. Rich with oxygen, it felt sweet and the atmosphere in the room lightened.

Reggie smiled at him as she rested her head on his shoulder. With her spirit down, but never out she said weakly, "Not bad Poindexter, but I could really go for pie right now." She giggled.

He joined her. Their laughter helped to restore her strength, but Chase still held her in his arms, rooted to the spot. They glanced around. In that moment, the library looked and felt just like any other room in the house. It was filthy and sorely in need of a face lift, but it was just a normal room.

In a voice that was almost her own, Reggie said, "I think we can go. We've won this round." For now, the thing was at bay. She didn't know why or how, and it gave her no sense of relief, but they'd done what was needed for today.

Chase didn't put her down until they reached the living room. She smiled when he put her back on her feet instead of on the couch. He knew her so well. Holding her elbows, he stepped back. "Are you okay?"

She nodded, and he said, "Good, I'll go get the pie."

* * * *

In the kitchen, Chase grabbed a chair and sat down heavily. He took a deep breath, waiting for his heartbeat to slow. Reggie couldn't see his weakness. She'd needed his support. She'd been magnificent, a fearless Amazon...no...with her coloring, more like a Valkyrie.

With a rueful grin, he knew that if asked he'd have to admit that when they'd been in that room, he'd played Robin to her Batman. He could live with that as long as she was ok. His grin turned into a full fledged smile. White hats one, black hats zero. They'd beaten that thing back for now. He'd take what he could get. With that realization came satisfaction. He felt better. Now where did he put that pie?

* * * *

Sitting on the couch with Pru at her feet, Reggie put a hand to her stomach. She'd called upon strength from her belly. How odd, she mused. Who would have thought to go there? Then she thought, maybe that's the best place for her to find strength what with her appetite and all. She took a steadying breath as that same stomach lurched. The nausea hit so fast and so violently, she barely made it to the powder room.

When she came back into the living room, Chase said, "I was just coming to check on you. Are you okay?" He looked at her, puzzled.

Strangely, she felt absolutely fine. Reggie's face was glowing. This was not the complexion of a weak or ill woman. She looked vibrant and healthy.

With a bemused smile, she said, "You know, if you'd asked me that question five minutes ago I would have said, 'No, I'm sick. Fix it.' But at this moment, I feel just great."

She saw the tray he'd brought in. He'd heated the pie and brought ice cream. *Was there ever a better man?* Reggie mused. "Yummy, pie."

He waited until they'd both got about halfway through the pie before speaking. "I guess we won that round, huh?"

She nodded, her mouth full. After swallowing, she said, "Yeah, but I don't feel triumphant. It was too easy."

"You call that easy?" Incredulous, he pinned her with a blue gaze, "Damn it, Reggie, what you did in there buckled your knees. If truth be told, it almost buckled mine too."

"He was strong. Yes, but not as strong as he was before. That concerns me. I would have thought that after what he did to Sam, he'd be pretty powerful right now."

Chase nodded. "You're right, either he's using his strength in a way we haven't discovered yet or he was holding back. I don't like the sound of either possibility."

Sipping the peppermint tea he'd been so clever to brew, she agreed with him. "We'd better find out which it is because I don't think we can afford to let him get the upper hand." She stood. "I'm going to talk to Constance."

She rushed out of the room and into the garden. He followed her. It was dark and the air was chilled, but this kind of cold Reggie could handle. This was the perfectly normal kind. It felt wonderful, in fact. Standing by the little iron gate, she concentrated on Constance.

"Don't let your victory go to your head," the obstinate ghost said in a singsong little voice.

"We won't," Reggie said sharply.

"He won't be able to keep you out of the library again," she said.

Looking around and not seeing anything, Chase spoke to the air. "Is he weaker?"

"No."

"Why did we succeed then?" Reggie could see Constance perfectly and looked at her intently, trying to gage her reactions.

"He wants you in the library. He's very confident that you'll make a mistake and he can take from you. That would give him a significant edge."

Chase said, "Well, there's where he's wrong. He's not taking anything from us except a one way ticket out of here."

Constance laughed at his fierce tone and said, "You please me, kinsman. Work together, children. Work together..." She faded away.

Reggie sighed with frustration. "I'm getting pretty sick of how she takes off just when we start to get something from her."

"Me too," Chase said.

Reggie cocked her head. "Chase, do you have plans for dinner? That pie just wasn't enough. I'm thinking, Italian."

* * * *

Sitting in a private booth at Luigi's, the best restaurant in one hundred miles, Reggie took a long sip of her iced tea. Casting a covetous eye at Chase's wine, she regretted promising Gillian that she'd abstain.

Correctly interpreting her gaze, Chase asked, "Do you want some?"

"No thanks. Gillian told me that I should cut out alcohol for the duration. Seems she thinks it's not a good idea for me to dull my senses."

He narrowed his eyes. "She didn't say anything about me, did she?"

Laughing, she shook her head, "No. I think you're safe, so go ahead aim for the Betty Ford clinic. I'm designated driver for the time being."

He looked at her askance. "Uh, I don't think so, Crash, but thanks for the offer."

The waiter arrived with their dinners. Reggie looked up at the smiling young man and said, "You know, Dino, I'm just not appreciated around here."

"I appreciate you. I have always appreciated you." He smiled and bowed.

"Yeah, of course you do. I have a fondness for food, and I tip extravagantly."

"And I appreciate it." He laughed and walked away.

Their meals were delicious. Eyeing Reggie's seafood pasta, Chase casually stabbed a shrimp and popped it in his mouth. Grabbing the piece of bread she'd buttered, he pointed his fork at her and said, "Very good choice."

"That shrimp is going to cost you, Poindexter. Give me my bread back." She swiped it out of his hand and said, "Butter your own." As she took a bite, he stole a piece of crab meat from her plate. He smiled triumphantly.

Reggie couldn't help but laugh at his delight. It was such a small victory. "Just you wait till dessert. That's my best event."

By silent consent, they kept their conversation light. They could talk on any subject. Reggie always had an opinion and was generous with it. Chase was not nearly so talkative, but when it came to facing off with Reggie, he held his own handsomely.

Stirring his coffee, Chase finally broached the subject. "You were brilliant today in the library, Reg. That last jolt you sent out was almost visible. If I didn't know better, I would swear you threw out little lightning bolts from your fingers."

"That's exactly what I was going for," she admitted. "I called on some power inside myself and threw it out like I was Storm from the X-Men."

"Well, it worked. Have you ever done anything like that before?"

She shook her head. "Never. It's a bit scary to think I have that in me, but I guess we'll need it to take on Vincent."

"Yeah. I did some more research today. It's not good. It seems he had a thing for young Asian women."

"Go on." She braced herself.

"Well, he always had an Asian servant girl. They kept disappearing, and he'd find another to take her place. It would have been easy for a slave trader. I could find no record of what happened to them. They vanished." He looked sad. "Now, it is possible that they went on to work for someone else. No one kept good records of servants and exactly who was who. They weren't considered important enough."

"They didn't go anywhere else. He killed them." She gritted her teeth. "That bastard killed them. Who knows what hell he'd put them through when they'd been in his service. Maybe death was kinder."

"I imagine it can be sometimes."

"Constance has to know something."

He shook his head. "I don't know. It seems he stayed clean once he came to America, or at least he didn't cause any concern in that direction. He probably just learned to hide it better."

"I can't imagine Constance turning a blind eye to this kind of depravity no matter how infatuated she'd been." She shook her head. "No, I'm willing to bet that she knew nothing about this. She was a Guardian. She couldn't have ignored that kind of evil!"

"I want to agree, but she's my ancestor, so I might be a little biased. We still need to talk to her about it though."

"I agree. But not tonight. I'm tired. That little session in the library took a lot out of me." Reggie rubbed a hand across her forehead.

"I'll get the bill, and I'll tip with outrageous abandon. How's that?"

She laughed. "You're so cute when you're spending money."

Chapter 18

Chase was quiet on the drive back to Bennett House. Reggie didn't mind. She enjoyed the silence. But she grew concerned when they walked into the house, and he still stayed mute. Chase wasn't one to waste words, but this was odd even for him, given what they'd been through together.

Concerned that she'd done something wrong, she started to ask him. She didn't get a word out because he said, "It's been a long day. We're both tired. Good night, Reggie." He turned and walked into the living room. Pita waited a second, looked at her with disdain, and followed him.

Reggie ascended the grand staircase trying to puzzle out why Chase had behaved so coldly. Did he regret last night? She sure didn't. He'd seemed pretty pleased with the situation when they'd breakfasted. In fact, he'd seemed fine throughout dinner. Their record for clear communication was not good. Damn him. She'd been looking forward to spending the night in his arms and letting nature take its course.

Getting ready for bed, Reggie reviewed their dinner conversation. Nothing in it would have driven him away, not that she could see. Slipping between the sheets of the enormous bed, Reggie turned and looked at the empty space beside her and felt lonely for the first time in her life. Tomorrow. She'd give him the night to get over his mysterious sulk, but come morning, she'd confront him and demand an explanation.

* * * *

Downstairs on the couch, Chase stared up at the ceiling. He'd abandoned the hope of sleep. It was no use. She'd hit a soft spot when she'd made that comment about him spending money. He knew she'd been joking, but in that one sentence, she'd pierced his balloon. He knew what it was like to sweat for every penny. She did not. In a way, Reggie took money for granted. She never spoke about it because it was never a concern for her. Her family's fortune was intact, and so was their reputation. Chase still struggled with the taint his stepfather had left on his family name. Robert Adams had owed everyone in town. He'd stolen from some and conned others. He had used his wife's good name to gain the trust of the people of New Crescent and had left Chase to make it right. He'd felt he owed it to his ancestors. Over the years they'd amassed a fortune and he'd let it slip through his fingers, taking it for granted.

Working like a madman, Chase had made amends with every single one of Adams's victims, but it had taken time. During that time, his self-confidence had taken a severe blow. It was hard to get it back no matter how hard he worked or how much money he made.

Last night with Reggie had been like a dream. It had felt so right. They'd fit together perfectly, like interlocking pieces created solely for one another. Now lying in the dark, he felt a deep despair. Would he ever make it right with her? He sighed. Pita meowed and slapped at him like he'd stepped on his tail.

Surprised, Chase sat up and looked about the dark living room. Pita crouched nearby, hissing at something he could not see. The room felt colder than it should. He sniffed. It was extremely faint, but Chase had a keen sense of smell, and he recognized the odor. Somehow, that thing in the library had slithered out in the darkness and was playing with his tormented thoughts. It would have been so easy. He'd felt drained to begin with. All that thing had to do was help him along. A strategic nudge in the right direction, and Chase could have slipped into a full fledged pit of despair.

He shook his head to clear it of Vincent's insidious manipulations. He laughed. "Nice try. But now I know your tricks. I won't be fooled again."

He stood and walked to the staircase with speed. He took the stairs two at time, hurrying to get to Reggie. Nonchalantly, Pita curled up on the warm spot he'd left behind on the couch.

* * * *

The soft sound of knocking surprised Reggie, but since she knew it could be no one but Chase, she welcomed it with anticipation. She didn't have to tell him to come in because he was already there. He moved to the bed with a grace Reggie envied. God, she loved to watch him move. He didn't say a word, and neither did she. He sat on the edge of the bed and leaned his head down. Apology, passion, and reverence were in his kiss. Luckily he'd never been one much for night clothes. He dispatched his pajama bottoms in one smooth motion.

It thrilled her to see that he was hard and ready. He didn't waste time, and for that, she was grateful. He paused only long enough to make sure she wanted him as much as he wanted her. He entered her in one sure thrust. She cried out with pleasure. He took the last of her cry with his kiss then groaned a reply. Their lovemaking this time was fast and hard and thoroughly thrilling. His voice joined hers when they found release. It had never been so easy.

When Chase rolled off of her, she immediately missed his weight. He pulled her close to him and sighed when she wrapped a long leg over his hip. They held each other for a long time simply enjoying the sensation of moist skin against skin.

Reggie looked up at him with a question in her eyes. When she started to speak, he put a finger to her lips, then replaced the finger with his mouth. He started all over again. This time, he stopped to enjoy the view along the way. Reggie felt like she was being worshipped and longed to return the favor, but he wouldn't let her. He needed her too much. She laughed out loud this time when she felt that wonderful pressure then release. He looked at her, puzzled for a split second, and then joined her.

He looked up at the ceiling and addressed no one in particular. "She laughs. I think I'm insulted."

She looked up at the same spot on the ceiling and said, "Who are we taking to?"

She started to laugh again, and Chase pounced. Straddling her, he trapped both her hands in one of his. "So you think this is funny huh? Well, I'll show you funny."

Damned if he didn't start tickling her. She fought back. The room was filled with their shared laughter.

Exhausted, she finally dropped down beside him on the bed. He slid her closer to him and spooned behind her.

"I'm sorry about earlier tonight." He was out of breath.

She was gentle. "Care to explain it?"

"Do I have to?" Over her shoulder, he looked down at her like a seven year old trying to get out of going to the dentist.

She surprised both of them by saying, "Not tonight."

He sighed. "Thanks. I think I had some help with my black mood."

She turned in his arms and looked up at him in inquiry. She rested a hand and her chin on his chest and said, "Now, this time, I'm afraid I'm going to have to ask you to explain."

"I couldn't sleep. I couldn't stop my mind from racing. I started to feel an overwhelming sadness. I know what you meant when you described it as getting the hope sucked out of you. At first I let it get to me and I did some weapons-grade brooding. Thankfully, Pita chose that moment to smack me across the face. I snapped out of it. Vincent had paid me a visit. The entire room was unnaturally cold, and I recognized the foul stench."

"Oh my God, he is getting stronger. If he can move freely about the house, I'm afraid it might be too late to stop him."

Chase shook his head. "I don't think so." She looked confused, and he explained. "You see, I learned something from my late-night visitor. I was able to shake him off pretty easily once I realized what was happening. He'd like us to think he's all powerful. I think he took advantage of my distance from you and gambled that I'd be too wrapped up in myself to notice his role in it all." Chase kissed the top of her head. "I was actually able to laugh at him. He retreated immediately, as if he'd been burned. Venturing out of the library, away from his energy supply, weakened him, and he had to slither back to his hole."

"Well that's a vivid image. I'd like to believe you're right," she said hesitantly.

"What's wrong?"

"I'm reluctant to get too cocky about our successes. It was pretty devious, what he did tonight. He played upon the distance you put between us."

With regret, Chase nodded. "It looks like. That thing is an opportunist. I was just being stupid, Reggie. I let my past seep in. You were at college. You weren't here much in the years after my mother's death." Absently, he stroked her short hair. "Did you know she died right in front of me?"

She shook her head, but didn't say anything. She let him talk.

"It was like she was hanging on just long enough to get it all off her chest. She and my father had a wonderful marriage, but when he died so young she grew lonely and let herself fall in love with the wrong man. My stepfather was a monster. I never liked him much, but I'd had no idea just how abusive he was. I was oblivious...wrapped up in my own life. My mother and Jade hid it from me. They were afraid of what I might do if I'd known and rightly so I guess. I'd have killed him." Reggie could see the truth of it in his eyes as he went on in a low but steady voice. "He never struck my mother anywhere I could see. He used Jade to help control her as well. My mom knew that as long as he was hurting her, he'd lay off Jade." Chase ground his teeth. The whole sordid mess was obviously difficult to relive.

"On her death bed, my mother actually apologized to *me* if you can imagine. She was in so much pain. The morphine they gave her made her sick, so she refused all but the smallest of doses. She wouldn't let go until I promised not to take action against Adams. Finally, I agreed, just to ease her suffering."

"I'm so sorry, Chase, I had no idea. No one told me." Reggie had tears in her eyes.

"I didn't tell you. The fewer people who knew, the better. Adams had so many shady deals and debts when he left that it was all I could do to make amends. The people of this town are miraculous. No one blamed me. They were all prepared to forget it all, but I couldn't let them. I had to make good."

"And you did. That's admirable Chase. It wasn't your job to pay for what your step father did."

"Strictly speaking no, I guess, but I had to do something. For so long, I'd been blind to what was happening around me. I also did it for Jade's sake."

"I know you tried to get custody of her."

He nodded. "Yes, but legally I didn't have a leg to stand on, so I did the only thing I could think of to help her. I cleaned up her father's mess. Jade is not my blood sister. She's more than that to me. She's the sister of my soul."

Tears fell freely from Reggie's eyes as she treated him to a watery smile. "She's lucky."

"No, I'm the one who's lucky. She's an angel." He nuzzled Reggie's neck, and she shivered in reaction. Was it possible to want him again?

He interrupted her musings, saying, "Tonight, I was stupid and filled with self-pity. You see, in the past, I haven't been much of a regular at Luigi's. I couldn't afford it before."

It dawned on her, and she blushed, feeling horrible. "And I made that stupid crack about money. I'm so sorry."

With a crooked finger, he tilted her head up. "You have nothing to apologize for. It was just a joke, and I reacted like an idiot. I think the whole thing with Vincent in the library affected me more than I'd realized. Please don't apologize."

She could tell he was serious. "Okay, I won't. I'll just do this instead." She dipped under the covers. When her mouth took over, he groaned.

* * * *

Outside in the garden, Constance smiled. They were where they needed to be. It was so difficult to talk to them without giving orders. She'd always been a little autocratic and more than a little impatient. She needed their help as much as they needed hers, but they had to exercise free will. If they were to succeed, her interference was forbidden. That didn't stop Constance from giving them a nudge in the right direction here and there. If they had genuinely resisted, she'd never have been able to push them. No, she'd just sped things up a little. If she hadn't, Chase would still be tongue tied and Reggie frustrated. What was going on up there in that big bedroom was much better. They gained strength in each other.

Chase had proved formidable tonight. She was proud of her descendant. He was a good man who deserved happiness. She understood his pain. He'd lost the women in his life who had meant the most. He still blamed himself. Not unlike the guilt Constance carried with her beyond the grave.

With raw hatred, she looked in the direction of the library. He was in there licking his wounds. Constance hoped defeat tasted bitter, and she willed him to choke on it.

* * * *

He raged. He knew his anger would dissipate his strength so he struggled to make it submit to his will. It wasn't easy. His fury was like a wild thing fighting for its very existence. He'd almost tricked the man, almost fed at the rich trough of his impressive strength. A potent stronghold resided within the man, Vincent could smell it. If only he could tap it. The woman too had power within her. The source of her power was the one thing that he truly feared. He had to recover from the day's debacle. He called to the child.

Chapter 19

Her three-inch heels made a satisfying *clack, clack, clack* as she walked down the hospital hallway. She loved that sound. It made her feel sexy and feminine, and that was always good. She was dressed in cashmere, her favorite fabric. Enjoying its softness, Reggie ran a hand up and down her arm. She'd dressed with care in a pink sweater and skirt. Sam had always liked her in pink, so today she wore it for him. It was a tremendous relief to get the call this morning from the nurse. He'd regained consciousness and was decidedly ill tempered. He'd begun to balk at his forced inactivity less than an hour after he'd come to. Reggie smiled. Sam was a man of action. He just wasn't built for confinement.

She smiled when she heard Travis Sinclair's voice. She should have known he'd be here. Chase was going to visit in the afternoon.

Reggie peeked her head around the door and said, "Are you decent?" She looked at Travis. "I don't mean you. You're never decent." She approached the bed. Bending at the waist, she kissed Sam's cheek. He smiled at her. His crooked grin was the only thing asymmetrical about Sam. Otherwise, he was so handsome that he didn't look real. Reggie could remember that smile when it had two missing front teeth, and still Sam Daniels had been the best-looking boy in town. It was hard to see him hurting.

"Ah, the sisterly kiss on the cheek. Is that what they mean by the kiss of death?" Sam said. He was sitting up, but he looked so pale it reminded Reggie of what might have happened. He could have been killed. Before she lost it and started to bawl, she called on her ever-reliable sense of humor.

In an exaggerated Southern drawl, she said, "Well, honey child, I do declare you are a sight for sore eyes." She struck a pose and smiled brightly.

"So are you, Reg. Thanks for coming, and in pink too. You certainly know the way to a man's heart."

Reggie started to tear up. Before she had the chance to blubber, Sam opened his arms, and she moved into them hugging him fiercely. Sam and Travis let her cry until she was done. Travis ran a hand through his hair as Sam patiently soothed her. He was a big man, and she was a whole lot of woman. There wasn't much room on that narrow bed, but somehow, they managed it.

As soon as she straightened, she turned to Travis and hugged him too. She sniffed, took a very deep breath, and started speaking as if she'd never shed a tear.

"What the hell happened?" Her voice was sharp. Tears were forgotten.

Travis smiled. "I was just asking the same thing when you breezed in all pink and particular."

"Well?" She pinned Sam with a steady look.

Sam shook his head. "Damn it, I wish I knew. I wanted to check out the house, find out what all the fuss was about. Neither of you were there, so I poked around on my own. I had no idea I'd wandered so close to the Big Bad until it was too late." He closed his eyes and leaned back. "I don't remember much else until I woke up here."

"Are you in a lot of pain?" Reggie asked.

He grimaced and admitted that he was experiencing some pain.

Reggie slapped his chest with the back of her hand. "Good. You deserve it, scaring us all like you did. If you had died, I would have killed you."

"She would have had to stand in line, Trust Fund," Travis said. "What did the doctors say about your leg?"

"Apparently, I should heal nicely. The surgery went well. I'm going to need physiotherapy once the cast comes off." Sam shrugged.

"Have your parents contacted you?" Reggie asked tentatively.

"Yes, Satan and Cruella called me," Sam said rolling his eyes.

She smiled. Now she knew he'd be okay. He was insulting his father and mother again. Sam loved his parents, but he didn't like them.

"I told them I was fine. You know their genuine concern has the life expectancy of a Spinal Tap drummer." He shifted in the bed.

Travis said. "Hmm, hospital sheets. They must chafe like sand paper after your fine linens."

Sam said, "Now that you mention it…"

"You're soft, Trust Fund."

"That may be so, and for the record, only where it doesn't count, but I think I should inform you that Gillian told me that you like honeysuckle in your bubble bath."

Travis looked sheepish. "I think it smells pretty."

"You're such a girl," Sam said.

"I guess this really puts a crimp in your share of the work on our haunted house for Halloween. Figures you'd find some way to get out of the real work. This was pretty drastic though, even for you," Travis said.

Reggie sighed deeply, enjoying their usual banter. The only thing missing was Chase. She loved these two men like brothers. When she was with them she felt invincible. They could handle anything as long as they did it together. Her romantic feelings for Chase weren't going to change that. She wouldn't let it. Knowing that gave Reggie comfort, and she joined the conversation with enthusiasm.

* * * *

After leaving the hospital, Reggie drove to the schoolyard. She'd called John Marks and asked him if she could stop by and talk to Todd again. She hoped to get a beat on his friend Aidan, the ringleader. Was he an innocent victim or a willing accomplice? She had to know.

She parked her car and made her way to a picnic table. She sat on the bench backwards and leaned her back on the edge of the table. She rested her forearms on the table and stretched her legs out, crossing them at the ankle. All modesty aside, Reggie knew she'd command attention from the other students. She waited for Todd.

"Hi, Reggie," Todd said shyly.

Reggie smiled at him and invited him to sit beside her. He took a seat. She could see a group of boys watching them with curiosity.

"So, how's it going?" Reggie asked.

"Fine, thank you."

"Are you completely recovered from that flu you had?" She turned her face up to the warm autumn sun.

Todd did the same. "Yeah. I'm fine, but I still feel really bad about what I did."

Turning her head and opening one eye she looked at the young boy and said, "I know you do, but like I said before, no one was hurt. Can you point out to me the boys who were involved? Which one is Aidan?"

Savvy enough to know that he shouldn't actually point anyone out, Todd said, "Aidan is the tallest…in that group over there." He nodded in the direction of six boys gathered around the bicycle rack. They all looked about twelve years old. Reggie didn't move as she continued to observe them. Aidan was the uncontested leader. The other boys obviously deferred to him. The center of attention, he was dressed in the latest cool gear, and was trying so hard to appear aloof. Reggie could tell his height was the result of a fairly recent growth spurt because his movements were so painfully awkward. He had the kind of looks that peaked in high school when foolish young girls thought that sneering dispassion was cool. As a man, Reggie thought, that same expression had the potential to make him look petulant and spoiled. Reggie was reluctant to admit it because after all, he was still just a child, but she didn't like him on sight. He reminded her of all those cocky young men in her past who had made her ashamed and embarrassed of her developing body.

"So what have you told the others about Bennett House?"

"I told them that I wasn't going near that place, and I didn't care if they didn't want to be my friends anymore."

"How did they react to that?" Reggie asked.

"Most of them already caught hell…er…trouble from their mom or dad." When Reggie stayed quiet, he continued. "Jeremy was the coolest. He was gonna have to go next, so he was real relieved. Aidan was pissed." Todd looked apologetic and said, "Pardon my language." Reggie gave him an understanding nod and urged him to go on. "His dad's a lawyer. He told him that the cops have no evidence, and they can't prove nothin'. He said that was as good as being innocent."

"You know that's not true, don't you?"

"Yeah. It turned out okay because none of the other guys were ever gonna go back to that house, so we kinda out-numbered Aidan. He pretended that he didn't care, but he hasn't been mean to me since."

"How does that make you feel?"

"I'm okay with it. I don't want to hang with him if he wants me to do bad things. After I stuck up for myself, the other guys were like, 'Way to go dude.'"

Peer pressure. Reggie was so glad she was finished with school. She just wished she knew then what she knew now. What woman hasn't said that before? "Todd, I'd like to meet your friends."

He looked at her with surprise. "Okay. They sure want to meet you." He stood up and jogged over to his friends.

It pleased Reggie to see that the other boys seemed to respect Todd. Maybe there was hope for them after all. It didn't surprise her that the boys quickly agreed to come and meet her. For a pubescent boy, she was Mecca in pink cashmere, and she knew it.

Todd introduced Reggie to his friends. His friendship with her gave him an extra jolt of street cred. Reggie took her time getting to the point. She didn't want to make them turtle. Finally, she felt the time was right.

"I'm working on Bennett House," she said. Aidan didn't react. "I know your parents have told you to stay away from there, but I don't know if they told you why." Reggie didn't wait for replies before going on. "Bennett House right now is very dangerous. It's not a good place for kids. As soon as it's safe, I'll give you all a tour, and then we'll go out for pizza, but you have to promise me that you won't go near the place until I give you the all clear." Everyone but Aidan was quick to agree. He simply looked away and shrugged.

Reggie didn't let up. "Aidan? That means you too. If you won't stay away for your own good, then remember Bennett House is private property. Trespassing is illegal. Your actions will have consequences."

Before Reggie got the answer she was looking for, the bell rang. The boys said a hurried good-bye, and she quickly thanked Todd for his help. The appraising look Aidan cast her way as he left shocked her. Reggie shivered as she walked to her car. That kid did not look at her with the eyes of an innocent. That jaded look he'd flashed her stuck with Reggie as she drove to Bennett House. Maybe they hadn't seen the last of him. The thought made her sick. He was just a boy. Where were his parents? Her stomach lurched again. She needed to eat.

Reggie pulled up outside the diner. When she walked in, she immediately spotted Chase. His size made him hard to miss. The tuft of hair at the back of his head stood straight up as if greeting her. She'd know that cowlick anywhere. She smiled and started toward him. She took two steps and froze.

He wasn't alone. She was exquisite. The sheen of her long, dark wavy hair rivaled the rich veneer Reggie had selected for the wood on the grand staircase. The petite woman's lips were full, and her eyes were exotic. Those beautiful lips and eyes smiled at Chase with obvious interest. She touched his hand as it lay on the table between them. Reggie lost her appetite when Chase put his other hand on top of hers.

Relieved he hadn't seen her, Reggie rushed out of the diner and into her car. She drove. For so many years, Bennett House had been her sanctuary. This time she knew she'd find no peace there. Now the house was intrinsically connected to her relationship with Chase. She hated feeling this way. The woman in the diner was the antithesis of Reggie and represented every little minx she'd ever envied. She laughed without humor. How ironic. She'd just been thinking about the insecurity she'd felt when she was younger. Logically, she knew that she was overreacting, but she couldn't control how she felt. After last night, she'd been preparing herself to come clean with Chase and tell him how she felt. Instead, seeing him holding hands with that woman in the diner, Reggie wrapped her feelings up tightly and filed them away under the letter B for big mistake.

She pulled into Gillian's driveway and said a silent prayer of thanks that Travis's truck was no where to be seen. She needed her girlfriend. As much as she loved him, Travis could never play that role. Gillian was the best.

Hank barked once. Gillian was already walking to the door when Reggie opened it. The door wasn't the only thing she opened. Once she sat down with Gillian, she told her friend everything, only pausing once or twice to take a breath.

Frowning, Gillian said, "You left without him even knowing you were there?"

Reggie nodded. "Of course I did. They looked pretty intimate. Besides I wasn't really in control of my emotions. So I took off."

"Yeah, Reggie, you do that don't you?"

"What? You would have stayed and had lunch with them? What if it had been Travis?"

"If I found Travis with another woman, I'd be shattered, but I wouldn't run away in a panic. I think I'd join them and proceed to make Travis the most uncomfortable man in the world. And I wouldn't stop until I'd ground him into dust and blown him away."

Reggie got into the spirit. "Better yet, grind him into a fine powder and make the woman snort him." The thought made them both laugh so hard they were breathless.

Finally, Reggie said, "Oh, that felt good, but it doesn't solve my problem. What do I say when I see Chase again?"

"Don't run. That didn't go so well last time. Have you ever thought of telling him the truth?"

Reggie looked at her suspiciously. "What truth?"

"That you're in love with him, silly."

"Would I have to add the silly part?" Reggie smiled.

Gillian shook her head, but her lips turned up into a smile. "You're doing it again you know."

Reggie looked confused. "Huh?"

"I've said it before. You use humor to get out of every jam. Oh, I'm not complaining. It makes you irresistible, and we all love you for it. You slip under a person's secret armor one quip at a time. You seem so confident and capable of seeing the humor in every situation. People are drawn to you. Why does loving Chase scare you so much?"

Reggie sobered and answered her. "I don't know really. We're amazing together in and out of bed. But there's a part of me that just doesn't feel worthy."

She shook her head and put up her hand to stop Gillian's objection. "I said something boneheaded at dinner last night. I was insensitive and made an offhanded comment that hurt him. Sometimes I'm just oblivious to everything but my own concerns. Gillian, I wanted to be a Guardian. I was supposed to be special. I failed, and I have no idea what I did wrong. I didn't deserve the gift of the Goode sisters. Maybe there's something wrong with me...inside." She pressed her hand to her heart as her voice broke on the last word.

Gillian hugged her close. Reggie appreciated Gillian's attempt to soothe her especially given Gillian's abilities. Using her gift, Gillian tried to ease Reggie's mind, and she succeeded, a little. But Reggie pulled away.

"My emotions are in overdrive. What's wrong with me? I'll be fine. Don't worry about me." She took a couple of deep breaths and shook her head.

"Where's Travis?"

"Nice segue Reggie, but I'll play. He's with Sam. I'd love to have gone with him, but as you can imagine, my ability to pick up the feelings of others can be a bit of a handicap in hospitals. I've talked to him over the phone. Travis has been with him since he woke. Apparently, it's absolutely hilarious watching Sam politely submit to the ministrations of just about every woman within one thousand miles. That includes Ernestine, by the way."

"And me, but I only ministered my irritation with him. Oh, I bet Ernestine gave him what for."

"Poor Sam. I honestly think she made him miss the coma. She was furious with him for going to Bennett House after she'd told us all to leave it to you and Chase."

Reggie rolled her eyes. "Yeah, Sam...duh! He should have known better."

"Well, he does now. Ernestine has vowed to visit him everyday until he's in physio." Gillian liked the idea and laughed.

Reggie joined her. "That should speed his recovery along nicely."

They laughed at Sam's expense. Reggie didn't feel guilty in the least. He could afford it.

Feeling a little better, Reggie told Gillian about Aidan. "Gill, do you think you could try to connect with him? Find out what he's up to?"

Gillian frowned as she thought about it. "Ernestine has been pretty adamant that I stay out of this. I'll ask her what she thinks. I may be able to get some info just by being close to him. From what you say you see in his eyes, I'm not too eager to touch him and get into his mind. Besides, I'm not sure you were meant to know what's going on with Aidan just yet. It's inconceivable to think he's Vincent's accomplice."

Reggie shook her head. "Yeah, and he's only twelve years old."

Chapter 20

Reggie breathed a sigh of relief when Chase's pickup truck wasn't in the driveway at Bennett House. She had a short reprieve, and it was appreciated. Pru was thrilled to see her. The little dog's enthusiasm came as no surprise, but she welcomed it anyway.

"Well, girl, I guess you need to go outside for a bit." Reggie opened the patio doors off the kitchen. Pru took off at the run. The heels Reggie wore hindered her ability to keep up. She tottered around the corner of the house and ran right through Constance.

"Pffft," Constance said in irritation.

"Can you spell that please?" Reggie said automatically.

Constance ignored her. "Pru is fine. She came running when she sensed my presence. What have you done now?"

"What do you mean, 'What have I done?' Why don't you ask, 'What has Chase done?'"

"Because it is you I've connected with, you I need to guide, and you who needs the help." She sighed and ran a hand over her ghostly hair. "Frankly, the question surprises me."

Reggie had had a trying day which had left her with very little patience for Constance and her insults. She pointed to a spot beyond Constance's shoulder and said, "Hey, what's that? Over there, I think it's a light. Go to it." She raised her voice with frustration. "Cross over, already!"

"It would serve you right if I did, but you need me. It is your destiny to face Vincent. I've done my part, in life. I still have work to do in death. I have to help you, and that's not easy when you work against me."

Reggie sighed and sat down heavily on a nearby bench. Running a hand through her short hair, she said, "I'm sorry. I'm agitated, and I'm taking it out on you. To what do I owe this visit?"

Constance narrowed her eyes and hesitated. Finally, she said, "You have to go into the library as soon as Chase gets home."

Reggie looked at her as if she'd just granted amnesty to Hitler. "Why do you say that? This is it, Constance. I won't blindly follow your instructions anymore. You're going to have to explain yourself."

"I do not recall you ever blindly following anyone, my dear. Perhaps you wish to rephrase that question." Constance too could be stubborn.

Reggie recognized her affect. Shaking her head, she said, "Okay, Constance, no offense meant. Please tell me what it is you need to say."

"I sense that all is not well between you and Chase, my kin. Did he not please you last night?"

"Knock it off."

"Patch up whatever is wrong between the two of you immediately, because Vincent will use it against you." There was no humor in Constance's voice as she spoke.

Reggie rolled her eyes and her voice dripped with sarcasm. She said, "Oh… well…in that case… If it was so easy to solve my problem with Chase don't you think I would already have done it?"

"No, my dear. I think you are looking for reasons to pull away from Chase. Talk to him. Ask him every question that comes to mind. Talk to him and then go into the library and force Vincent to retreat."

"And we have to do this today? It's starting to get dark." Reggie pointed towards the fiery sunset.

Constance didn't bother to look. Instead, she pressed the issue. "Yes, it is getting late, so you must do this as soon as possible. I can feel Vincent's vulnerability. It won't last long. Talk to Chase. Clear this up. Talk to him…talk to him…" And she was gone.

Chase came home well after the sun had set. By the time he walked into the kitchen, she'd been pacing so long that she was ready to spit rusty nails and run naked down Main Street. Just the casual way he looked at her set her off, and as he greeted her, she sat at the table fuming. She didn't have a choice. There wasn't much time. She was going to have to vent her anger if they were to face Vincent with any success. Reggie figured there wasn't time to pussyfoot around, so she got to the point.

"I thought about eating lunch in the diner today. I even considered joining you, but you were otherwise occupied." Her inner struggle put a light in her eyes and a sharpness in her voice.

Chase's eyes widened in reaction, and he looked at her with surprise. He said, "You should have joined us. Jackie would love to meet you face-to-face."

Reggie furrowed her brow and narrowed her golden gaze. "Jackie? That was Jackie Blake, Pat Somers's agent?"

"Yup." He started to grin.

"Well, why didn't you tell me!" She huffed about the kitchen opening and closing cupboards with a bang in impotent frustration. He'd defused her rising anger like a kid popping a birthday balloon, but her adrenaline was amped up, and she was ready for a fight. Reggie hated waste. She took a deep breath and began.

"Didn't it ever occur to you that I might have wanted to meet the woman? I have a million questions for her that are so much easier to communicate in person. There's the four other bedrooms to furnish, paintings to select for the walls in every room except the dining room. Television, what about television? Do I go out and purchase televisions. Does she want an entertainment system in any of the bedrooms? What about the kitchen? People are putting TVs in kitchens these days. Personally, I wouldn't advise that. Don't get me wrong, I love TV just as much as the next guy…okay…a little more than the next guy, but is it really necessary in the kitchen? I mean, I could get distracted and mistake baking soda for icing sugar. Now that would totally wreck a cake. Mmm…speaking of cake. I didn't eat lunch." This time when she opened a cupboard, she had something in her hand when she slammed the door. She opened a bag of potato chips with a pop.

Chase was smiling now. "Maybe the next time Jackie Blake is in town, I'll introduce you. I didn't know she was coming. She just showed up."

Looking into the bag of potato chips, Reggie selected the one she wanted and said, "She wants to jump your bones."

"Yup." He said.

"Have you ever been the jumpee?" She tried to keep her voice casual.

"Nope." He stood up and approached her as she stood next to the stove. Reggie looked at him with a frown. He looked into the bag of chips and took out a handful. He rested a hip against the countertop and waited for her reply.

Without looking at him, she read the back of the bag and took another chip. She said, "Have you ever noticed that everything tastes better deep fried? It's like, deep fry a jalapeno pepper and even *I'd* consider eating it."

Chase laughed, but said nothing.

Anger spent, Reggie looked at him with embarrassment. "You were holding her hand. It looked pretty intimate."

"Jackie is a toucher."

"And you? Are you a toucher?"

"When it comes to you I am." He pulled her into his arms and trapped her mouth with his. He tasted of salty goodness, and Reggie channeled all her excess energy into her enthusiastic response.

They didn't make it out of the kitchen. Reggie had a fleeting thought that having sex on her client's kitchen table might be unprofessional, but at the same time, Chase unzipped his pants, and she stopped thinking at all. God, he was good in the kitchen.

* * * *

Sitting comfortably half naked in his lap at the table, Reggie sighed. "I think Constance would be proud of us."

"To hell with Constance, *I'm* proud of us." He said against her neck.

She shivered, and goose bumps flooded her body. "I hate to mention this to you, Poindexter, but Constance told me that we have to face Vincent again today."

"In the dark? After sunset? Isn't he stronger when the sun goes down?" Chase said.

Reggie shook her head. "No, I think that only applies to vampires."

Chase looked at her with concern, "Do you feel up to it?"

"I do now. Had you asked me when you first came home, my answer would have been very different." She grinned at him.

If he were a physically flexible man, he would have patted himself on the back. Instead he chose to self-congratulate verbally.

"I am so good! Careful, Reggie, now I know how to handle your temper. It might get a little awkward if I have to find a closet or phone booth for us at strategic locations all over town, just in case you get angry." He looked at her and wiggled his eyebrows, with an exaggerated look of excitement on his face. "But hell, I'd be willing to try."

"I don't think that will be necessary," she said as she pulled the bag of chips away from him, wrapped them up, and returned them to the cupboard. She wrinkled her nose at him. "I'm going to change. Pink cashmere and heels are not the best choice for the modern-day ghostbuster…oh great, now I've got that song running through my head," she muttered as she picked up discarded clothing and walked away. Reggie sang a little off key. "Who you gonna call?"

They shut Pru and Pita in the master bedroom to keep them out of harm's way. Reggie could almost feel Constance in the room protecting them. She smiled her thanks as she closed the door.

She met Chase at the bottom of the grand staircase. Her heart rate increased. It could be attributed to the adrenaline rush impending battle caused. But Reggie thought, *Who am I fooling?* He looked searingly hot standing there looking up at her. It was the sight of him that made her heart race.

Pushing her hormones aside for the time being, she rushed down the stairs. She wanted to get this over with. She took hold of Chase's hand, and said, "I trust you Chase. You'll watch out for me."

He looked down at her intently, "I will. I trust you too, and I know you'll watch over me too." They kissed and headed toward the library.

* * * *

The gagging smell no longer permeated the hallway leading to the library. Chase and Reggie exchanged a look when they noticed that fact. It gave Reggie hope and she held on to it for dear life. Reggie's confidence took a cautious step up.

The room was still sadly dilapidated and the careless waste made Reggie sad, but she refused to let that sadness become anything other than a passing emotion. She didn't want to hand out even the tiniest treat to Vincent. She could feel that he wasn't as strong as before and that pleased her.

The air in the room was still thick and heavy. It was hard to breathe at first, but after a few minutes, they both started to get used to it. They'd brought battery-powered lanterns with them. Reggie didn't relish the thought of walking into the library in the pitch black. Outside, the harvest moon shone brightly, but there was no evidence of it here. All the windows had been boarded up. Reggie looked forward to transforming this room. To give this feeling a little more weight, she said in a light and happy voice, "Chase, this is such a beautiful room. I can't wait to restore it. I have all kinds of ideas. I don't think I'll maintain everything because it used to be far too masculine. I want the library to mesh the male and female with subtlety."

Chase picked up her cue. "That shouldn't be hard to do. In fact if you'd like, Duncan and his men could gut the place and start from scratch."

The hissing started, and Reggie and Chase knew they'd touched a soft spot.

In a loud, but steady voice, Reggie said, "This room will be the center of this home. Everyone will be welcomed. I'll fill every shelf with great literature. The lower ones will have all the classic children's tales." She smiled brightly at Chase and fought the urge to give that yawning nothingness even the slightest bit of her energy.

For his part, Chase appeared to be doing the same. The only part of Reggie that was warm was the hand held by Chase. Fortunately, she'd anticipated the cold. She wore just about every sweater she owned, layering them. As she'd put them on, she'd smiled to think the sweaters might also provide some padding should Vincent get physical.

The longer they spent in the library, the more Reggie could feel her strength waning, and for a second, she considered how easy it would be to let it all go, to give up. She longed to stop struggling. She had no special power, so what was she trying to prove? It was pathetic really. Not so long ago, she'd been kidnapped by someone she'd trusted. Her judgment was suspect. She'd been a fool. Chase had helped rescue her and hadn't stuck around long enough to discuss what had happened that day, to examine their feelings for each other.. Now she was in love with the man, and he didn't love her back. She was going to dry up inside before long. She may as well surrender now. Her life was a mess, and she wanted to give up. Her shoulders drooped.

She turned to look at Chase and could tell he was feeling the same hopelessness. Seeing him so sadly vulnerable broke Reggie's heart, and all she wanted to do was comfort him despite her own despair. She squeezed his hand to remind him that he was not alone.

That one small act saved them. It was almost intangible, but something deep inside Reggie held on to that compassion and worked to cast off the insidious depression hammering at her.

What the hell? Reggie thought. *If that worked, how about this.* She took Chase into her arms and kissed him, not with passion, but with all the love she had in her heart for him. He responded at the first touch of her lips. The hissing in the library became almost deafening, but they ignored it. They pulled back, their lips mere millimeters apart, and they smiled. His grin kissed hers. Their strength returned.

In a firm, confident voice, Reggie called out to the entity, "Get out of here. This house is for the living. You are an abomination and we will clear this room of everything you cling to. We will gut you. Go now!" The last words were said with such power they almost rattled the foundation, creating their own low level earthquake. Reggie looked around in confusion. Had that voice really come from her? It must have, because Chase stood looking at her with astonishment.

The hissing was gone. So was the smell. For the first time, Reggie felt warmth in the library. They'd done it! She wanted to jump for joy, do something impulsive in celebration. She ran to the curved staircase to slide down the banister. Chase tried to stop her but wasn't quite fast enough.

Her shoe hit the second step and slipped out from under her

Chapter 21

She landed heavily and banged her head hard on the banister. Chase was beside her immediately.

"Can you stand?" he said with concern.

Reggie laughed with embarrassment. She stood and dusted herself off. "Ah, slap stick comedy, not the most sophisticated, but I must have looked pretty funny. It's okay to laugh Chase. I guess the nickname Crash still holds." She laughed again. "Let's get out of here. I would love some ice cream." She took hold of Chase's hand and, with a huge smile, pulled him out of the room.

Sitting on a stool at the kitchen island, Reggie rubbed her hands over her face. When Chase moved to the freezer for ice cream, she put up a hand.

"Don't bother with the ice cream. I'm not interested. I just needed to get out of there, and I didn't want it to look like we were retreating. We couldn't appear weak in any way." She rubbed her backside. "Now this is going to leave a mark."

Chase hugged her close. "You were magnificent, Crash, even when you fell to the floor. I don't know how you did it."

"To tell you the truth, neither do I. I knew the smell, the hissing, and the cold had gone. I figured Vincent had retreated for the time being. I wanted to celebrate in an obvious way." She felt the bump on the back of her head and said, "I didn't account for the greasy filth that covered every inch of the place thanks to Vincent. When I fell, I could feel his pleasure at my expense. So I pretended to find the whole thing very amusing. I needed him beaten."

"You were brilliant. You almost fooled me."

She looked at him with disbelief. "Almost?"

"Yeah, almost. You hit bottom heavily. I knew that had to hurt both your pride and, well, your derriere. I think it was a stroke of genius to act like you'd found the whole thing funny." He opened the fridge, turned to look over his shoulder at her, and said, "Don't bother to tell me you're not hungry, you will be soon. I'll make us both something to eat. You go take a nice hot bath, maybe take the edge off your aches and pains."

Reggie groaned with gratitude. "That sounds wonderful. Thanks." As she walked away, she thought about what fragrance she'd use in the tub.

Chase hollered. "Anything but honeysuckle. That scent will remind me of Travis forever more, and I just don't want to go there."

Reggie giggled and decided she'd sink into a hot bath scented with relaxing lavender.

* * * *

When she came back down to the kitchen, she could smell chicken baking and sighed. "Thank God, dinner is almost ready. I'm starved."

Chase was sitting at the island working on a laptop computer. He immediately closed his file and logged off, giving her his undivided attention.

"I hope I didn't interrupt anything."

Chase shook his head and smiled at her flannel wear and fluffy slippers, "No, just some business I needed to attend to." He opened the oven door and took out the chicken. "Have you made any progress on arranging for telephone, Internet, and satellite service?"

"Yeah, I've got all that taken care of, but I need to know where I'm putting everything before they come. That will be one of the last things I do. I want Pat Somers's final approval before I proceed." She helped him to set the table.

Over dinner, Reggie and Chase talked easily. By mutual agreement, they did not discuss what had happened in the library. When they finished, Chase suggested they take their dessert into the living room and light a fire.

While Chase fussed with igniting the fire, Reggie looked out the French doors. Bennett House was built on ocean-front property, but the sightline to the water had been obscured by years of overgrown trees and bushes. Chase and his men had been working to clear a path, but it was a huge job, and they didn't want to impact on Mother Nature too much. Only on the second and third levels of the house could one see the ocean in the distance, but Reggie knew it was there and drew comfort from it. Bennett House would be incredible once she and Chase got through with it. But then it would belong to someone else. Reggie turned from the window. "You know, I still haven't met Pat Somers yet. Have you?"

He nodded but didn't elaborate.

"What's she like?"

"I don't know. Regular. What's a romance novelist supposed to look like?"

"Whoa there, information overload. Best not to gossip so readily, Chase." She rolled her eyes. "You're such a guy. Now a woman would be able to tell me just about everything about her. I'll bet if Gillian had been in your place, she'd give me a physical description so good I could pick the woman out of a police lineup." She shook her head in mock disgust. "Okay, Mr. Magoo, just tell me this, did she carry a big bag? I've always imagined that romance novelists carry huge handbags." She shrugged. "I don't know why."

Chase smiled. "She didn't carry a huge handbag, at least not that I could see."

"Is she as taken with you as Jackie Blake is?" Reggie tried to look unconcerned.

"Not that I noticed."

That meant the woman had to be either happily married, lesbian, or dead. Reggie smiled happily and ate her dessert.

"How was your bath?" Chase asked.

With her mouth full of chocolate cake, Reggie nodded and took a huge gulp of her milk. "Glorious, thank you. It was a very smart suggestion."

He leaned toward her and sniffed. "Lavender." He lifted his arm to the back of the couch. She leaned against him and put her head on his chest. He put his arm around her and pulled her close. She fit perfectly in that particular part of his body as if it had been molded to her specifications.

She sighed with contentment.

Chase pinched the flannel on her arm and rubbed it between his fingers. "New flannel?"

She looked up at him and blushed. "Not really, I just haven't worn them before. Some women have a weakness for lingerie. Besides shoes, flannel jammies are my weakness. Sorry."

He laughed. "No need to apologize. I know what's under all that flannel. It helps to keep my imagination fresh. Reggie, you don't have to dress sexy to turn me on. You can pretty much take my arousal as a given…when you're in the room, when you're outside…downtown…in the county…okay…on the planet."

Reggie snuggled closer and said, "For a man who's never been much for words, you use them beautifully."

She turned her face to the fire. Finally, the excitement of the day seeped in, and she dozed off.

* * * *

The next morning, Reggie found herself alone in the massive bed in the master bedroom. She turned and looked at the pillow beside her. Chase had slept with her. Good. She stretched until her bones cracked and then snuggled back under the covers and savored the warmth. She could stay here all day except that her stomach growled so fiercely it made her nauseated. When she looked outside, she could see heavy gray clouds gathered. It looked pretty bleak. Rain fell in a steady rhythm and showed no inclination to stop anytime soon. Sighing, she slipped on her robe and walked with Pru down the back staircase.

Chase wasn't in the kitchen, but he'd left a muffin and a banana on a plate for her. She opened the door and said, "I know, Pru. The weather sucks, but out you go."

Reggie watched Pru pick her way around the garden. She peeled the banana and took a big bite wishing she could spend the day in bed. Her head pounded from her little adventure the night before. She didn't even want to inspect the bruise she knew she had on her butt, figuring what she didn't know wouldn't hurt her.

Her spirits hadn't lifted much after her shower. She dressed in beige and wandered about the house making lists of what she still had to do and taking notes of creative thoughts as they occurred to her. If she worked it just right, she might not need to leave the house at all. The thought appealed to her even more when she heard the wind outside. Looking out at the little gate that Constance favored, Reggie wondered if ghosts got wet.

"We don't, you know," Constance said softly.

Reggie turned in the direction of the voice. "Don't what?"

"Get wet. We are not affected by the weather in such a way. I can sense the dampness and cold, but I don't actually get wet or suffer from the cold." Constance said.

"Ah, but you don't much like the rain or you wouldn't have come inside today." Reggie said.

Constance laughed. "No my dear, I knew you weren't likely to venture outside today so if I wanted to talk to you I had to come inside." She looked around. "You've done wonders with the place. I don't know if you intended to or not, but you've put your own stamp on it."

Reggie frowned. "It's not my house, but I guess every designer puts their own stamp on everything they do."

"Well, it's far more beautiful than it was in my day." Constance looked sad.

"What was it like coming to this house as a new bride?" Reggie asked tentatively, not really expecting an answer.

"While Vincent was building Bennett House the entire town was energized. It was exciting. He was such a mystery, and the house was so grand. It fired my romantic imagination. I think I was almost half in love with him before I even set eyes on him. My father wouldn't tell me anything about this exciting stranger, so I was left to fabricate his life story."

Constance shook her head with regret. "New Crescent was so boring to me, and Vincent Bennett brought the outside world with him. I was eighteen years old, beautiful, and inexperienced…ripe for the picking. My power was irresistible to him."

Constance paused a moment lost in silent reflection. Reggie listened to the rain and waited. "I entered this house with such anticipation. We'd eloped. The very word sent exhilaration through my veins. My friends were so envious, and when you are young, the admiration of others can mean so much."

"You eloped, so your wedding night was spent where? In Boston?"

Constance looked at her as if just remembering she was there. She shook her head. "No, my husband didn't touch me until my first night in Bennett House. I had a virgin honeymoon. Every night I'd go to bed and prepare for my husband, but I woke every morning alone, untouched. Vincent wouldn't discuss it. He told me that I was too precious to spoil thoughtlessly. By the time he brought me home, I'd given up the hope that I'd ever be a true wife. I told no one. I was ashamed. Foolish child, I thought he'd tired of me, so I went to extravagant lengths to temp him. It shames me to remember." She blushed crimson and looked away from Reggie.

"I'm so sorry, Constance." She could think of nothing else to say.

"It was my own fault. My father disapproved of the match and wouldn't speak to me after the wedding. My mother cried whenever she saw me. I came to understand that my father blamed himself. Instead of telling me what he knew of Vincent Bennett, he sought to protect me from his depravity and held his tongue. He could not have known I would be so headstrong as to elope with the man."

"It sounds like your parents loved you very much."

Constance nodded. "They did. And because of that, I couldn't go to them when I learned the truth about my husband, because I knew it would only cause them more pain. I suffered in silence. I was a Guardian. I had a great power." She took a deep breath. "Vincent Bennett came to me our first night here in this house. I welcomed him when he came to my bedchamber, but he didn't want that. He wanted my tears and my resistance. He hurt me. That night, I slept in sheets soaked with my own blood."

Reggie moved toward Constance as if to hug her. Realizing she could not comfort the woman, Reggie froze and said, "Oh my God, Constance."

When the ghostly woman looked at Reggie, there were tears on her cheeks. Ghosts could cry. They could feel pain, and it sounded in her voice when she spoke again.

"He was so cruel. You see, as a Guardian, my power was sweet. My virginity was like ambrosia to a man like him. He took so much from me that night."

Listening to her sorrow, Reggie felt utterly helpless. She longed to soothe her but knew she couldn't. No one could. Finally, she said, "Constance, is there anything I can do for you?"

The face Constance turned to her showed signs of tears but held great determination.

"Yes, Regina Stanton, you must destroy Vincent Bennett or die."

Chapter 21

"She said what?" Chase was incredulous.

"She said I would die," Reggie said with a forced laugh. "Believe me, I wish I'd heard her wrong, but the look on her face pretty much convinced me that I heard her perfectly well."

"Get your rain coat. We're going to see Ernestine. She has to be able to tell us more, give us some direction."

Reggie peered outside. It was still raining. With a long, suffering sigh, she said, "Okay. Give me a sec." She walked out of the kitchen to fetch her raincoat.

Chase drove while Reggie shivered in the seat next to him. He'd turned on the heat, but it hadn't seeped into her damp limbs yet. He looked over at Reggie helplessly.

"I should have warmed the car up before you got in. Sorry."

She shook her head. "No, it's not that. I think I'm nervous about what Ernestine is going to tell us."

Chase grabbed her hand and placed it on his thigh. He covered her hand with his. He said, "Ernestine loves you, Reggie. She'll do whatever is best for you. For us both."

"I know you're right, but she can be pretty cryptic and I'm not sure I'm up for that right now."

Chase said, "Leave Ernestine up to me." She was happy to do so.

* * * *

They caught Ernestine as she was heading in to dinner. They smiled in greeting, and she said, "You can take me out for dinner. It's fish tonight. You'd think living in New England they'd know how to cook fish."

Chase and Reggie exchanged glances. They let Aunt Ernestine pick the restaurant. Molly's Famous Barbeque was busy but Ernestine was well known and much admired, so they got a booth without too much fuss.

They each ordered, and when the waitress walked away, Ernestine said, "So you know a little bit about Constance's marriage." She shook her head. "Such a tragic tale, unusual for this town. Guardians are supposed to see to it that such horrors never happen in New Crescent. It is supposed to be a sanctuary."

Reggie said, "But Constance was a Guardian herself. How could she have let that happen to her?"

Ernestine frowned. "Haven't you been listening to her? She was young, cocky, and foolish. Surely she's come to understand that much in all these years."

"Yes, she has. I was just wondering if there was another reason," Reggie said.

"Oh, there are other reasons, but we rarely understand them. Things happened as they were meant to happen. Constance McCann Bennett was not meant to be happy...to have children or to live a long life. She knew it, too."

"What do you mean? Are you saying that Constance knew her fate all along?" Chase asked.

"Constance had precognition. She could see into the possible futures each act would yield. She knew it had to happen the way it did in order to get you two where you are right now." She laughed at Reggie and Chase's astounded faces. "Such a thing surprises you?"

"You're kidding, right?" Reggie said. "Of course it surprises me. I'm not a Guardian. I have no special abilities. I was passed over. That was bad enough, but to have to take on an evil such as Vincent on my own is...well..." She shrugged. "Not fair!"

Ernestine gave her a sharp look. "What makes you think you face him alone? Have I not told you never to go into that library without Chase? You are not alone, and don't belittle yourself, young lady. You have special abilities. You've just been too blind to see them."

She stopped talking when the waitress brought out their food. Ernestine waited until she left before continuing. "Stop feeling sorry for yourself. You have so much, yet still, you obsess over what you don't have. It isn't that you've been denied the things you've wanted most of all. It's that you don't appreciate the things you have." She slapped the bottom of the ketchup bottle. A dollop of red dropped reluctantly on her French fries, and Reggie couldn't help but think of blood.

Noting Reggie's expression, Ernestine said, "Knock it off."

"Hold on, here, Aunt Ernestine," Chase said. "Reggie has been shouldering this burden with amazing fortitude."

Ernestine narrowed her eyes at him. "And you. You, too, need to appreciate all that you've got and stop living in the past. If you want it, state your intent and go for it. You're heading in the right direction. Quit pussyfooting around, man!"

Aunt Ernestine lowered her voice and said with urgency, "Constance is right, Reggie. You must rid the town of Vincent Bennett and his evil. You have what is necessary to defeat him. It's all just a matter of timing now. I'm sorry that's all I can say at this time."

The old woman refused to talk about it again for the entire meal, despite Chase's persistence. Instead, she brought up a different but related subject.

"The people of New Crescent are gearing up for Halloween. They do tend to act a little strangely around this time of year. Horace from the hardware store swears he saw a vampire in his neighbor's house. Mrs. Frickett, your old grade-school math teacher is encouraging him, saying that this town has always had vampires. She claims she was bitten by one back in the eighties." Ernestine smiled knowingly, "We all know Jasper Cambert gave her a hickey the night his wife kicked him out for drinking all the elderberry wine. As if any self-respecting vampire would go near Alma Frickett..."

Reggie shared a smile with Chase. Then she sobered and asked, "Have you heard anything about the school? Is that strange flu still infecting kids?"

Ernestine sighed. "No, there hasn't been a case since you clamped down on young Lex Luthor and his minions. There have been reports of bullying though, first time ever. Travis has had to break up a couple of fights at Kally's Roadhouse, too."

She shook her head. The muted light in the restaurant turned her white hair to quicksilver. She swallowed.. "It's no coincidence that Vincent Bennett is getting stronger just as Halloween approaches. At this time of the year, the veil between our worlds thins. Vincent Bennett has failed with you two. He's had to cast his net a little farther from home. These fights and disagreements are just little incidents, but he feeds on them nonetheless."

Chase said, "It's all coming to a head isn't it?"

Ernestine raised her eyebrows and ate a french fry in silence. He looked at Reggie.

"We're running out of time," Reggie said.

After dinner, they dropped Ernestine back home and as she turned to leave them, she said, "Look inside yourself, Reggie. You never know what you'll find there." As she walked past Chase, she grabbed his hand and squeezed, pulling him down so she could kiss his cheek. When she did, she whispered, "Don't give up. You've already won. All you have to do is see it."

The trip back to Bennett House took them past the elementary school. Reggie looked at it with nostalgia. Ernestine had been right. She'd had a happy childhood. She and her friends never had to deal with the kind of problems Todd and his friends did. In the darkness of her car, she exchanged a smile with Chase. It seemed he too was reliving fond memories.

Their expressions changed to alarm when they heard breaking glass. Chase slammed on the brakes and made a sharp right turn into the school's parking lot. He started to tell Reggie to stay in the car, but she'd already jumped out. The rain had stopped, leaving huge puddles on the football field, and it occurred to Reggie that she'd get soaked running through it. She wished she'd worn jeans instead of beige wool–cashmere slacks.

Reggie and Chase ran toward the sound of laughter behind the school. The boys must have heard them because all four of them took off in different directions. Reggie raced after the one she thought looked like Aidan. She had to slow her pace when she hit the soaked football field because she lost her footing and slid in the mud. The kid had the same problem. He lost his footing and fell into a deep puddle. Reggie was convinced she'd catch him once he was down, but he was agile and jumped to his feet almost immediately. He made for the darkened forest. She knew she'd never find him in there, but she had to try.

The dense growth of trees blocked all light. She opened and closed her eyes trying to adjust to the thick blackness. Eyes open or closed, it made no difference. She was as good as blind. She could see nothing, but she could hear noises. Unsure of the direction the sounds came from, Reggie stopped dead. Damn it, the kid had the eyes of a cat on a carrot diet. The sounds of his footsteps faded in the distance, and Reggie tried to figure out which way he went. Finally giving up, she turned around and carefully retraced her steps. It wasn't easy, and she prayed to God that for once her sense of direction was reliable. She heard Chase calling her name and gingerly headed toward him.

Chase was empty-handed as well. The boys had too big a head start, at least that's the story Reggie and Chase agreed upon. They walked back to the school. Reggie was covered in mud. Chase had chosen to follow a kid who had darted toward Main Street so he was wet but not muddy.

Together, they inspected the damage. Three windows were broken, and obscene phrases and drawings were spray painted on the wall. Reggie looked at Chase with sadness.

"How do we get that off the walls?" Reggie pointed at one of the most explicit drawings. "Young children shouldn't see such things."

Chase shook his head and dialed Travis's number with his cell phone. They waited for the sheriff. Reggie was glad she'd already had dinner.

* * * *

The next day, the sun shone so brightly it dried up the puddles left behind by the rain. Bennett House was quiet. Work on the renovations was still on hold. It was too dangerous. Reggie marveled that she and Chase were the only ones who could remain at the house with Vincent active. Constance protected them. Reggie was sure of that. She could feel her otherworldly presence the last time they'd ventured into the library. Ernestine had advised her to go with her gut. Reggie put a hand on her belly and said, "Okay. Go with my gut."

She looked down at her hand and, in an impatient tone, said, "Well, gut...say something!" Her stomach lurched, and she felt sick. "Not what I had in mind."

Taking a seat on the living room couch, Reggie took deep steadying breaths, waiting for the feeling to subside. So much for her gut, she thought. Maybe Ernestine and Constance were wrong. Was it possible? She'd never known Ernestine to be wrong about anything significant in her whole life.

The old lady sucked at trivia, but she was an oracle when it came to the big stuff.

Gillian. She'd ask Gillian for advice. Maybe she'd be able to help. She stood up and called for Pru.

The inside of her car was still muddy from the night before. Reggie grimaced and wondered what that was going to cost her. She had to see to that soon. She'd been so occupied with Bennett House that she'd neglected everything else. When was the last time she'd seen her parents? Sam was home from the hospital, and she hadn't even visited him. Reggie reminded herself that there was life beyond Bennett House and that she'd have to live it. She pulled into Gillian's driveway.

Hank greeted Pru with enthusiasm and Gillian smiled at Reggie in welcome.

"Hey there, what's up?" She frowned at the look on Reggie's face.

"I think I need some girlfriend time. Do you mind if I hang out here with you for a while?" Reggie asked.

"You know you don't have to ask. Did you want to talk about something in particular?"

Reggie nodded. "Yeah, I do, but do you mind if we just hang for a bit? I think I need to forget about Bennett House and the Big Bad for a couple of hours."

Gillian smiled gently at her friend. "I'm all yours. Travis is working on the haunted house. Sam's there too, but I'm sure he's just there to make sarcastic comments because with that leg, he's pretty useless. Chase is expected as well. So I guess we are all taking a break from the Big Bad today."

It was a relaxing day. Reggie and Gillian never ran out of things to say to each other. They laughed a lot, often at Travis's expense. *Nothing beats a woman friend,* Reggie thought. Even the most sensitive man could never replace a girlfriend. She understood that and every day she felt gratitude for her friendship with Gillian.

Reggie said, "So I guess Travis hasn't got it right yet, huh?"

Gillian laughed. She knew exactly what Reggie was referring to. The whole town knew that Travis and Gillian would be married. It was just a matter of time. It all rested with Travis. Gillian had insisted he get it right. He had to ask her properly in order to get the answer he sought. So far he'd failed miserably. The town had a pool going. Everyone was making bets on when Travis would finally get what he wanted. Reggie had yet to get in on the action. She hoped to get inside information before putting her money down.

Gillian giggled. "So far, he's put a ring in my soup. I almost broke a tooth. He tied a string around my finger while I was sleeping and waited for me to wake up and pull it, and I don't know what he'd planned." She nodded at Reggie, "Lame, I know but worse…he'd tied it so tight the string left a red mark on my finger. Sky writing? He tried that too, but the guy he hired got my name wrong, and Travis ended up asking Gilligan to marry him. Do you have any idea how many people in New Crescent know the *Gilligan's Island* song?"

She paused and waited for Reggie to stop laughing before continuing. "He put a ring in a bubble gum machine and had to take Cindy Wilton for ice cream every day for a week before she'd give it back. She thought it was pretty. He's written me the most hilarious poetry. Who taught him how to spell? Jethro Beaudine?" Both women cracked up and started to imagine even more hilarious ways Travis could bungle the simple act of asking the woman he loves to marry him.

"I swear, there's a genius to his incompetence," Gillian said.

"He's made it performance art." Reggie giggled. "He really is the best, though, isn't he? You gotta admire his persistence."

Gillian nodded. "So, feel like talking now?"

Chapter 23

Reggie told Gillian all that Constance had said about her life with Vincent Bennett.

Horrified, Gillian said, "Oh my God, that poor woman. What an evil man."

"Yeah, and Chase and I are expected to defeat him. Constance even said my life depended on it."

Gillian frowned, "Really? She shouldn't have said that."

Reggie paused and looked at her friend with suspicion. "What should she have said, Gillian? What do you know?"

"Last summer, Ernestine told Travis that if he didn't stop the rapist, he would not survive it. Pretty dramatic huh? But true. Failure would have destroyed Travis. In a way, he would have died, I guess. Could that be what Constance meant?"

Reggie shook her head, "No way. She meant that it was a matter of life and death. And you know? I believe her. I've felt the evil in that room. If it's ever unleashed Gill, there's no telling what damage it would wreak"

Gillian nodded and the expression on her face was serious. "You could be right. Ernestine's been teaching me about what being a Guardian entails. I wasn't born here, so it's all so new to me." She shrugged humbly and said, "According to her, there are towns like New Crescent all over the world, places that act as a buffer between the supernatural world and the natural world. These towns attract people with special abilities, people like me." Gillian put her hand on her heart and said, "We feel at home here the moment we cross the town boundaries. But Guardians have a special mission. We are women who accept responsibility for the town's safety. We guide the people of our town and help them to make good decisions so that we can stand firm against the forces that would destroy all that is natural and good."

As a card carrying member of the Old Families and an expert on New Crescent and it's position in the scheme of things, Reggie already understood all that Gillian was saying. But the passion in Gillian's voice was so compelling she sat silently and listened to her friend's tirade.

"People must be protected from evils such as Vincent Bennett. They're unprepared for the kind of power he can wield. He will unleash a kind of Hell on earth, should he succeed. Outsiders cannot possibly conceive of the forces from which we protect them. It's our job. New Crescent is the first line of defense. Sadly, Constance failed to do her job. She is now tied to that monster until he's destroyed. She's had to keep him in check for hundreds of years." Gillian bent and hugged her dog Hank, and she spoke as much to him as she did to Reggie. "Once loosed, Vincent could infect so many others, I'm afraid to even imagine the numbers."

Gillian stopped speaking and Reggie stayed silent for a moment. Finally, she said, "What you said about Constance makes sense. I couldn't figure out why she stuck around. I guess she didn't have a choice. She's been a Guardian even in death. How tragic."

"She needs your help just as much as you need hers. It's a symbiotic relationship. Use it to your advantage and force Constance to tell you everything. She's the only one who can do it."

Reggie shook her head uncertainly. "She's so reluctant. Her pain is so fresh. Even after so many years, Constance still suffers every day."

Gillian nodded. "She was too young to be a Guardian, but after all this time, surely she's matured enough to tell you all she knows."

"I guess that's my next task. Make Constance tell me her entire story. I can feel that time is running out. I don't know how, but I'm sure Chase and I will have to do this thing soon." Reggie hugged herself and ran her hands up and down her arms to stimulate circulation. She felt cold.

"How's Chase during all of this?"

"He's been wonderful. We're not fighting anymore."

Gillian smiled knowingly "Is that a good thing?"

"You have no idea."

* * * *

Back at Bennett House, Reggie didn't waste time. She had a mission. She walked through the garden and stopped near the iron gate. She didn't need to call Constance because she was there waiting.

"You knew I was coming, did you?" Reggie's voice was firm.

Constance just nodded.

"Tell me more. Chase uncovered rumors of Vincent and his possible involvement in the disappearance of a number of Asian servant girls. Do you know anything about that?"

Constance flinched, but didn't say anything.

"We're running out of time. Halloween is next week, and you know how significant that day is. Vincent will use it to his advantage. I need to be ready." Still Constance said nothing. "Damn it woman, tell me what you know about the servant girls!" Reggie was losing patience.

"He liked them young." Constance's voice was hollow. "Some weren't yet fourteen. He'd traveled widely and used his considerable wealth to satisfy his sick impulses. The Orient was a rich feeding ground for a man such as my husband. Those poor girls were completely helpless. Even the authorities turned a blind eye."

She turned away from Reggie but kept talking. "He'd been doing such things for years. It wasn't so easy in New Crescent. People here would have done something had they known. When he was here, he was careful to be discreet. I got pretty close to one of the girls. It wasn't easy because they were all so frightened. I don't know what her parents called her, but she told me 'Mr.Vincent' called her Mai." Constance shook her head sadly, "She didn't even have her own name. This exquisite child was his undisputed property and she knew it. Once I'd understood my husband predilections, I knew Mai wouldn't survive his attentions for long. I put a stop to it."

Reggie waited for her to continue, but she stayed silent. Finally, Reggie asked, "You had so little power over Vincent yourself. How did you stop him?"

The sorrow in Constance's face when she replied was heartbreaking and Reggie let her take her time responding. She felt a twinge in her belly when the ghostly woman spoke at last.

"I was with child." Her tears fell unchecked. "After that first night, my husband never visited my bedchamber again. He'd achieved his goal. I carried his child. We both knew it almost immediately. I could see my future, my child, his instrument."

Reggie was struck speechless. Without mercy, Constance told her story. "I told my husband that I would kill his son if he laid a hand on Mai again. He went mad with anger, but I knew he'd dare not touch me for fear of hurting his son. My delicate condition gave me a small advantage. I then contacted my father's lawyer, and we found a good home for the girl. I instructed him not to tell anyone, even me where he'd placed her. He was a kind man. I knew I could trust him with Mai's future."

"I'm so sorry, Constance…I…"

Constance ignored her and ruthlessly continued. "I knew what his seed would become. I was no longer a Guardian, but I could still see what would be. What my actions would yield. If I didn't die in childbirth, my husband would see to it that I would never raise my own child. He would kill me to ensure that I had no influence in the child's life. It occurred to me that I lived only while I carried his seed."

"What about the other Guardians? Couldn't you go to them for help?"

Constance hissed at her in anger. "Fool! I was my husband's property! No one could interfere. Vincent wouldn't risk hurting the child, but he still controlled everyone in this house. When I tried to leave, he sent men out to bring me back and made me watch while he whipped a young servant in my place. After that no one dared help me. I was watched every second of every day. I tried to get a message to my family, but my messenger never returned. I could not ask another innocent to risk their life for me."

"So what did you do?"

"I incubated his seed. At first, I refused to think of it as mine. The child was a parasite that would lead to my death. I tried to stop eating, but the thing inside me demanded sustenance, and I was too weak to resist."

Reggie looked at Constance with horror. The ghost sneered at her. "I disgust you, don't I, Regina? Don't judge me too harshly. I was a victim of my own destiny. I couldn't hate my child. Every day he grew inside me I knew a love unlike anything else I'd ever imagined. My dreams were filled with the exquisite joy of feeding my son from my breasts. My instinct to love and protect him was primal and beyond my control."

She started to keen. This was not the quiet, discreet expression of a remembered grief. This was the gut wrenching assault of fresh loss.

There was nothing Reggie could do to console her, so without a word she waited for Constance to calm down. Her own tears, she wiped from her face with the back of her hand.

Constance drew her dignity around her like a cloak. She straightened her shoulders and held her head high. In a flat tone, she addressed Reggie.

"Is there anything else you'd like me to relive for you?"

"No! Constance, I didn't know. I had no idea of what you'd endured. How could I have known?"

She just looked at Reggie blankly.

"I'm more sorry than I can say, Constance, but at the risk of sounding cruel, I have to remind you that that was a long time ago. Somehow, you managed to neutralize Vincent until now. You have to help me end all of this. Maybe then you can cross over and be with your child."

The fury Constance aimed at Reggie was equally self-directed. Her image flared and blinded Reggie for a split second. Dizzy, Reggie lost her balance and reached for the stone bench to break her fall. Landing hard on one knee, she cried out in pain.

Constance's image softened and grew hazy. Reggie could hear the regret in her voice as she faded away. "Forgive me, forgive…forgive."

Using the bench as support, Reggie regained her footing and limped into the house. All she wanted was a long hot bath…and maybe some cookies. She hesitated in the hallway…food or bath…bath or food?

Chase saw her as she stood indecisively motionless in the hall. Concerned, he asked, "Reggie? Are you okay?"

She smiled at him. "I will be. I hurt my knee."

He was on his own knees in front of her in the blink of an eye. Idly, Reggie wondered if his position was just what would get Travis the answer he sought from Gillian on the whole marriage question. She winced as Chase touched her bruised flesh.

"Ouch!"

"Sorry. I had to determine if anything was broken."

She looked crossly at him. "Nothing's broken except my silence."

He stifled a snort. "Where were you heading?"

She sighed. "I want a hot bath and a cookie."

Trying not to laugh at her, Chase said, "I'll carry you upstairs and run you a bath. I'll give you fifteen minutes and bring up milk and cookies. Okay?"

He was so sweet, she wanted to cry, but all she did was nod at him. He swept her into his arms with ease. She loved him just a little more for that. And he took her upstairs.

In the bathroom adjoining her bedroom, Chase started the bath. He turned to her and asked, "Do you need help with your clothes?"

She shared her smile with him. "I think I can manage just this once, but can I have a rain check?"

Chase laughed. "As you wish." He walked out. When he started back down the stairs he hollered, "And remember, no honeysuckle, unless you aim to render me impotent."

Carefully, she shed her clothes. Her knee hurt, but she felt tension in her entire body as well. She'd been taking quite a beating these past few days. Constance's revelations were horrific, and her stomach lurched as she remembered all that she'd learned about the Bennett marriage.

She couldn't wait to talk to Chase and get his take on what Constance had revealed, but Reggie wondered how she'd find the words to describe an eighteen-year-old girl's pain. Steam rose from the tub, and she tested the water with one hand. She liked it hot but not that hot. She turned the cold water knob a fraction of an inch. Avoiding the honeysuckle bath bubbles, she reached for lavender with a fond smile.

The water reached the perfect temperature, and Reggie eased herself into the tub. She was just moaning with pleasure when Chase came in with a tray.

"Yup. I've heard that sound before." He held a chocolate chip cookie to her mouth.

She swallowed a mouthful of cookie. "Yes you have heard that sound, but you haven't heard what I learned from Constance just now."

Chapter 24

Her bath water was tepid when she finished telling Chase what Constance had revealed. He was silent after she stopped talking. Reggie sat up in the tub and started to get out. Her tears were a little warmer than the water she soaked in, and she knew it was time to get out.

Chase wrapped a white fluffy bath sheet around her and helped her to dry off. It felt wonderful to be so pampered, and it surprised Reggie that he could be so nurturing. How little she knew about him, even after all these years. Wrapped in her terry robe, Reggie stretched out on the bed. Both Pru and Pita joined her.

"I pushed Constance hard today. It wasn't easy. She was almost mad with grief, and I can't blame her. What did she ever do to deserve such a fate?"

Chase looked sad. "What makes you think our fates are earned?"

Reggie sighed. "I guess you're right, but it's all so horrible." She put a hand on her tummy as her stomach churned with anxiety. "How does knowing all of this, help us to beat Vincent, except that now we're both a whole lot more motivated?"

"I don't know, but have you ever wondered why Vincent stays in the library while Constance moves about pretty freely?" Chase asked. She frowned at him, and he said, "I think there's something in the library he's protecting. Maybe it's the key to the source of his power."

"Makes sense, but what do you suggest we do about it?"

"Why not ask Constance? She's finally opening up to you. Maybe she'll help us search the library."

Reggie played with the belt on her robe. "I could try. If we're going back into the library tomorrow, I'd appreciate Constance's backup."

Chase sat on the edge of the bed beside her reclining form. He too played with the belt of her robe.

She smiled up at him and said, "I feel a rain check coming on. I would appreciate some help with my clothes."

He grinned and dispensed with her robe smoothly. He worshipped her body with his eyes, his mouth, his tongue, and, yes, even his teeth. She writhed in response and tried to pull at his clothing, but he forestalled her. He wasn't finished yet. His mouth traveled down her body, and she arched her back and thrust her hips up to meet his talented mouth. My God, the man was an artist. She lost all conscious thought as sensation shattered her control and she cried out her release. He looked at her with such an expression of triumph on his face, Reggie took it as a challenge and proceeded to undress him.

* * * *

In the middle of the night, together, they raided the refrigerator and hauled their score up to the bedroom where they picnicked naked on the massive bed.

After biting into his peanut butter sandwich, Chase said, "We're gonna leave crumbs. I just want to go on record that you can't kick me out of bed for it."

"I'll try to remember that."

"I got some good news today."

Reggie smiled. "Well, don't keep me waiting. What news?"

"Jade's coming home."

Reggie remembered Chase's stepsister and how close he'd been to her. In their youth, Jade had trailed after her older brother like a puppy. Because Chase didn't mind, neither did the rest of them. Despite their own immaturity, Reggie, Travis, Chase, and Sam understood what being included in their group meant to the little girl. She was included in everything. Jade Adams had been a chubby little adolescent eager to grow up. Animals loved her, and she loved them right back. She could calm even the most agitated dog or cat despite her inexperience. It was a wonder to watch her with an animal who was frightened or in pain. She had a magic touch. Finally, Jade was coming home. It made Chase so happy, and Reggie said a silent word of thanks to her young friend.

"Jade's coming back to New Crescent. I think that's wonderful, Chase. It's been a long time since I saw her last. When was it?" Reggie tried to recall.

"My mother's funeral, I guess."

Reggie nodded. "Yeah, I remember her pale face. She was devastated, and it showed in every part of her body. Those beautiful green eyes looked huge and so sad." She turned to see the pain in Chase's face.

"I'm sorry, Chase. I didn't mean to be so insensitive." She hugged him close.

He smiled at her and shook his head.

"It's okay. It's the truth. Jade was devastated when my mother died. I'm just relieved she's finally coming to live in New Crescent again."

"Will she live with you in your house?"

Chase nodded, "She'll live in the bungalow. I'm going to give her my bedroom. Women need more space."

Reggie nibbled on a celery stick and said, "How observant you are. Jade's, what? Five-feet-three tops. She's almost two feet shorter than you, but she needs more room." She laughed at him.

Chase shook his head. "Jade comes with a menagerie of animals. I've lost track of the last tally, but believe me, she'll need the room."

"So when are Jade and the ark of animals going to arrive?"

"I've asked her to wait until you and I destroy Vincent. She's so gentle and sensitive I don't think it would be good for her to be here right now."

Reggie said, with a teasing lilt in her voice, "So I guess I'm not gentle and sensitive then."

He shook his head vehemently, "I didn't say that. You're stronger, one of the strongest people I've ever known." He took her head in his hands and kissed her before he continued. "You doubt yourself but you shouldn't. Sometimes your bravado is utterly false. I've seen through you for years."

In a mocking tone, she said, "My, how Clark Kent of you. Does that mean you have x-ray vision?" She frowned at him. "Have you been peeking at my underwear?"

He laughed. "I see through that too, Crash."

She looked unsure, and he explained. "Your sense of humor is your armor. Nothing hurts you if you can laugh at it. It took me a long time to understand that about you."

"So you've been trying to figure me out have you? Tell me what else you know about me." Stretched out on her side, she propped her head up with her elbow.

"You like bubble baths and long walks on the beach. Oh, and piña coladas and getting caught in the rain." He laughed.

She pushed at him playfully, "Not fair!"

"I think it is. I'm tired, and I need to get some sleep. Care to join me?"

She snuggled down beside him and said, "Since you ask so nicely."

* * * *

The next morning she dropped by her parents' place just in time to help make breakfast. While she cooked eggs and bacon, she filled her parents in on what progress she'd made on the house.

Her father said, "It sounds like you've done a great deal of work, but why are you stalled now?

"We can't get past the library. There's some sort of energy in there, and Chase and I are trying to figure out some way to exorcise it."

"What does Ernestine say about it?"

Her mother sounded suspiciously nonchalant. Anne Stanton was never able to hide anything from her daughter.

"Ernestine has told you everything hasn't she? I should have known." Reggie said.

"Yeah you should have. We'd much rather have heard it all from you. Ernestine can be a little vague. She talked about destiny, fate, power. You know how she gets. Suffice it to say, we understand that this is something you have to deal with alone." Her father frowned. "Your mother and I don't like it, but we understand."

"Thanks, Dad," Reggie said. "I don't think I could turn my back on it even if I wanted to. I love Bennett House, and that fact alone would make me want to investigate the spirits I feel there."

Her mother looked confused, and Reggie explained. "Yeah, you heard me right. There are two spirits there. One is Chase's ancestor Constance McCann Bennett."

Her father said, "I didn't know that Chase is related to the Bennetts."

"He isn't, Dad. Constance McCann and Vincent Bennett had no children on record. She either miscarried or died before giving birth to their first child."

"What's she like? I've always wanted to see a ghost. You'd think I would have, living here in New Crescent, especially since I'm so willing to see one, but nope," her mother said.

Reggie laughed. "Constance McCann is stubborn, secretive, impatient, manipulative, precocious, and sometimes humorous. She drives me crazy. Since I have no physic ability, I have to practically beg her for information, and believe me, she's stingy with that."

"Does Chase see her too?" her dad asked.

Reggie shook her head. "No, he's never seen her, but he can hear her. So far, it seems I'm the only one who can see her. Chase can see the change in the atmosphere when Constance manifests, but he hasn't actually laid eyes on her. She has the most tragic story. She can still feel the pain poignantly, so it's hard for her to talk about. It's almost as painful to listen to. She relives it every time she tells the story."

He mother patted her hand. "Patience has never been easy for you."

"I know. I'm going to contact her today and ask for no new information. Chase and I thought we'd give her a rest from that. We're hoping to search the library, and we need her help to keep Vincent busy while we do it. She's been keeping him at bay for hundreds of years. Surely she can do it for a couple of hours more."

"But Ernestine said he feeds off a person's life force now since Bennett House has been reopened. Are you sure you should go in there?" Her mom shuddered. "It's so horrible."

"That's why Chase and I have put a stop to work on the house for now. We are trying to make it harder and harder for him." Reggie said. "We've warned everyone to stay away from the house because it's dangerous. Most of the people working on it were from New Crescent, so there were no questions. They could feel something there and were glad when we put a halt on the work. Chase and I have to do this, Mom."

"What about the owner? Does she know about this?" Her dad sounded so protective.

Reggie paused for a moment and said, "Chase has been in contact with the agent, Jackie Blake. He's met Pat Somers. It seems she has complete faith in Chase's judgment. For someone who is investing a fortune on a house, she sure is blasé about how her money is spent. If I were a dishonest person I could take advantage big time."

Her mother smiled proudly. "But you're not dishonest dear, so everything is fine. Did Chase tell you what Pat Somers is like?"

"He was useless." Reggie pouted.

Her father was quick to defend Chase. "What's to say? Unless she's a suspect for a crime, personal descriptions are pretty useless these days. People can't be trusted to pick up important details." He picked up a piece of bacon and took a big bite.

"Yeah, well, Chase is particularly bad at it. I'm glad he didn't have to provide a physical description of my kidnapper or they never would have found me."

Her parents exchanged an uneasy look. Reggie could joke about an experience that was the most terrifying of their lives. Their brilliant daughter had been kidnapped by a man who had viciously raped and beaten three women. They went out of their minds with worry. When they'd received the news that she was okay, they collapsed with relief.

To Don and Anne Stanton, Chase McCann was a hero.

Her dad said, "Don't be too hard on Chase, my girl. He knows you'll soon meet Pat Somers, and you won't need a description from him. Ernestine told us that Chase has to help you to fight this evil spirit."

Reggie nodded. "Yes, apparently neither of us can do it on our own. In fact, I feel more powerful when he's with me. I trust him."

Her mom put her hand over Reggie's. "We do too, and that's the only way we would promise Ernestine that we'd stay out of it."

Her husband agreed. "Chase is a good man. He didn't have to, but he cleared up the complicated schemes and cons that his stepfather had started all over town. He saw to it that people got their money back with interest. He was just twenty-one-years old, had just lost his mother and his sister. He was completely alone in the world. In my book Chase McCann is a good man."

"We had him over for dinner every week during that time," Her mother said. "He was so tired, I thought he'd fall asleep in his soup bowl but, he always insisted on helping me with the dishes. His mother raised him right.

He even stopped by here the day after you left for Europe this summer to make sure you were okay."

Reggie was surprised. "Why have you never told me this?"

Her mom took a dainty bite of scrambled egg and then said, "You never asked, and we figured if Chase had wanted you to know he'd tell you. The two of you have never been strangers."

Reggie shook her head bemusedly. "My parents. Anything else about your relationship with Chase that I don't know about?"

Her parents exchanged looks and started to think. Finally, Her dad looked at Reggie. "No."

Her mom hurried to say, "Unless you count me teaching him how to cook." She smiled happily at her daughter.

Reggie shook her head with astonishment. "Who are you people? You got any more secrets you wanna get off your chest? I'm not adopted, am I? Dad, please don't tell me you try on Mom's clothes."

They laughed. Reggie loved the sound of her parents' combined laughter. They had a wonderful marriage. Reggie would never settle for less than what they had together and she understood that was a tall order.

He father smiled. "Well, actually…" He paused for effect and was delighted when Reggie looked at him with horror. "For Halloween, your mother's going as me and I'm going as her. Does that qualify as trying on your mother's clothes?"

Reggie picked up a crisp slice of bacon and pointed it at her smiling parents. "Let's never speak of this again."

Chapter 25

Reggie and Chase stood in the garden and waited for Constance to appear. It didn't take long. The air changed, signaling her appearance and Reggie got right down to business.

"We want to search the library today. We need your help to keep Vincent busy while we look around."

Constance didn't seem to mind Reggie's direct approach. She smiled at her and said, "What makes you think you'll find anything?"

"We're not sure, but he's stayed in that room since this thing started. He's protecting something. If we find it, we'll have a better idea of how to destroy him." Reggie said.

"Just how do you suggest I keep that monster occupied? Do you have any idea what that would entail?" Constance approached them. She didn't float exactly but she didn't walk either. She moved in the ghostly blink of an eye.

She stopped just an inch from Chase and said, "And what do you think of this, my kin?"

Chase couldn't see Constance, but still he took a step back. "It's time we started to clean house. I know there's something in that library Vincent cares about and we have to find it."

Constance laughed. "Oh my dear, you are passionate." She paused a long time and Reggie was getting prepared to press the issue when Constance finally said, "I'll do it."

"You...you will?" Reggie said.

"Don't sound so surprised. I'm aware of the passage of time. All Hallows' Eve is just next week. He'll use that day to his advantage if he can. You need to weaken him as much as you can before that time."

"Constance," Chase said gently, "do you know how to distract Vincent and not damage yourself?"

"Sweet of you to ask, my boy. I haven't communicated with my husband for years. We know of each other's existence, but we keep the status quo. Without the help of others we are evenly matched, stalemated for all eternity."

Reggie frowned. "Can you keep him occupied long enough for us to search the library?"

Constance nodded. "I can try. Don't be surprised if you feel strange elements in the air. The room could run cold. You may see sparks. Don't be alarmed. Just go about your business."

"How will we know if you can't hold him off for us?" Reggie asked.

"I will speak. You may not hear me clearly, but when you hear my voice say your name, Regina, get out of there." She smiled and added, "Go with your gut. Is that the expression?"

Reggie sighed. "Yeah, it's familiar to me."

Chase looked at Reggie and frowned. "Constance, why are you cooperating with us now?"

"I don't know what you mean." Her ghostly voice sounded defensive.

"You haven't connected with Vincent in hundreds of years. Up until now, getting help from you has been like herding cats. You're going to help us today, face off with your husband. Why?"

Reggie could see Constance start to fade, and she yelled, "Stay!" Her stomach lurched, and she felt nauseated but stood her ground. Constance reappeared. Reggie sent a self congratulatory look to Chase.

Figuring it best not to press her luck, Reggie spoke gently. "Confronting the man responsible for all your pain will not be easy, but we'll do it together. If you get into trouble, say Chase's name, and we'll try to help. Chase brings up a very good point, Constance. We need to know why you're willing to help us today. Let's not have any surprises."

Constance looked mutinous, but she finally answered. "It was not easy to tell you my story yesterday. It tore me apart. The pain is still so acute. It haunts me, and it always will, until I face him, the evil responsible for so much despair. Feeling that agony of grief and guilt again helped me to face the fact that the time has come. I can't do it alone, but we may be able to do it together." She gave them a ghostly smile. "I'm afraid. My failure has resounded through the decades. It is hard to have faith in myself again."

Reggie said, "We have faith in you Constance. You've suffered enough. We can do this together."

She nodded and said. "I will be there when you need me to be." She was gone.

Chase and Reggie were silent until they reached the kitchen. Chase poured them each a glass of water.

Reggie said, "So she's not as sure of herself as she pretends, who knew?"

"Does she remind you of anyone?" Chase laughed.

She frowned at him. "I suppose you mean me."

"If the Manolo fits."

"What do you know of Manolo Blahniks?" She narrowed her eyes and waited for his answer.

"I've seen *Sex in the City*." He said defensively.

"Ok Mr.Big. Let's talk strategy."

Chase's cell phone rang. For a second, he looked like he might ignore it, but finally he answered it. Reggie tuned him out. She had no interest in listening to his one-sided conversation. Instead, she mentally ran through strategies they could use to search for hiding places in the library.

"That was Sam," Chase said.

He had her attention. "What did he say?"

"His parents are friends with a certain Aidan Spencer's father."

"Todd's Aidan?"

"Yeah. Sam says the dad's a jerk, but we knew that already. All Sam's parents' friends are jerks. It seems Aidan's the product of the passion between Jason Spencer and his latest trophy wife. Neither are model parents. They think they love their son because they give him everything he wants." Chase took a deep gulp of water and went on. "Aidan's been expelled from several private schools. He's made trouble everywhere. It sounds like he's a bully just like his father."

Reggie ran her hand through her hair and rested her chin on her elbow. "And the perfect pawn for Vincent. I wonder how many times Aidan's been here after we made it clear it was trespassing."

"My guess would be, every night," Chase said. "I'm going to stake out the library windows again tonight. I guess that means you will too, huh?"

She laughed and didn't bother to answer him. His question was rhetorical.

"Let's just get through today. How do you think we should approach the search in the library?"

He lifted a finger and pointed at a roll of architectural drawings. "Those are plans of the existing house. I had a draftsman draw them up for us. The other roll is a copy of the original plans for Bennett House. I got them from the town's archives. I think we should compare them and see if there could be any hidden rooms or tunnels…well, you know what I mean."

Reggie favored him with a bright smile. "That's a scathingly brilliant idea, Poindexter. I'm glad you're on my side."

They spread out the plans on the dining room table. It was the largest surface available. Poring over the drawings, it didn't take them long to find possible hiding places. The east side of the room looked most promising. There was at least a six-foot discrepancy between the two plans.

Chase looked at her. "Well, it looks like we start working on the east side. Are you ready?"

Reggie nodded. She wore work boots, jeans, three layers of sweat shirts…and a very determined look on her face.

* * * *

The hallway outside the library still reeked. It made Reggie think of unnatural death and putrefied flesh. Her stomach wanted to rebel, but she forced it to behave. She exchanged a look with Chase. He could smell it too, and he didn't like it any more than she did. The air got thick and clammy as they approached the double doors leading into the library, but they pretended not to notice.

Reggie didn't have to call upon Constance. She could feel her presence. She wasn't with them in the hallway but rather was outside the windows away from the rancid smell. Chase opened both doors with minimal effort. Reggie remembered how hard it had been for her to open those very same doors the first day she arrived at Bennett House just weeks ago. Was Vincent's power depleted? Maybe he could no longer keep them out because he'd had no one from which to feed. Reggie mentally corrected herself. No, that would be too easy. Vincent Bennett was tricky. It made sense to her that he'd pretend to be weak and catch them off guard. They could not afford to underestimate him. He was still stinking the place up.

The air inside the room was thick and damp. Reggie felt an irritation at the back of her throat as she breathed it in. She coughed.

Forcing her voice to sound normal, she said, "It really is a beautiful room. And think how much more beautiful it will be when we're through with it. I have all kinds of ideas for it."

Understanding Reggie's attempt at normalcy, Chase joined in, "I can just see it. Fire blazing, dog sleeping by a club chair, and the *Masterpiece Theatre* music."

Reggie could feel resistance in the air, but stubbornly refused to acknowledge it, pretending it was so inconsequential that she didn't even notice it.

In a lighthearted voice, she said, "I think the first thing to do is take some of the boards off the windows and let the sun in. The fresh air might help get rid of that funky smell."

They moved toward the windows. Reggie helped as Chase removed the boards, she chattered on, filling the room with cheerful observations about nothing. She was uniquely qualified. She refused to let a single negative thought enter her mind.

The outside air swept in like Mother Nature's broom. It didn't quite succeed in ridding the library of the rancid odor, but it sure helped. Reggie could breathe again without gagging. Her stomach settled, and she sent a silent prayer of thanks to who ever was listening—Constance maybe? Everyone kept telling her to follow her gut but lately her gut hadn't been much help. She looked down at her abdomen and thought, 'thanks for nothing.' She took deep breaths of the fresh sea air outside, hoping to settle her stomach. She watched Chase do the same.

Reggie could feel Constance just outside the windows they'd opened. Her power was palpable. Still Vincent didn't react to their presence. To someone who didn't know better, the library felt almost normal, if a little musty. On closer inspection, however, every surface in the room was covered in the same greasy dust Reggie had slipped on the last time they'd been in the room. It wasn't natural. It came from him, Vincent Bennett. Everything that came from him was twisted, sick, and just plain wrong. She figured that the strange greasy film was best described as a physical manifestation of an evil presence. Reggie wondered if they'd ever be able to wipe the room clean. 'Yes of course they would', she told herself. At the same time, she was reminded of how sly and cunning Vincent could be. His first attack would be subtle, maybe it would start as a question. Yes, he wanted them to question themselves. He played on a person's insecurity and chipped away at it so he could feast on their despair. Locking eyes with Chase, Reggie shut down all her self-doubts. She could feel her strength grow.

"Okay," Chase said, "let's start with the east side. You start here"—he pointed—"and I'll start at the other end. We'll meet in the middle." He kissed her before he left her side. She could feel the jolt of power their contact created.

They tapped their hands against the wall every two inches hoping to hear a hollow sound. Meeting Chase in the middle, Reggie pursed her lips. She refused to frown. She wouldn't even give him that much.

"Anything?" she asked Chase, hopefully.

"Nothing hollow."

Narrowing her eyes, she asked, "You didn't answer my question. You didn't find anything hollow, so what have you found?"

Chase grinned and took her by the hand. Reggie was assaulted by a strong whiff of Vincent Bennett's signature fragrance. The Big Bad was rattled. They were headed in the right direction. Reggie spared a look outside and saw Constance focusing on something she couldn't quite see. *Handy to have your very own watch ghost,* Reggie mused. She could tell that Constance had engaged Vincent and was struggling for control. The temperature of the room fluctuated between comfortably mild and icy cold, and she could swear if she touched metal she'd conduct electricity.

Chase guided her to a section of mahogany wainscoting and told her to knock hard on it. She did as he asked. It didn't sound hollow to her and she looked up at Chase and said, "So?"

"Now, knock here." He pointed to a section about three feet away. She tapped her knuckles on the wall. "Notice the difference?" He smiled expectantly.

"There's something behind this panel," she said, the excitement evident in her voice.

The force hit fast and hard. It knocked the wind out of her lungs leaving her gasping for air. When she took deep gulps of air, she wanted to gag. The air was almost gray with that horrible stink. She held a hand out to Chase.

Chapter 26

Chase got a good grip on Reggie's hand and pulled her towards him. Their touch helped to restore her strength. She took a breath and grimaced. Chase nodded, understanding immediately why she made such a face. His upper lip curled in response and Reggie laughed with genuine amusement.

"Good Elvis impression, Poindexter," she said as she regained her center of gravity.

He smiled back at her fighting the overwhelming odor. "Thanks, but I have to admit it isn't intentional. It's not something I could recreate on command."

They were both struggling to breathe through the strange air that filled the room. Reggie looked outside and saw Constance. She was still focused and had a determined look on her face, but Reggie could feel her strength waning. Chase followed her glance but couldn't see anything out of the ordinary.

Reggie held fast to his hand and headed in the direction of the windows. "Come on, Chase, let's let more air in here. We could take down a few more boards." Together, they fought their way through the heavy air. It was like pushing her way through quick sand and it depleted her strength. By the time they made it to the windows, the room was filled with a grayish mist. Its atmosphere looked like something out of a bad horror film and Reggie tried to think of it that way. It made it feel less threatening.

Prying another board off, they stuck their heads outside and breathed in the clean air. Reggie spoke to Constance. "Are you okay?"

Constance nodded but didn't look Reggie's way. She was concentrating on something even Reggie couldn't see. Reggie realized that breaking her focus even for a split second may unleash Vincent's power. Once those floodgates were open, she feared what he'd be able to do. She popped her head back inside.

"I can't see her, Reg. Is she okay?"

Reggie nodded. "She's just playing with him. Everything is under control. We can do this." She turned her face up for his kiss. When his lips touched hers, she felt the butterflies in her stomach take flight. Her giggle was genuine and Chase looked down at her with bemusement. "Shall we take down another board?"

"Sure thing. Let's get some help from Mother Nature herself. Out with the unnatural, in with the natural." Laughing, she made sweeping gestures with her arms. Chase just smiled at her.

Without warning, the mist disappeared. All was still and quiet in the room. Reggie and Chase looked at each other in wordless anticipation. Something was coming. This couldn't possibly be the end. Could it?

Reggie took a breath and began to speak. She didn't get the words out. A massive force threw her against the wall. She hit solid mahogany like a fly hitting a windshield. Sinking helplessly to the floor, Reggie winced at the pain in her shoulder. Her left arm hung at an impossible angle. She knew it was dislocated and she bit down hard to keep from crying out. The same force that had sent her flying had also thrown Chase. He sat against the opposite wall, his legs in front of him. He must have hit his head because he opened and closed his eyes and shook his head as if trying to clear his vision.

Chase didn't much waste time. On his feet, he ran to Reggie and helped her to stand. He kept his hands off the side with the dislocated shoulder and put his arm around her helping to prop her up.

Forcing the stammer from her speech, in a steady voice she said, "That was exciting. He'll have to do better than that." She gathered her strength, calling upon that unused reserve she had stored somewhere deep in her belly. She pushed back with force. They heard a deafening bang, the house shuddered in its wake. The air cleared again. They could move easily, and ignoring her throbbing shoulder, Reggie walked back to the east wall. Chase joined her. There was something behind that wall. They just had to find the way to access the opening. They tried everything they could think of and still it wouldn't budge. Reggie looked outside and saw Constance. She was still concentrating on some invisible foe, but she made an almost imperceptible gesture with her hand and Reggie understood.

Using her right hand and gritting her teeth against the pain in her left side, Reggie traced the shape of the baseboard. She felt triumphant when she found a tiny notch in the smooth wood. Carefully, she mimicked Constance's subtle hand gesture. The panel popped open. She almost collapsed with relief. Chase pushed the panel aside and they looked inside.

The nook was just big enough to hold an average sized man. Chase had to bend his head in order to enter. He went first. Reggie leaned her uninjured shoulder against the panel and watched as Chase's flashlight illuminated the shelves. Books. This secret room held about thirty dusty old books. Chase used a thumb and wiped the greasy grime off a leather spine. *The Dark Path Volume I* was embossed there. Chase cleaned off a few more books with the same title but different numbered volumes.

Chase shone the flashlight on the opposite wall. More shelves. There were no books on this side of the secret room. Instead there were hundreds of unlabeled glass bottles of varying sizes, every one filled with unrecognizable, but truly repulsive contents. Reggie dared not speculate on exactly what the bottles contained, but she could have sworn she saw a human toe.

Through gritted teeth, Reggie said, "Damn it, I was thinking of having toe for lunch today. We were all out."

Chase laughed. "We have to get you to the hospital. I can't clear this thing out in one trip, so I'll grab what I can for now. We'll have to save the rest for later."

Reggie agreed. She'd been stoic long enough.

* * * *

Her shoulder ached without mercy or respite. She had indeed dislocated it and it still hurt like hell now that it was relocated. The emergency room doctor gave her a prescription for pain killers and Reggie waited in the car while Chase had it filled. Maybe she could take a half dosage just to take the edge off the pain but still be clear headed. She needed to discuss this latest discovery with Chase. She longed to open the books Chase had taken from the secret room. Had they found the source of Vincent Bennett's power? Could it be something in one of those disgusting bottles? The thought of analyzing the contents of each container made Reggie shiver in revulsion. She was glad she wasn't a scientist. She wasn't fond of goo.

She hoped Constance was okay. They'd left the library in such a hurry that she hadn't had the chance to find out. Pain killers or not, that would be the first thing she did upon returning to Bennett House. Contact Constance. She shook her head and leaned it against the cool smooth passenger side window. She smiled. Months ago, she would have laughed at anyone who told her that one day soon she'd be concerned about the health and welfare of a two-hundred-fifty-year-old stubborn, tragic, and rather endearing ghost. Her life had taken quite a turn.

Chase returned to the car and handed her the pills and a bottle of water. "Take them now."

She shook her head. "No. I'm okay. I'd rather be level-headed when I connect with Constance."

His voice had a sharp edge to it. "You're not connecting with anyone except your bed. The doctor said with the proper treatment there would be no lasting damage, but it must hurt like hell."

She smiled wanly. "It does, but I don't want to lose momentum. I need to make sure Constance made it through and find out whatever she can tell us about her end of what happened today."

"That can wait until tomorrow." Chase was firm.

Reggie wasn't impressed. She sat up straighter. "No, it can't wait until tomorrow. Time is running out. I'll do what I think is best."

Chase said nothing. She looked at him with suspicion. Did he do that on purpose? Make her just angry enough to forget about the throbbing pain in her shoulder? Good one.

Returning to Bennett House, Reggie walked immediately to the little iron gate in the garden. Chase followed close behind.

"Constance?" She called. "Can I speak with you please?"

They heard a little laugh. "Aren't you polite?" She teased.

Happy to hear the ghostly but snide voice, Reggie smiled. "Yeah, every once in a while I try polite on for size, but it chafes."

Constance ignored her. "Did the physician mend you?"

"I'll be all right. How are you?"

Constance shrugged, "There is no physician who can mend me. I am as I am."

Reggie rolled her eyes and looked at Chase. She said, "You know what I mean but hey, I'm glad you have the energy to be difficult."

Constance smiled but said nothing.

Chase said, "Thanks for your help today. We found the hidden room."

"I'm glad. It was not pleasant facing my husband again, but I am stronger when I work in concert with you."

Reggie smiled. "We make a good team."

She gave them both a ghostly frown and said, "Do not think this is the end. We won a battle today. The next will not be so easy."

Reggie's golden eyes widened, "You call that easy? Well you don't have to breathe to stay alive. We do, and let me tell you that stuff he's spewing out is toxic."

"You both did well today. Go rest." She made dismissive motions with her arms.

Chase, of course, couldn't see her, and he said, "I'm going to stake out the library windows tonight. He'll need energy, and I'd rather he not get it from a misguided kid."

Constance shook her head. "As you wish." She was gone.

"She's gone, isn't she?"

"Yeah. Let's go inside. I could eat something."

Chase gave her a measuring look. "Good idea. You shouldn't take painkillers on an empty stomach."

Reggie shook her head. "You know, I don't think I'll take those pills." When he started to object she put a hand up to quiet him. "Gillian told me to abstain from alcohol until this thing is over. I'm sure she'd put pain killers on the restricted list."

"I forgot about that." Chase said.

"I almost did too. I need to keep my wits about me now more than ever. We've got a hold of something Vincent treasures. He didn't want us to find that room. That makes me think those books and those heebie-jeebie bottles are important."

"Agreed. I'll fix dinner."

In a conversational tone, Reggie said, "Yeah, my mom told me that she taught you how to cook."

Wary, he said, "And?"

"Did she show you how to make her macaroni and cheese?" She looked hopeful.

He laughed. "As a matter of fact…"

* * * *

Tempted by the huge bathtub, Reggie showed self-discipline and stepped into the shower instead. She didn't have time for a long soak. Chase was preparing dinner after he grabbed a quick shower, so she didn't have much time. If she ran a bath, she might never get out, and at this moment, her most urgent need was food.

Dressing in comfortable pants and a sweat shirt Reggie looked down at her little dog. Poor Pru. She didn't understand why she'd had to spend a good portion of the day locked up in the bedroom with Pita. Reggie and Chase didn't dare let them run loose while they were engaged with Vincent. The little dog and cat were perfect targets for his sport. Emotionally, both Reggie and Chase were bonded with the animals. Although Chase pretended otherwise, Reggie knew he loved that cat and was touched by its loyalty to him. No, they had to keep the animals away from the library and the power it housed. The best way to do that was to shut them up in a bedroom as far away as possible. It was no real hardship so Reggie didn't have much sympathy for them. She'd finished work in all the bedrooms, but that one was especially beautiful. Not quite as luxurious as the master bedroom, the smaller spare bedroom had character. Painted in periwinkle blue with white trim, the white-washed vintage furniture suite suited the room to a tee. It would make a wonderful little girl's room.

Reggie's stomach growled, and she obeyed. The kitchen smelled glorious. If she were a character in a Looney Tunes cartoon, she'd be floating in the air, bewitched by the aroma. Reggie wasn't a cartoon, so she just closed her eyes and breathed deeply in appreciation.

Chase was seasoning a salad when he saw her walk in. He smiled and tossed her a cherry tomato. "How do you feel?"

"Better, thanks." She said before she bit down decisively on the round tomato. Its guts sprayed her mouth and she swallowed with satisfaction. "Mmm." She said and licked her lips. Jealous, Chase bent and kissed those very same lips. She responded eagerly. When the oven timer went off, it startled them both. He smiled down at her a question in his blue eyes. Reggie decided it wasn't just food she was hungry for.

Chapter 27

All appetites satiated, they poured over the books they'd managed to haul from the secret room in the library. What they found defied description. These were English translations of very dark magic. Blood magic, Ernestine would call it. So powerful that only the most committed of servants could wield its forces without destroying himself. Reading the rituals and incantations made Reggie sick. She felt cold and Chase put an arm around her.

"You don't have to read anymore, Crash. I think we got the gist of what these books are and what they represent."

Reggie rested her head on his shoulder and sighed. "I think we need to get these books and all those gross little bottles to Ernestine as soon as possible. I don't want to see them ever again. I hope to hell we don't have to understand all of this before we can defeat the Big Bad. You know, like when Travis was with the FBI and had to get into the mind of a serial killer in order to catch him."

Chase ran his thumb down her cheek. "I know what you mean. Let's hope Ernestine can handle this for us. Let her be the scholar and we'll be the warriors."

He glanced outside and said, "It's past the dinner hour. I need to set up my stakeout of the library windows. Now they're not boarded up, who knows how tempting they might appear to a kid who likes to ignore the rules."

"That and Vincent has to be tweaking for a fix right about now."

Chase nodded.

Pushing the books away from her, she stood and said, "I need to wash this disgusting spew off my hands. I'll meet you outside."

Chase looked at her, an expression of incredulity on his face. "Are you crazy? You need to get some rest. I can take care of this on my own."

Stubborn, she stood her ground. "Sorry Poindexter, we're in this together. How many times have we been told we're stronger as two? I'm joining you."

"Reggie, let's think this through logically—"

"Logically? In order for us to discuss this logically, you'd have to be either a girl or a Vulcan." She looked him up and down. "I know you're not a girl, and you can't possibly be a Vulcan because they mate only once every seven years or so...sorry, Spock, but you're way over your quota. I'm going on a stakeout."

"Vulcans mate only once every four years," Chase corrected her.

"Ah huh, geek test!" She walked out of the dining room and went looking for warm clothes and for something to sit on. She didn't relish the thought of hunkering down in the mud, uncomfortable and miserable.

She met Chase outside. He'd selected an advantageous location for the stakeout. "Since we're supposed to do this together, I blocked off every other approach to this side of the building. Don't worry. It doesn't look intentional like manipulating a rat in a maze. It's just that this is now, the easiest way to get to the library windows. He'll have to go past us."

She smiled at him. She almost laughed when she saw how prepared he was. He'd set up two small folding lawn chairs. There was a blanket on each. He'd brought two thermoses. Reggie assumed they contained coffee. She was delighted.

He put his hands in his pockets and showed her an assortment of candy bars. She threw her good arm around him and brought his head down to hers so she could land a kiss of gratitude on his lips.

Despite all Chase's preparations, the stakeout was excruciatingly boring. They had to stay quiet but alert. Quiet wasn't Reggie's forte. She dozed off a few times, her head resting on Chase's warm chest. At long last, when the sun rose, Chase stood up and stretched until his bones cracked. Reggie winced at the sound.

"Now you go to bed. I'll drive the books over to Ernestine and swing by the school to make sure Aidan Spencer is in class. If we know where he is we know he's not here playing host body to the Big Bad."

Reggie shook her head. "I should do that. It'll be easier for me to recognize Aidan."

Chase shook his head. "I know Aidan's teacher. I'm going to ask her for a favor. She can let us know when or if Aidan disappears."

"Convenient that, knowing his teacher thing," she mumbled as she walked away.

* * * *

Chase tied the books up with care. He wanted them out of the house just as much as Reggie did. Touching them made his skin crawl. He wasn't looking forward to hauling out the rest of them, not to mention those bottles and he knew they'd have to do that soon, maybe even today.

He pulled his truck into the visitors' parking lot at the school. The bell hadn't rung yet, and he could see the grounds filling up with kids. He smiled. He wanted to have kids. He planned on being a dedicated father. Chase believed if he was going to do something, he'd better do it right and he fervently believed parenting kids was the most important job of all.

He walked down the hallway and paused outside Sue Hanks's classroom. It was decked out for Halloween. She looked up when he opened the door and smiled brightly at him.

"Hi, Chase, what brings you here this morning?"

Avoiding the kids' desks, he leaned a hip against the teacher's desk. He got right to the point. He asked her to keep an eye out for Aidan and make sure he didn't cut school. Sue asked for an explanation, and Chase admitted that he couldn't give her one at the moment, but he told her to call Travis if she needed corroboration.

She shook her head. "I trust you, Chase. I'll give you a call if I lose Aidan at any time during the day."

The bell rang. Chase thanked her and quickly left the building. He loved kids, but he wasn't sure if he liked them en masse.

His next stop was Ernestine's place. It was still pretty early, but since the day was fair, he knew where she'd be. Carrying the stack of books, he walked the path and found her sitting on her favorite bench feeding the birds.

Her feathered friends flew off as he approached. Ernestine looked up, not a glimmer of surprise in her eyes. She was prepared for his visit.

He showed her the books. She shook her head. "I never knew these texts were ever translated into English. Vincent Bennett was well traveled indeed. The owner would not have given these up for any price. His blood, spilled on the books, would increase their power." She frowned. "Vincent would have had to kill the previous owner himself. He could never trust something this important to a subordinate no matter how loyal. He would have to make sure the power passed to him and only him."

"There are more. I counted thirty in total." Chase sighed. "There were hundreds of glass bottles filled with I don't know what. They were found with the books in the secret room in the library.

Ernestine nodded knowingly. "Of course, he'd have kept them close. Don't let anyone else get their hands on those books or those bottles. They're very dangerous to someone who cannot understand them. Bring me everything from that room as soon as possible. I know what must be done with them. Gillian can help me."

"It wasn't easy getting this stuff, but if you need everything, we'll get it done. Hopefully, once you've disposed of it, we'll have cut the head off the snake."

Ernestine touched his frowning face and said, "Be careful, I don't want anything bad to happen to either of you. And you're beyond my protection."

* * * *

When he returned to Bennett House, he ignored all the paper work waiting for him and slowly walked up the grand staircase. He smiled down at Pita, who had greeted him at the door.

"You still here?" he asked as usual. "Well, okay, you can stay, but just this once."

Reggie was sleeping on her back. She instinctively cradled her injured arm in her sleep. Pru lay at the bottom of the bed and lifted her head an inch to acknowledge his presence, then went back to sleep. Chase took a very quick shower, dried off and joined Reggie in the bed. She murmured in her sleep and cuddled up beside him. He could hear Pita's soft purr. Chase McCann was home at last.

* * * *

A couple of hours later, Reggie woke up. Chase still slept beside her. She decided to let him sleep and bring him food for a change. Carefully, she slipped out of the bed. She wrapped her terry cloth robe around her impressive body. Her fluffy slippers made her clumsy as she descended the back staircase to the kitchen.

She opened the door so Pru could run in the garden for a bit. Reggie looked around the kitchen. It was pretty well stocked. She wondered if Chase had raided his own kitchen to outfit this one for the length of their stay. He'd even brought a waffle iron. Her mouth watered at the thought. Reggie figured, how hard could it be? Surely waffles were just pancakes with little square craters to hold extra syrup.

She was proud of her progress when the doorbell interrupted her. She paused for a second to admire its rich tones. Perfect. Not too loud or jarring but not too whimsical or weak. The bell rang again before Reggie was able to make it to the door.

Jackie Blake stood on the threshold. Reggie was mortified. It was just past noon, and she was still in her bathrobe and burning waffles in her client's new home.

Petite and poised, Jackie Blake smiled knowingly as the door opened. She was the perfect contrast to Reggie. Small, dark-haired, delicate boned and immaculately groomed. Jackie Blake made Reggie feel like a troglodyte. Her manners were impeccable, and Reggie wanted to smack the woman as she stood so composed and patient in the doorway.

"Hi, Jackie, to what do we owe this pleasure?" At ease, Chase walked down the grand staircase while rolling up the sleeves of his light blue shirt. He looked like the ultimate man of the manor. Reggie wanted to smack him too. He got that do-you-smell-something look, and Reggie raced to the kitchen, but not in time to save her first batch of waffles. Discouraged, she threw away the physical evidence and started anew. It wasn't going well when Chase and Jackie walked in a little later and found her talking to the waffle iron, her language mildly profane.

He stood beside Reggie. "Regina Stanton, I'd like you to meet Jackie Blake."

Jackie couldn't have been nicer, and Reggie grudgingly warmed up to her a little, but she still didn't like the way Jackie touched Chase's arm every now and then. Chase showed her around the entire house while Reggie went upstairs to shower and change. On principle, Reggie refused to dress competitively. She pulled on a pair of threadbare jeans and a yellow T-shirt. She stuck her tongue out at her reflection in the mirror and marched out.

She could hear muted voices on the third floor and followed them. Chase was doing most of the talking. Jackie said very little, so eager she was to approve of everything Chase showed her. He had her in the palm of his hand. She was obviously there to catch a sneak peek at their progress, but Chase had charmed her so thoroughly she asked few questions. She loved everything. Tour complete, Jackie stunned Reggie by hugging her and saying, "Congratulations, the house is so beautiful. It was such a pleasure to meet you."

Okay, so she was rather sweet. Her pleasure sure seemed genuine so Reggie rewarded her with a heartfelt smile. She grew tired of being cranky, it took up too much energy.

"It was a pleasure to meet you too. I'm so sorry for my earlier state. You see, we didn't get much sleep last night."

As soon as she'd said it she regretted it. She'd made it sound like they'd spent the whole night having sex in their client's bed. She sputtered. "Oh dear, that sounded so much better in my head."

Before she could explain, Jackie laughed with genuine amusement. "Thanks for showing me around. I hope to see you both again soon." She walked out, smooth as silk.

After Reggie heard the engine of her BMW start up, she started to laugh. Chase joined her.

She put a hand up to her mouth. "Can you believe I said that?" She cracked up all over again. "The woman must think I'm crazy. Note to self—sleep…good, experimental cooking…bad."

"I wouldn't worry about it. Jackie's cool. Nothing shakes her composure. That's one of the things that makes her such a good agent." He took Reggie's hand. "Come on, I'll show you how to make waffles." He pulled her toward the kitchen.

Chapter 28

Over fluffy, golden waffles, Chase told Reggie about Ernestine's reaction to the books. She wasn't surprised.

"Well I guess we go back in there today and get the rest." He looked like he wanted to object, but she shook her head. "It has to be today, Chase. He'll be weak after yesterday, plus we saw to it that he wasn't able to recharge last night. It won't be pleasant, but I know that with a little assistance from Constance, we can do it."

She didn't wait for him to agree. Instead, she started for the garden in search of Constance.

Constance was cooperative and Reggie was right. They had very little trouble clearing out the secret room in the library. The bad smell still wafted around and they could hear a faint hissing sound, but they felt no supernatural energy pushing back at them. The whole operation took under two hours. It wasn't an enjoyable afternoon, but no one got hurt this time.

They boxed up all the contents with meticulous care. Reggie called Ernestine and told her how many boxes they had for her. She asked that they take everything to Gillian's and that she'd see them here. It seemed fitting that they all meet at Gillian's house. It had once been owned by Ernestine herself. The house had known its fair share of unexplained phenomena, and it was all coming full circle.

In Gillian's driveway, Reggie was grateful that Travis came out and helped Chase unload the boxes from the truck. She hated touching those books and those bottles. Even with the gloves she'd worn, she could still feel its unnatural residue.

Once inside the house, Reggie was happy to see Sam there. He had a set of crutches propped up on the chair beside him, but he looked well.

Reggie hugged him carefully . "Am I glad to see you!"

"Right back at you, Reg," Sam said.

Travis had already picked up Ernestine and the books Chase had dropped off the day before. Before they started unloading everything, Reggie said, "Careful, guys, this stuff is covered in some sort of gunk that defies description. You may want these." She tossed some gloves on the table.

Gillian smiled at her friend. "Good thinking, Reggie, but I have my own." She held up her hands and wiggled her fingers. She wore gardening gloves with little daisies on them. "Believe me, I'm reluctant to touch that stuff. Who knows what horrible images I may tune in to. I've never picked up impressions from inanimate objects before, but I'd rather not test that theory today."

Ernestine said, "Gillian, I'd rather you not touch any of this stuff even with gloves until I've checked it out." Gillian frowned and started to object, but Ernestine shook her head resolutely. "Trust me, you'll go through everything in time, but not right now. You are just coming into your powers as a Guardian. You're more vulnerable to this kind of magic than you know."

Gillian looked about to argue and Travis stepped in. "Gilly, you can't take this lightly. Look what that thing did to Sam. If Aunt Ernestine says you're too vulnerable, believe her."

They stood facing off against each other for a few more seconds in silent battle. Finally, without a word, Gillian stepped back. Travis smiled at her. Once again witness to their unique psychic communication, Reggie felt goose bumps form on her arms. It was incredible to see them do it. In that moment, Reggie knew in her gut that Gillian would someday be a great Guardian and that Travis would be her protector. Reggie felt the butterflies in her stomach react and in response, put a hand on her tummy.

They started with the books. Ernestine pressed her lips together firmly, creating a thin straight line of her mouth. She looked apprehensive and nodded to the boxes holding the bottles. Chase opened the first one for her. She looked inside and immediately turned to Reggie.

"Reggie, you and Chase are done here. We'll take care of all of this."

Reggie couldn't believe what she was hearing. "What are you talking about? We risked our lives to get that stuff, and now you want to shut us out? No way!"

Chase moved to her side and supported her stand. "You can't ask us to just drop that stuff off like a bunch of old clothes."

Reggie had never seen Ernestine look so severe when she said, "Go! Both of you! Leave this with me." She looked at Travis and Sam for assistance.

Sam said, "I don't blame you guys for being upset, but Ernestine knows what she's doing. In fact, she's the only one here who does right at this moment."

Travis ran a hand through his perpetually mussed hair and appealed to Chase and Reggie, "Please?"

Reggie turned to Chase and saw the answer in his eyes. She said, "Okay, but we go under duress. You have to call us if you find out anything. We won't be left in the dark." She called to Pru and walked out of the house.

Before Chase could say anything, Ernestine took his hand and said, "Look after her. She doesn't like feeling useless. I will let you know what I find."

He nodded. He kissed the old lady's wrinkled cheek and walked out to his truck.

* * * *

The following week the Town of New Crescent pulled out all the stops in preparation for Halloween. The Sinclair house was buzzing with activity as Travis's parents got ready for both a party for the children and a ball for the adults. Saturday was October 31, and there was an air of excitement all over the town.

As the day drew near, Reggie grew more and more tense. She still hadn't heard anything from Ernestine. She'd talked to Gillian, but she too had been shut out. Bennett House was suspiciously quiet. They'd stopped work on the house until after Halloween, but Reggie wondered if they'd been too cautious. They'd cleared out the books and bottles containing the sum of Vincent's knowledge of dark magic. She hadn't felt Vincent's presence since. She'd tried to contact Constance a few times but failed.

Sadly, Reggie wondered if Constance had taken her earlier advice and crossed over into the light. It bothered Reggie to think she'd left without saying good-bye. Constance was stubborn, impatient, and often rude, but that didn't mean Reggie wanted her gone. She needed closure before bidding farewell to the irascible ghost..

Reggie was coming to the realization that there really wasn't much reason for her to stay at Bennett House much longer. The thought of leaving the house gave her a twinge. That was nothing compared to the desperation she felt at the thought of leaving Chase. What do they do now? She knew that Chase was feeling the strain as well. They still shared a bed, and they still had amazing sex, but there was so much left unsaid between them. Reggie didn't know where to start. Finally, she'd decided that after Halloween, she'd arrange for the work to start again on the house and she'd move out. The thought brought her no satisfaction, only despair.

For weeks, Reggie had been preparing for some sort of epic struggle with Vincent. It was a tremendous letdown when there had been no such final battle. They'd won, but Reggie didn't feel much like a champion. Their story ended with a whimper, not a bang, and she moped around the huge house feeling dissatisfied and irritated.

Chase had told her that even Aidan Spencer's behavior had improved. That thought made Reggie happy. The poor kid got a rough break with parents such as his. She fervently hoped that he'd rise above what his parents had taught him. She made a point of taking Todd for ice cream again despite the cooler weather. He reported to Reggie that he and Aidan were getting along okay, but they were no longer friends. Todd had made his stand and was not backing down from it. He made Reggie proud

* * * *

Halloween day dawned gray and grim. The skies looked ominous threatening rain all day. The weather didn't help Reggie's melancholy. She tried hard to shake it. After all, she'd always loved Halloween at the Sinclairs'. When she been a child, she'd joined all the other kids and finished up her trick or treating with a visit to the Sinclair estate where she could count on doubling her haul of candy. Once she'd grown, Reggie always attended the adult party. She could remember how excited she'd been going to her first. She'd dressed as a fairy. In retrospect, Reggie laughed at the idea. She'd have made a much more convincing Amazon, but back then, she hadn't yet been ready to accept that she'd never quite fit the profile of a fairy.

Chase had left early to help Travis with the last minute touches on their haunted house. Since Sam was pretty much immobile, they'd found the perfect role for him to play. Dressed as a mad surgeon, Chase would ghoulishly operate on Sam in front of the children. Reggie didn't even want to think what horrible things Chase planned to remove from Sam's bound body. The kids would love it.

Reggie's costume was pathetically easy to prepare so she drove to the Sinclair estate in good time to help out with the set up. She left the haunted house to Chase, Sam, and Travis, instead she got a beat on the DJ and headed toward him. She smiled when she saw the look on his face when he laid eyes on her. Fatally attracted but terrified at the same time, he looked like a rodent caught in the headlights. Reggie had indulgent affection for him. Peter Jabonowitz was almost a foot shorter than she was, and he looked up at her with a kind of titilated fear on his face. A woman of her impressive proportions dwarfed a man his size, but he soldiered on and appeared to enjoy their interactions. Reggie admired his courage.

She smiled with genuine pleasure. "Hi, Peter. It's good to see you again. I'm here to help." She hugged him with enthusiasm then grabbed his elbows when his knees started to buckle. He was a sweetheart and just the sight of him cheered her up.

Peter didn't need much help. He'd provided the music for the last Sinclair party, so there wasn't much Reggie could do. Once they finished setting up, Reggie smiled at him and turned to head into the house. "See you on the dance floor Peter."

Inside, Travis's mother Ruth Sinclair was finishing the set up for the kids' party in the game room. Most years, they used the great room, but since both parties were on the same night, the kids got bumped to alternate digs. From the game room, it was an easy walk to the guest house, where the haunted house awaited them, so it worked out great.

Just before it got dark, Reggie used a guest bedroom to change into her costume. She wrapped bandages all over herself and used red food coloring and corn syrup to suggest oozing blood. The sling cradling her dislocated shoulder added authenticity. Using the mirror, she gave herself a black eye and drew stitches on her forehead and cheeks.

She was ready just in time. Toddlers and the younger children started to trickle in with their parents. Reggie knew most of them. Playing the gracious hostess, she wished everyone a happy Halloween. She pointed out all the goodies to the little ones and with a word of caution directed them to the haunted house. She could hear the nervous laughter and the delighted squeals as one monster after another jumped out at them. From what she could tell, Chase, Travis, and Sam had done a marvelous job. Now it would be expected every year. She knew they'd try to top the previous one every year. With a sigh, she wondered what her life would be like next Halloween. Pat Somers would be living in Bennett house and what would she and Chase be doing?

Soon, she was greeting older children. The little ones had all gone home with their loot. Recognizing Todd and his friend Jeremy, she told them to take their time through the haunted house. She knew they wouldn't want to miss a single thing. As the hour grew later, the monsters became more menacing. In keeping with the age of their audience, the guys stepped up the blood and gore to more appropriate adolescent standards.

Around ten, Reggie heard the last peep out of the haunted house. Her feet were killing her, and she flopped onto one of the chairs in the game room. Chase had told her that once the haunted house was over he planned to go back to Bennett House and change into a more comfortable costume and meet her back in the great room for dancing. She hadn't danced with Chase since that fateful night he'd kissed her when they were so young. She wondered how it would feel tonight. Would people be surprised to see them together? They'd made no secret of their relationship, but they hadn't announced it either.

Taking a deep breath, Reggie stood up. She walked to the door and started to turn off lights when she heard a deep laugh. She spun around and saw Aidan Spencer standing behind her. He didn't appear to be wearing a costume. Reggie narrowed her eyes trying to get a better look at him in the dim room.

He stepped closer, and Reggie saw what she wished she hadn't. The vacant look in the young boy's eyes made her stomach drop and turned her blood to ice.

Chapter 29

On the way back to Bennett House, Chase smiled recalling some of the kids' reactions. He was glad they'd toned it down for the younger crowd. It pleased him that they'd made no child cry, but had made a lot of them squeal with delight. The sound of their laughter made him happy.

Walking through the front door, Chase once more imagined the grand old house filled with laughing children. It was his fondest wish to live to see that. Instead, he could only expect to hear the sound of Pita's meow of welcome.

All was silent. For a second, Chase worried that the cat had finally taken him at his word and walked out just as unexpectedly as he'd come. He called the cat's name, the name Reggie had given him.

"Pita, kitty, kitty, where are you?"

Silence. Sam had told him once that some people did terrible things to cats on Halloween. Chase felt sick at the thought. Quickly, he walked through the house opening doors and calling to the cat. There was no sign of him.

With a sinking heart, Chase approached the library. Knowing that Vincent fed off the pain of other living creatures, Chase forced himself to hope that Pita was ok. With a great push, he opened the double doors. The smell assaulted him at once. It felt more concentrated than ever and Chase struggled to breathe.

Pita lay limp just outside the door to the secret room. He and Reggie had left it open in the vain hope of airing it out a little. Chase ran to the still cat. He didn't make it. Just as he was half a foot away, Chase was thrown back and off his feet by an invisible force. The attack left him breathless and he struggled to get up off the floor. His heart raced as he fought the energy field that held him down. It crushed his chest. Chase heard a snap and knew he'd broken a rib. It hurt like hell, but he continued to fight against the weight mercilessly pressing down on him.

Unable to get up off the floor, Chase's mind raced. He could see Pita's body move almost imperceptibly as the cat breathed. He said a prayer of thanks. At least he was still alive.

The strange force he knew to be Vincent, had him pinned to the floor, but Chase couldn't give up. Staying flat against the floor, he started to worm his way over to Pita. It was slow going, and he broke out into a cold sweat struggling against the pain of his broken rib and the weight crushing him. The hissing started, and Chase's skin crawled, but it got worse when he heard the laughter.

* * * *

"Aidan?" Reggie asked.

The boy who had once been Aidan didn't respond. He looked at her blankly. His eyes glistened, but held no life; his childish lips were red and wet; saliva dripped onto his chin. Reggie shuddered.

"What do you want?" she asked. Still no answer. "Vincent?"

He blinked at her and started to laugh. The sound was unnatural, deep and gurgling. More saliva dripped from his mouth. His eyes rolled back in his head, and Reggie was sure he was going to drop to the floor as he swayed.

Reggie's stomach reacted. The kid's breath smelled foul, and as he laughed, spittle sprayed Reggie. Frantically, she wiped it away.

With horror, she realized that they'd been fooled by Vincent. He hadn't weakened a bit. He'd been waiting until this most hallowed night to make his move, and they'd been stupid enough to fall for it. Somehow, they'd missed it all. That secret room couldn't have held his spirit. It was a red herring.

She commanded Pru to stay with the boy. Leaving Aidan behind, she sprinted toward the haunted house. There was nothing she could do for the kid alone. Racing at full speed, she almost ran Sam down. He tottered on his crutches for a moment and said, "Whoa there, Crash…"

He didn't get anything else out as she demanded, "Where's Chase?"

"He went back to Bennett House to change into his costume. What is it?" He was alarmed and he let go of his crutches to grab Reggie by the upper arms.

"There's a kid in the game room with Pru, get him to a hospital. Give me your keys, I've got to find Chase." Without hesitation, Sam put his keys in her hand.

She was already running to his car when she yelled, "Thanks."

She drove Sam's car like a madwoman. She was grateful that he hadn't broken his right leg or she'd have lost valuable time trying to find another car. The Mercedes handled beautifully, taking the corners at the speed she demanded of it.

Finally, she squealed to a halt in front of Bennett House. To Reggie, the drive had taken forever, but in reality, it couldn't have taken more than ten minutes. She'd barely come to a stop before she threw the car into park and raced for the house. She didn't take the time to shut the door to the car or the house.

The hallway that led to the library was so cold that Reggie could see her breath, but she didn't care. The doors jammed. She threw her weight against them and grunted when she hit resistance.

She yelled at the top of her lungs. "Chase! I'm here. I'll get to you."

She almost cried when she heard his voice, "Reggie! I'm pinned. I've got Pita. He's barely breathing, but he's alive."

Reggie rolled her eyes and yelled back, "Are *you* okay?"

"Yeah." She knew he was lying. She needed a distraction, something to make Vincent turn his attention away from them for a second so she could break through the doors and help Chase.

"Constance! Damn you, help us!"

She threw herself against the doors again ignoring the pain in her shoulder. This time they seemed to give a little so she tried again. Success!

She ran to Chase just as he was trying to sit up. He groaned when the effort reminded him of his broken rib.

Reggie kneeled beside him. "Liar! You're hurt!"

He smiled at her, and the butterflies in her stomach danced.

"I'll live now that you're here."

Reggie shook her head and helped him to his feet. It wasn't easy because he didn't want to let Pita go.

"He's in shock, I think. He needs warmth." Chase said.

They heard a loud bang and saw Constance bathed in a bright white light.

Despite his predicament, Chase gasped in awe. "I can see her!"

In a voice that reverberated in Reggie's heart, Constance addressed her husband for the first time.

"Vincent Bennett, evil aberration, today, you have no more secrets. I've kept my guilty silence too long, and that's given you power over me. My own guilt has been my curse, but no longer."

Reggie and Chase saw a huge electric spark, and they heard a snap. Constance addressed them.

"Please, forgive me. There is so much to forgive." She wept but miraculously managed to keep Vincent at bay. They could hear an inhuman raging and spitting as he struggled against the power Constance used to contain him.

Reggie said, "Constance, you've punished yourself long enough. There is nothing left to forgive."

She cast a sad look at Reggie and shook her head. "No. You must know the truth. I loved my baby more than life itself, and I was prepared to make any sacrifice for him, but I had seen my son's destiny. He would be far more powerful than my husband had ever dreamed. Combining our power was unnatural, and it created an evil beyond what this world could hold."

Constance looked so sad that Reggie started to cry for her. "You shed tears for me, my dear? I knew you would, but there is so much more to tell. Then we'll see if you can still cry tears for my sake."

They could still hear Vincent's hissing and snarling. He wasn't going without a fight. Constance ignored him and continued her confession.

"I knew I would die in childbirth. I was not meant to have children. I knew that fact as a young girl and I rebelled against it. I felt power in Vincent and hoped he'd change my destiny." She laughed without humor, "I was a fool. Finally, I was forced to accept my fate. I was prepared to die, but what would happen to my son? Every day my body nurtured his, and I loved him more and more. Regina, you know what I mean." She pierced Reggie with her stare. Pita moved in Chase's arms.

The butterflies in Reggie's stomach fluttered, and for the first time, she understood what they were trying to tell her. This power, this unexpected power she had within herself, was life. She touched her belly and knew. She was carrying Chase's child. She'd conceived the first night they'd made love. With knowledge came power, and Reggie was full.

Her face glowed with it, and she nodded at Constance to continue.

"I knew I had only one option." Constance shuddered "I killed my baby."

Reggie shook her head. "No! No, you didn't Constance! You cannot kill something that was never meant to be. You took your own life to save your child to save all of us…your children."

Constance whimpered. "Is there forgiveness for such a sin?"

Chase said, "Forgive yourself, Constance, and let it go. I am your blood, and I live because of you. We all do. You saved us by taking your life and freeing your son from Vincent Bennett's madness."

Reggie smiled at him. He got it. She said, "Tell us everything, Constance."

In a somber tone, she told the rest of her story. "On the eve of my labor, I walked into the garden with one of my husband's foul potions. I drank it. I knew it would kill me and my son instantly." They could hear Vincent snapping as he fought against Constance and Reggie's hold on him.

"He found me hours after my death, and by the light of the rising sun, Vincent Bennett, the monster I'd married, cut my dead baby from my body. He holds it still. His own diseased bones were laid to rest along side my son's. Our child's corporeal body is the source of his power. Find them and bury them before this night ends."

Chase set Pita on the floor gently and grabbed a piece of solid wood that once belonged to the banister. He moved into the secret room. He looked over his shoulder at Reggie, and with all the strength he could muster, he struck the floor. The floorboards cracked. Chase gasped from the pain the contact had caused him. Reggie ran to his side. Together, they pried off the floorboards.

A gust of wind blew through the room dusting them with fine particles of the rich earth they'd uncovered. Reggie and Chase knew what they'd find, but still they gasped when they saw the bones of Vincent Bennett holding the tiny bones of the child who was never meant to be.

Reggie touched the tiny bones and felt an echo inside her womb. Reggie and Chase turned to see Constance crying tears of joy. In her ghostly arms, she cradled her gurgling baby boy. They saw a flash of bright white light, and Constance faded away.

Confused Chase looked around the room. The smell was gone, the cold was gone, but he could still hear the faint sounds of hissing.

In a commanding voice, Reggie said, "Vincent Bennett, you are vanquished. This world is not for you. You are forbidden to return." In an ear-shattering scream, he was gone.

The room changed. The mahogany wood gleamed, and that strange greasy residue had vanished. Despite its years of abuse, the library looked beautiful in that moment. Joy bubbled up inside Reggie, and she hugged herself and laughed.

Chase made a small noise and alarmed, Reggie turned just in time to see him wince.

"Come on Poindexter, it's the hospital for you." She stroked Pita's head and said, "And you too."

They recognized the emergency room doctor. He greeted them as friends. He smiled and said, "I was wondering when you guys were going to show up. It's been days."

Chase did in fact have two broken ribs. But otherwise he was fine. The doctor still insisted he spend the night. This time Reggie stayed too. She wasn't giving him the opportunity to bolt like the last time she put him in the hospital.

She'd called Sam and told him what had happened and that she and Chase were okay. He promised to get Travis to help him remove the remains in the secret room, to bury the child's and burn the man's. She also asked him to come and get Pita.

He laughed and, in a very mild tone, said, "Sure I'd love to, but, Reggie, where is my car?"

Chapter 30

The next day dawned bright and sunny as if in apology for its foul mood the day before. Reggie watched the sun rise from Chase's hospital room. She fit right into the atmosphere of the place since she hadn't taken the time to change out of her Halloween costume. Finally, she divested herself of most of the bandages. She still had traces of fake blood and smears of fake stitches all over her, but she didn't care.

She hadn't left Chase's side since he'd succumbed to the pain killer the doctor had prescribed. Reggie wasn't giving him the opportunity to leave against his doctor's orders. She'd sit on him if she had to. A hospital room may not have been the most suitable location for their discussion, but Reggie was long past caring. She'd lived in limbo and didn't like it much. They needed to clear the air. Besides, she had to tell him about the baby. She touched her abdomen. She felt so much love that her chest swelled and her eyes teared up.

She heard a noise behind her and turned from the window to see a pale Chase smiling at her. They said nothing for a moment and Reggie was afraid that she'd lost her courage. Relying on old favorites, she started to talk.

"Chase, I'm glad you're awake. Sam and Travis have taken care of the remains in the secret room. Pita is fine. You have two broken ribs, but there isn't much they can do for ribs, so you just have to be very careful for the next six weeks. Aidan doesn't remember a thing about Halloween night, but Travis is going to have a talk with his parents, just in case. Gillian will be a great help to the kid if they let her. Vincent is gone. We did it!"

She stopped talking only long enough to take another breath. Chase waited for her to go on because she always did.

"I'm pregnant." Reggie said. Chase was dumbstruck. "And the baby is yours."

Chase responded with spirit. "Of course the baby is mine! As soon as I can get released from this place we'll find a justice of the peace and get married." He pushed the button for the nurse.

Reggie sat in the chair close to his bed and shook her head. Chase frowned and waited.

"I can't marry you, Chase."

"Why the hell not?" He spoke so explosively that he could be heard in the hallway. A passing nurse turned her head in surprise, then kept walking.

Reggie stood her ground. "I can't marry you just because I'm having your baby. I won't start a marriage that way. A child deserves two parents who love him and each other."

Chase looked beaten and said, "Reggie, I can make you love me. Look, we're already good friends, and the sex is amazing for us." He took one of the hands she had clasped in her lap and brought it to his lips. "Just give me a chance, Crash. I love you so much. I think I've loved you forever. I just always seemed to miss my chance with you. I'll make it enough for both of us for now. Please, Reggie, I beg you, just give me a chance."

Reggie was speechless. She started to sob. Chase threw the covers aside and pulled her onto the bed beside him. "Please don't cry, Crash. I'll make it right." He pulled back to look at her face when her shoulders started to shake.

He frowned at her in confusion. Sure she was crying although not with regret or sorrow, but with joy. Her shoulders were shaking with laughter.

"You love me!" she cried. Her tears mixed with her hardy laughter. Chase's frown deepened.

He shook her and yelled, "Are you on drugs? Yes, damn it, I love you! I love you! I'm in love with you! I don't see what's so funny about that. I swear, sometimes, Reggie, you can be so dense that you elevate it to an art form. Of course I love you! What do you think all of this was about?"

The nurse poked her head around the door. She raised her eyebrows when she saw Reggie stretched alongside Chase in the tiny bed. "Is something wrong here?"

Both Reggie and Chase looked at her and yelled, "Go away!"

The nurse gave them a knowing look and shut the door, leaving them alone.

Reggie pulled away from him and rested on a forearm savoring the look on his face. His eyes showed, love, frustration, desire, hope and an irritation that Reggie found irresistible. She started to enjoy herself. "Are you saying you'll make me marry you?"

He narrowed his blue eyes at her. The color had returned to his face. "If I have to."

She shrugged and said, "Well, okay then."

He looked at her with disbelief. "What did you just say?"

She smiled and brightened the room up with her joy. Taking his beloved face in her hands, she said, "I love you Chase. I'm not sure when it started but it's real, and strong and endless. You are everything I want in life, a friend, a sparring partner, a lover…you are my mate, the father of all my children. Let's have six."

He hugged her so tightly he winced. She giggled and hugged him back ignoring his grunt of pain. He could take it.

Chase closed his eyes tightly. When he opened them, again there were tears at the corners of his eyes. "That night at Ernestine's birthday party so many years ago. I thought you knew how I felt. You'd just broken up with your boyfriend, and you were vulnerable. I'll never forgive myself for taking advantage. You needed a friend that night, and I failed you. I hated myself, and I had to get away from you before I lost all control. I left you there on the dance floor all alone. I'm sorry. I had hoped to explain, but then my mother died and my world changed forever."

She nodded. "When you kissed me that night, I didn't want you to stop. You made me feel something I'd never felt before or since…or at least since you kissed me again. Last summer, when I saw that gun pointed at your chest, I knew I didn't want to live in a world that didn't include you. When I saw you sneak into the farmhouse to rescue me, I thought I'd explode with joy."

She frowned and punched him in the arm. "Why the hell did you leave the hospital before we could talk last summer, you big dope?"

"Jade's father died, and for the first time ever, she called and told me that she needed me. I can't go into the details right now, but her father had died rather unexpectedly. As you know, he was an unsavory character to say the least. I came back as soon as I could, but you were gone. I cursed myself a million times for letting you get away."

Reggie smiled. "I cursed you two million times. It's a wonder you're still in one piece. I thought for sure some part of your anatomy would have fallen off or something." She kissed him. "Now I'm so glad I'm lousy at magic."

He smiled and said, "You think?"

Tears ran like wavy little streams down her cheeks. "Chase, we're having a baby. We conceived the very first night we made love. I think Constance knew it would happen. Everyone kept telling me to look inside myself to find my strength. When our lives depended on it, I did and found our child there. You and I alone couldn't defeat Vincent. We needed the baby to help us do it." She touched her belly and kissed him softly. "He's strong, Chase, a miracle. For so many years, I despaired that I hadn't inherited the gift. Well, Chase, you are my gift. You give me my power. I could feel it pulsing through me yesterday."

Chase was silent. Reggie was used to it, so she just rested her head on his chest and reveled in her love for him and his for her. When he spoke, she heard it first from his chest, and she looked up at him with a frown.

"I haven't been exactly honest with you." He heart jumped into her throat, and her stomach clenched as she waited for his explanation. He took a deep breath. "I don't know how to say this but, I bought Bennett House."

She looked confused. "From Pat Somers? Why would she sell? She just bought the place. How did you..."

Chase took another deep breath, squeezed his eyes closed, and said, "I'm Pat Somers." He opened one eye and waited for her reaction.

This time, Reggie was silent. She tested his words in her mind. *Chase is Pat Somers, and he's kept it from me all this time. Should I be angry? It is a betrayal in a way...Oh, what the hell, the man loves me, who cares?*

She smiled at him. "Care to explain that tasty little tidbit?"

"My stepfather left my mother's estate in such a mess that I had to find a way to fix things. I couldn't continue living in this town knowing that I owed money to so many. You'd gone on to college as had Sam and Travis. I missed you so much, Reggie." He kissed her forehead. "I have a good imagination. What do you think I'm doing when I'm so quiet at times? I had such outrageous fantasies about you that I finally put them on paper. I sent my first novel to a literary agent, Jackie Blake." He smiled at Reggie's cross expression when he mentioned the name. "She liked it and sold it. I've been writing ever since. Now you and Jackie are the only people who know."

Reggie punched him on the arm again. "Damn, Poindexter, but you can write!"

He laughed. "Thanks. Last summer when I almost lost you, I swore that I'd never let you go again, but I did. I knew in time, you'd be back. This is New Crescent. You belonged here, so I tracked down the Bennett who still owned the house and bought it. Jackie helped me stay distanced from the sale, and I asked her to hire you. Sorry for the subterfuge, but I couldn't think of anything else to do. I wanted you to make the house over the way you wanted, but I wasn't sure how to tell you how I felt. I had no idea how you'd react."

He hugged her again and grunted when his ribs protested, but he kept talking. "That house is my wedding present to you, Reggie. It's yours, it always has been, and it always will be. Can I live in it with you and our children?"

"Yeah, but let's make it legal as soon as possible. I'd like to beat Travis to the altar."

"Good idea." He nuzzled her neck and she melted. Pressing against him, she could feel his arousal. He groaned but not with pain this time.

"Crash, I know that with you, I'm a sexual god, but don't forget I have broken bones here." In a pathetically wimpy voice, he said, "Be gentle with me."

She wasn't, but he didn't seem to mind.

* * * *

Later that day, Reggie hosted her first party at Bennett House. It was ad hoc and informal, the very best kind. Her parents, Travis's parents, Ernestine, Sam, Travis, and Gillian attended. They were all impressed with the work Reggie and Chase had done transforming the place.

Chase waited until they were all gathered around the dining room table before he made the announcement.

He stood up with care, favoring his broken ribs. His six-feet-seven inch frame was enough to command attention anywhere, and this was no exception. All eyes turned to him in anticipation.

"It's wonderful to finally have you all here in this house, but nothing makes me happier than to tell you that Reggie and I are in love, and we're getting married."

His audience burst into laughter. Chase and Reggie exchanged confused glances. That wasn't quite the reaction they'd expected.

Taking pity on them, Gillian spoke up. "Guys, it comes as no surprise to us. We've known for ages how you feel about each other. Sorry, but you were the last to know." This time Reggie and Chase joined their laughter.

After they'd eaten, they adjourned to the living room. Reggie checked to make sure all her guests were comfortable before she slipped outside. She walked to the little iron gate and thought about Constance.

After about thirty seconds, the air changed and Reggie looked around in anticipation.

"Congratulations on the coming nuptials."

"Thanks, Constance. None of this would have happened without you," Reggie said with humble gratitude

Constance nodded. "True, but what choice did I have? It was my destiny."

Reggie heard a noise and turned. Ernestine and Gillian had joined her. They smiled at Constance like they would an old friend. They could see her. Gillian said, "Have you told her yet?"

Constance shook her head. "No. I was waiting for you to get here."

Reggie looked at them with suspicion but said nothing. She waited.

Constance said, "I'm sorry Regina. It's my fault you did not inherit your gift on your fourteenth birthday. I needed it."

"What?" Reggie was bewildered.

Ernestine explained. "My dear, Constance held your power. She needed it to keep Vincent inactive for so many years. She knew the time would come when she'd have to contact you and share her burden." Ernestine gave Constance a disapproving glance. "She's stubborn and unpredictable, but she's still a Guardian. And tonight, she passes that mantle on to you, where it belongs. Together, we'll decide what must be done with Vincent's books, but we must destroy all contents in the bottles carefully. I'm sorry if you thought we were pushing you away and keeping things from you, but you had to stay away from the bottles for your own safety. Your power was in its most fragile stage."

Gillian took up the rest of the explanation. "Reggie, the power you felt in the library yesterday will be with you always. You just have to learn how to use it. Constance will be here for you. She's a Guardian. She can crossover to this world at will."

Reggie's emotions overwhelmed her. How was it possible that she could be gifted with so much? She wanted to cry, but laughed instead. "You mean she's gonna be annoying me for the rest of my life? Can't they make an ointment for that?"

They laughed, and Constance said, "I will help you hone your abilities, and I will see your children grow to be a great hope for this world."

The three women and the ghost formed a circle. The wind caressed them as they joined their power. Thunder was heard in the distance.

Chapter 31

They married at Bennett House or, rather, McCann House, as it was newly christened. They tried to have a small gathering but realized their wedding was something they wanted to share, so they threw open the doors and invited everyone. The entire town of New Crescent celebrated the event and filled the house.

Reggie's favorite disk jockey donated his services for the night. Peter looked at Reggie with a bittersweet smile, and she dragged him out to the dance floor. He closed his eyes and reveled in the experience. Before the song ended, he rushed over to attend to his duties as DJ. The music started again. Travis and Gillian took the floor, but he didn't take her in his arms. Instead, he knelt in front of her and said, "I love you Gillian. Will you marry me?"

The room was silent. Peter paused the music. The wedding guests all waited in suspended animation. Gillian grabbed him by the scruf of the neck and hauled him to his feet. "Oh no you don't. This is Reggie and Chase's day. You're not going to steal their thunder. You can do better than that. Now dance with me like you mean it." She looked over her shoulder and addressed the crowd. "Whoever put their money on today, you're out of luck." Their audience laughed and began daning again.

Eating her second piece of wedding cake, Reggie turned to her husband and said, "Chase. When are we going to tell them about the baby?"

He shrugged. "Why bother? They probably knew before we did."

They smiled and waved at Ernestine and Gillian, who looked at them with a secret knowledge in their eyes. Reggie could swear she caught a glimpse of Constance standing beside them. With her baby held tight in her arms, she too was smiling.

THE END

HTTP://MARYLOUGEORGE.BLOGSPOT.COM

ABOUT THE AUTHOR

Mary Lou George lives within driving distance of Toronto. She's worked in the design studio of a major art museum for over twenty years. The creative atmosphere there has helped to keep her imagination fertile and her humor well exercised. In her personal life, she's surrounded by family, friends and an animal or two or three. It's no surprise that her stories include four legged characters. She comes from a long line of earth mothers who've always believed there's a little bit of magic in each of us and that working hard for the happy ending is always worth the effort.

BookStrand

www.BookStrand.com

LaVergne, TN USA
24 May 2010
183759LV00006B/144/P